"Why
Roads
funeral. And then six months later
you showed up here, as if nothing had
changed."

"That is not fair," he snapped, rising to his feet.
"Everything had changed."

"Not for you! You'd barely been home in years—"

"I lost my brother!" He cut her off. "My best friend!
You think you're the only one who has grief to
manage? You're not alone in this, Erin. You're not the
only one who misses him."

"But don't you see?" she murmured, the words raspy.
"You'd already left years ago. You had all this time
and distance already. How can you possibly know
what it felt like to lose him, without a choice?"

"But I do know." Burke's words sounded hard to his
own ears. "You forget that I lost both my parents
without a choice. And then my brother, too."

Erin's jaw clenched, and he could tell she was
holding back what she wanted to say. He knew the
expression well.

When she finally spoke, she said nothing more about
Gavin but rather warned him, "Just don't get so close
to Kitt that you break his heart when you leave."

With that, she turned on her heel and headed back
inside, leaving him to wonder just whose heart she
was really worried about him breaking.

Dear Reader,

Grief is a tricky thing. It has no timetable. It will catch you unawares, lulling you into a false sense of security one hour, only to strike you savagely with the reminders of your loss in the next.

Grief is no stranger to the characters in *The Way Back to Erin*. With the death of her husband, Erin has had to dig her way through the years that have passed, remaining strong for herself and Gavin's son, Kitt. When she faces the threat of losing the Moontide Inn, which has been her home and safe haven for years, her grief is rekindled. Her struggle to reconcile her shattered dreams with the return of Burke, a love she laid to rest many years ago, is at the heart of this story.

When my editors suggested the title to me, something settled in my spirit. *The Way Back to Erin* encompasses so much of what this book is about. Not only is Burke finding his way home and back to Erin after his own losses, but Erin is finding her way back to herself, defining who she is without Gavin, who was the foundation of her existence for so long. What she learns is this:

Grief will tie you up, cut you deep and hold you down. But it will not keep you there forever.

For whatever you have personally lost, I am sorry. And I hope that sooner rather than later, you find your way back home.

If you'd like to share your story with me, I would love to hear from you. Contact me through my website at cerellasechrist.com, online via Facebook or Twitter, or by mail at PO Box 614, Red Lion, PA 17356.

Cerella Sechrist

HEARTWARMING

The Way Back to Erin

—

Cerella Sechrist

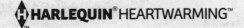

ISBN-13: 978-1-335-63349-1

The Way Back to Erin

Copyright © 2018 by Cerella Delbaugh Sechrist

This edition published by arrangement with Harlequin Books S.A.

For questions and comments about the quality of this book, please contact us at CustomerService@Harlequin.com.

Printed in U.S.A.

Cerella Sechrist lives in York, Pennsylvania, with two precocious pugs, Darcy and Charlotte, named after Jane Austen literary characters. Inspired by her childhood love of stories, she was ten years old when she decided she wanted to become an author. As a former barista, Cerella is a coffee snob who can spend hours discussing the finer points of a good Italian roast. She's been known to post too many pug photos on both Instagram and Pinterest. You can see for yourself by finding her online at cerellasechrist.com.

Books by Cerella Sechrist

Harlequin Heartwarming

A Song for Rory
Harper's Wish
The Paris Connection
Gentle Persuasion

To Haley Sechrist: sister-in-law, fellow barista, "buffet buddy," TV fan, cake lover and general partner in crime (remember to hide the evidence, especially when it involves cookie crumbs!)

Thanks for all the coffee, conversations, tears and laughter. But especially for being family.

Acknowledgments

Much gratitude to editor extraordinaire Karen Reid as well as Victoria Curran and the rest of the Harlequin Heartwarming team for all their hard work and support. You all have shaped Findlay Roads into the best little fictional town in Maryland.

Special thanks to my fellow Heartwarming authors, who are some of the most supportive and encouraging people I have ever met, with extra kudos to my blog partner, Loree Lough, for the phone chats, brainstorming sessions and support, and to Kate James for her patience, organization and general superwoman skills. You all warm my heart.

Additional thanks to fellow author Lisa Lawmaster Hess for our Starbucks writing sessions and helping my characters find their way through this story.

Finally, to my family and friends, who always provide me with the best character fodder. I love you all.

CHAPTER ONE

WHEN THE CLOUDS first rolled in, Burke had felt disappointment. Thirty minutes later, he wondered if the weather had known what was coming well before he did and had conspired to provide an appropriate backdrop to the day.

As he stood there with the June rain pouring down, soaking through his tuxedo and slipping down the back of his neck, he shivered. The guests had retreated, taking shelter in the tent where the reception was to be held. He felt like he should take charge, make an announcement, tell them to go ahead and enjoy the dinner that had already been bought and paid for. But his father-in-law...no. He brought that thought up short.

Allan Worth would not be his father-in-law after all. Not since Tessa had failed to show up, disappearing from the Delphine Resort where their wedding was being held.

She was gone, as completely as the sun. The rain pelted his face, but he stubbornly remained outside, welcoming the hammer of the elements. It soothed his disappointment, his embarrassment, his confusion.

Tessa didn't want to marry him. Or so the note in his clenched fist claimed. It was a paltry offering with no excuses. Just two simple lines.

I can't marry you. I'm sorry.

Burke raised his eyes and looked toward the portico of the hotel where his and Tessa's closest family members and friends congregated. Paige, Tessa's oldest sister, was gesturing wildly. Though he couldn't read her lips, they were moving at a fast clip, probably worrying more over the blow to the family's reputation that a runaway bride would deliver rather than the fact that Tessa had disappeared. Harper, Tessa's other sister, had her arms wrapped around their mother and was staring at her cell phone screen, as though willing it to ring.

Allan Worth was nowhere to be seen. Tessa's father was likely doing damage control among the guests, apologizing for the inconvenience, offering refreshments. Like Burke should be doing. But he didn't have the strength to face the expressions filled with sympathy, the strange condolences for someone who hadn't died yet had disappeared just the same.

He shifted his gaze from the small crowd on the portico and caught sight of Molly Callahan, Tessa's niece by marriage, playing tag with several other children, oblivious to how the rain stained their fine dress clothes. His lips tugged upward at the sight, and he wished he could abandon his dark mood and join them.

He searched the group of children for his nephew, Kitt, and wasn't surprised when he didn't see the little boy among them. Ever since his father's death two years before, Kitt had become a very serious child. Running through the rain wasn't something he'd take part in.

Burke moved his eyes back to the portico and found his nephew seated at Great-Aunt Lenora's feet, the old woman's hand absently stroking his hair. She leaned down and said something to the boy, but he didn't respond.

Burke's heart twisted anew. Not for his own loss but for his nephew's. Would Kitt never laugh again?

Then again…would *he*? Between his brother's death almost two years ago and now Tessa's defection, he didn't think there was much to smile about these days. His eyes continued to scan the group gathered on the portico, the kids scattered around the lawn, and the guests huddled in the tent, drawing into the center to avoid the rain that was blowing in through the open flaps.

It wasn't until he saw her approaching that he realized he'd been looking for her in particular.

Erin. His brother's widow, braving the downpour to get to him. Funny that no one else had bothered.

When she reached his side, she held out an umbrella, and he almost—but not quite—laughed at the sight. She'd picked her way across the grass, letting the deluge soak her, and hadn't opened the umbrella. What good would it be to either of them now?

"Aunt Lenora says you should come in out of the rain."

He could only blink in reply. Erin took a step closer.

"Burke, I'm sorry. But she's not coming back. There's no point in standing out here, waiting for her."

"I'd rather be out here than in there—" he gestured toward the tent "—where they can all stare at me."

Erin took his hand, the warmth of her fingers startling him. His own were chilled straight through to the bone.

"No one's staring, Burke. You have nothing to be embarrassed about."

Her words penetrated, and he laughed, an empty, bitter sound. "I've just been stood up by my fiancée on my wedding day, which was already ruined by this freak rainstorm. I kind of think I have *something* to be embarrassed about."

Erin's eyes sparked. "Well, I imagine standing out here in the rain like an idiot only makes it worse."

His jaw sagged. "You know, most people would be feeling sorry for me right about now."

She sighed. "I do feel sorry for you, Burke. But I don't pity you. Tessa's not a cruel woman. If she didn't want to marry you, then I suspect she had a good reason. Now, are you coming in out of the rain or not?"

He swallowed, shifting his gaze from Erin and to the arbor that had looked so festive and fresh only an hour earlier. Now, the boughs of greenery were sagging, dripping water in rivulets down the white columns. The flowers had lost quite a few petals, beaten from their stems by the rain and littering the ground in a soggy mess.

"I have nowhere to go," he said, more to himself than to Erin. He'd lived for so long without a home that he hadn't realized how much he was looking forward to finally settling down.

All of his possessions were boxed up in Tessa's garage. He was supposed to move in with her after their honeymoon. He felt a pang at the realization that he wouldn't have a home after all.

"You can stay at the Moontide," Erin told him. "Aunt Lenora already said so."

"I can't stay at the inn," he replied, almost defensively.

Erin frowned. She was a mess, the rain having washed her mascara in black lines down her cheeks. He felt a twinge of guilt that she was standing out here, in the rain with him, when no one else had bothered.

"Why not?" she demanded.

He couldn't explain it to her, couldn't give voice to his feelings on the subject. There were so many reasons for him to stay away from the bed-and-breakfast. Despite the fact that it had been his permanent home for four years as a teenager, he had never felt like he belonged there. And even less so now, knowing it was the house where Erin and Gavin had made their home, even though his brother had been deployed in the army for much of that time. Maybe it shouldn't have mattered, given that the inn was over two centuries old and had housed hundreds, maybe thousands, of guests during its lifetime. What was one more?

But it wasn't that simple. Not for him.

While this internal argument ensued, Erin's fingers tightened on his, the heat of her skin briefly bringing some feeling back into his own.

"It's either the inn, or we ask Allan to put you up in the Delphine."

This snapped some sense back into him. "I am not going to ask my fiancée's father to put me up at the resort he owns after she ditched me." He coughed. "*Ex*-fiancée," he corrected.

Erin frowned. "You said it yourself, you have nowhere to go."

He closed his eyes at the reminder. How had he ended up here? Just an hour ago, he'd had everything he ever wanted—he'd been about to become a husband, hopefully within the next year or two, a father, and he'd finally felt a sense of belonging. At peace. Settled.

But now all his dreams had washed away

with the coming of the rain…and Tessa's desertion.

The Delphine and the Moontide were the only two hotels in town. The Lodge had boarded up its doors last year. So he could either drive an hour outside of town and use his credit card to put himself up at a motel on the outskirts until he could figure out his next move, or he could go begging Allan Worth for a free room at the Delphine.

He was sure his father-in-law—correction, his ex-fiancée's dad—would have let him stay in the suite he and Tessa were meant to have for their wedding night, but no way did he want to set foot in that room now. Nor did he want to stay at the Delphine at all, where the staff and Tessa's family could take note and whisper about him behind his back.

That only left the Moontide.

Erin stood there patiently, letting him sort through his options before she spoke up once more.

"It would make Aunt Lenora happy," she pointed out. "She's always said that the years you lived there were some of her happiest."

He hadn't lived at the Moontide since he was eighteen years old. Other than a handful of visits, he hadn't spent any length of time at the bed-and-breakfast since he and Gavin had lived there as teenagers.

"She's missed having you under her roof," Erin added.

He swallowed, not daring to voice the question that rose unbidden.

And you, Erin? Did you ever miss me?

He quashed the thought as quickly as it came. There was no point in thinking along these lines. He had spent several long years burying that question as deeply as he could. The only reason it surfaced now, he told himself, was because he was feeling vulnerable and betrayed. But he would not even consider the subject because it no longer mattered.

His heart protested, whispering, *It does matter. It's always mattered.*

But he ignored his heart's cry and tugged his hand free of Erin's.

"All right. If Lenora has a room to spare, I'll come to the Moontide."

Erin looked at him so intently that he shifted away from her.

"But only tonight, Erin. Just until I get things sorted out."

Erin didn't argue with him, and no matter

how hard he tried to bury the feeling, part of him wished she would.

THE UNEXPECTED STORM had blown over, but it left behind a few threadbare clouds and an unseasonal chill in the summer air. Erin laid out Kitt's long-sleeved pajamas and left him to dress for bed before checking in on Burke.

Her brother-in-law had collapsed onto the bed in the Galway Room, one of the Moontide's middle-size bedrooms, as soon as they had returned home from the Delphine.

As she peeked inside the door he'd left ajar, she could see he hadn't moved from where she'd left him, and the gentle rise and fall of his chest told her he'd fallen into a sound sleep. She moved into the room and opened the armoire, pulling out one of the family afghans, knitted years ago by Aunt Lenora's grandmother.

She buried her face briefly into the soft, worn cotton, inhaling the scents of lavender and cedar from the armoire's interior before she unfolded it and stepped toward the bed. She draped the blanket over Burke's sleeping form, arranging it carefully, the same as she did for Kitt when he fell asleep on the couch while reading.

She lingered in the room, tidying up small details like centering the pair of porcelain songbird figurines sitting slightly askew on the fireplace mantel, pushing the ceramic pitcher and basin on the bedside table away from the edge and tugging a stray cobweb free of the wooden desk chair.

At one time, Aunt Lenora kept a girl on the payroll to come in twice a week for detailed cleaning of the rooms at the B&B. But in the last year, the inn's revenue had dropped so much that she'd been forced to try to clean the rooms herself. At eighty-nine, scrubbing floors and washing windows had taxed the older woman to her limits. When Erin had come upon her one day, leaning on the wardrobe in the Killarney Suite and heaving for breath, she had known it was time to take over.

The next day, she'd given Connor her two-week notice at the restaurant and began working at the inn full-time. She booked the reservations (though there were fewer than there once had been), made the morning breakfast (and lamented how much food was wasted), kept up with the piles of laundry that a B&B generated and cleaned the rooms, all while raising Kitt on her own and keeping an eye on Aunt Lenora.

The older woman had reluctantly given over much of the B&B's maintenance to Erin, but that didn't mean she'd retired. On any given day, Aunt Lenora could be found outside in the garden, tending to vegetables and flowers or crawling up into the attic to go through the expansive mementos stored in its rafters.

Erin had found her there just last week, after hours of searching. She'd fallen asleep in the attic's drafty environment, curled up in a pile of blankets with her arms wrapped around an album. After waking Aunt Lenora, Erin returned to the attic to restore order and found the album lying open.

It was a scrapbook of Gavin's life with pressed clippings of his high school wrestling career, a copy of his graduation program, the *Findlay Roads Courier*'s article about his time in the army and then, at the back, his obituary.

Erin hadn't needed to read the words. She knew each one by heart.

Sergeant Gavin Daniels passed into eternal rest this past week at the age of thirty-two.

She and Aunt Lenora had decided to leave

the specific details of his passing out of the paper, for Kitt's sake more than anything. It had been bad enough that her son had lost his father. She wanted to shelter him as much as possible from the senselessness of Gavin's death by a drunk driver.

The obituary had gone on to list Gavin's various accomplishments in the army before detailing what Erin considered the most important part of his life's summation.

Gavin leaves behind his wife, Erin, and his son, Kitt, as well as a great-aunt, Lenora, and a brother, Burke, along with many friends who will forever miss his spirit, laughter and kindness.

In the stifling air of the attic, Erin had started to cry, and even now, recalling the words, she had to blink back tears. That final statement had been truer than she might have known. She missed Gavin more with each passing day.

Her grief was cut short as Burke groaned in his sleep, and Erin turned back toward him. His face was lined with emotion, his brow furrowed in slumber.

She bit her lip, her feelings a tangled mess. On the one hand, she felt sympathy for the way the day had gone. He and Tessa had seemed like the perfect couple. She was petite and blonde, cute and sweet, and a lovely foil to Burke's tall, muscular physique, brown hair and blue eyes. They were easy around each other. Burke would often drape an arm around Tessa's shoulders as she leaned into him. The sight had always pierced Erin with a pang of envy, and she told herself it was the residual grief of losing Gavin.

But after today, she was forced to admit she wasn't so sure that was the only reason. Because at the root of her jumbled emotions about this day, there was one she hadn't expected to feel.

Relief.

She was relieved that Tessa had fled, pleased that she wasn't going to be Burke's wife. And that feeling frightened her. She had buried whatever she once felt for Burke. She'd convinced herself her feelings for him were long dead. She had loved Gavin, had married him, borne him a son, had been faithful during his years deployed overseas with the army and had grieved him every single day since his death.

And yet…she couldn't ignore how her heart had thumped with joy when it became apparent that Tessa had bolted.

Burke stirred, curling his fingers into the afghan she'd placed over him. She felt herself flush as she watched him.

She shouldn't have felt relief. She shouldn't have been happy about what he'd lost. She shouldn't be feeling anything for Burke at all, except to think of him as Kitt's uncle, her brother-in-law. She had loved Gavin. She still missed Gavin.

But as Burke sighed in slumber, she felt that same rush of relief once more. Biting her lip in frustration, she quickly turned and hurried from the room, down the hall and refused to look back.

CHAPTER TWO

BURKE SURFACED FROM sleep slowly, some elusive memory chasing him toward wakefulness. He kept his eyes closed, trying to orient himself. The bed beneath him was soft, much more comfortable than the flimsy mattress he was used to on the boat.

That's when he remembered. He'd sold the boat, the most permanent home he'd had in the last fifteen years, because he'd planned to move in with Tessa after the wedding.

But there had been no wedding. And he no longer had a place to call home. He was surprised to feel a twinge of disappointment at this realization. He'd never settled before in his adult life. Moving back to Findlay Roads and buying the boat had been the closest he'd come to putting down roots. He'd convinced himself that roots were overrated, and he'd done his best ever since his high school graduation to stay on the move, never lingering too long, never growing attached. Because he knew what happened when you grew attached to things.

Tessa was proof of that.

Why had she bailed on their wedding yesterday? He thought back on the last few weeks, leading up to their big day. She'd been distracted and perhaps a little moody, which was unusual—Tessa was one of the sweetest people he'd ever known. She was kind and encouraging, warm and welcoming. But he'd chalked it all up to stress over planning the wedding. Now he realized that she must have been having doubts, feeling the pressure of committing to him. And clearly she'd decided a lifetime as his wife was not for her.

He felt a pang of disappointment at the thought. He could have loved Tessa for the rest of his life. He *did* love Tessa, he quickly amended. But now there'd be no forever for them.

As he wallowed in this realization, he eventually began to prickle with awareness. The room around him was silent, but he sensed sunlight filtering through the windows. He had yet to open his eyes, blocking out reality for as long as he could. But he began to feel there was someone in the room with him.

He thought of Gavin, his older brother,

who had lived in this house, the same as he had, during high school. And after Burke had moved on, Gavin stayed, marrying Erin and making his home here at the inn, in between his stints of army deployment.

For a fleeting moment, Burke wondered if maybe Gavin was here with him, if his spirit still walked the halls of the B&B. But he knew better. Wherever his brother was, it wasn't here.

Still unnerved by the sense that someone was in the room with him, he opened his eyes. His nephew, Kitt, sat at the end of the bed, his blue eyes intent on Burke. He smiled at the little boy. Kitt ducked his head and didn't smile back.

It bothered Burke. He'd only met the kid once before he'd moved back to town. Gavin's son had been all of three years old at the time, but Burke remembered him as a round-faced, smiling child. That little boy had slight resemblance to the one before him now. This Kitt was subdued, his face already losing its cherubic roundness. He was far too serious for a six-year-old.

Then again, Burke could relate. His and Gavin's parents had died in the fire that had destroyed their home when Burke was ten years old. After that, he'd also lost his ability to laugh. It was Gavin who had kept him afloat, Gavin who had remained optimistic despite years of being shuffled from one family member to another. Burke had survived only because of his older brother.

But Kitt had no older brother. The thought pained Burke, both in his grief for Gavin and sympathy for his nephew.

"What's up, little man?"

Kitt shrugged and scooted farther down the bed. Burke couldn't quite make out his nephew's expression, both from his lowered head and because of morning shadows in the room.

Burke didn't press him to respond. He remembered his own childhood, the dual experience of self-inflicted isolation and the longing for someone to care.

He glanced around the room. This had once been his bedroom, long ago. But after years of being absent, Aunt Lenora had converted it into the Galway Room. He found he liked the changes. He hadn't had many mementos growing up. When he'd lived here, the room had been sparse, the way he preferred it. But now it had a homey, lived-in quality that made him homesick in a contradictory sort of way.

"Is your mom around?" He didn't know why he asked the question, other than the fact that thinking about his years in this house always led his thoughts to Erin.

Kitt gave a half nod and wiggled off the bed. Burke thought maybe he intended to leave, but he only moved a few feet away and settled on the floor.

Burke sat up and rubbed the pads of his fingers against his eyes, trying to focus. He sniffed the air and smelled the tantalizing aroma of coffee. At first, he thought maybe the inn was entertaining guests today, but then he remembered that Aunt Lenora had closed the B&B this weekend in order to attend the wedding without distractions.

"Have you had breakfast yet?" Burke asked Kitt. The little boy shook his head, though he still didn't look up.

Burke sighed, wishing there was some way to draw his nephew out of his uncommunicative shell. Then, to his surprise, Kitt spoke up.

"Mom's making blueberry pancakes. She said they're your favorite."

Burke was startled, not only by the sound of Kitt's voice but also that Erin had remembered, after so many years, that blueberry pancakes were his favorite breakfast food.

"She's right. I love blueberry pancakes."

"So did my dad."

This soft announcement, barely whispered into the stillness, gave Burke pause. "Yeah, I had to eat fast whenever our mom made them when we were kids."

He hadn't thought about that in years, family breakfasts gathered at the table. Those days had passed lifetimes ago. And to remember them brought more pain than pleasure. But he noticed that Kitt had lifted his head to watch him after this statement.

His little face was as somber as ever, but he looked curious now. "What else did he used to do when you were kids?"

Burke experienced a tug of grief. He didn't allow himself to go back to these days. His childhood had been a precious, beautiful thing, and then it had been his greatest source of pain. But he hated to refuse the rare question from his nephew, so instead, he changed the subject.

"Tell you what? How about we go get some of those blueberry pancakes, and we can talk about what it was like growing up with your dad some other time?"

Kitt hesitated but then seemed to decide this was a fair offer. He nodded his head and stood to his feet, padding toward the door. Burke swung his legs over the bed and quickly realized he was still wearing his dress shirt and tux pants from the day before. He frowned, but a glance around the room revealed no other clothing. He'd have to find out what happened to the luggage he'd planned to take on the honeymoon.

And then he supposed he'd have to make time to collect the belongings he'd moved into Tessa's house over the last couple of weeks. He wondered if she'd be there.

It was strange. Though he felt regret and disappointment in Tessa's defection, he wasn't experiencing the heartache he should have felt at the loss of his fiancée. Shouldn't he be more devastated? Unable to sleep or eat?

But he'd just woken from hours of uninterrupted slumber, and his stomach was rumbling loudly, prompting him toward the blueberry pancakes. Of course, he was sad about Tessa as well as feeling the sting of rejection. But heartsick? No, he didn't think he felt quite that badly.

He wasn't sure what this said about him, nor his relationship with his former fiancée. Maybe he was still in a state of denial, numb to the reality of what had *not* taken place.

Or maybe Tessa had seen something he hadn't and broken things off because she realized he didn't love her as well as he should.

ERIN LICKED A stray splatter of pancake batter from her knuckle and then focused on pouring more of the thick liquid into the skillet. She reached for the container of blueberries, sprinkled a few juicy orbs onto the wet dough and waited.

"Are they ready soon, Mom?"

Erin jumped at the sound of Kitt's voice. She hadn't heard him enter the kitchen. But then, he moved like a ghost these days. Just the sound of his voice was a rare and precious thing.

"Almost. Did you wake up your uncle?"

"He did."

Burke's voice startled her more than Kitt's had. But then, it had been a long time since there'd been a man in the inn's kitchen. Not since Gavin...

"Do I smell coffee?"

She turned her attention back to the pancakes and gestured in the direction of the coffeepot. Burke passed by her, stirring the air. The hairs on her arm stood on end from his proximity. The reaction left her uneasy. She'd spent years learning to temper her emotions where Burke was concerned. She was not prepared to give up that hard-won control just because he had spent one night at the inn.

It didn't help, though, that he looked a little like James Bond in his rumpled tux.

Erin resolutely kept her back to Burke as she finished cooking the pancake and put it on a plate. From the corner of her eye, she saw Kitt find a seat at the table. There was a large dining room off the kitchen for guests at the B&B, but this smaller table was reserved for family meals.

She sensed more than saw Burke carry a mug of coffee to the table and sit.

"Where's Aunt Lenora?" he asked.

"Lenny's sleeping," Kitt said, using his nickname for the old woman.

"Yesterday took a lot out of her," Erin explained.

Burke didn't say anything as Erin poured more batter on the griddle and then carried the platter of finished pancakes to the table. Burke reached for one of the plates she'd laid out earlier and stabbed a pancake, serving Kitt first and then taking three for himself. She moved to the pantry and retrieved some syrup before returning to the stove.

"Kitt, after breakfast, it's time for chores."

Her son didn't respond, nor had she expected him to. Kitt didn't make a fuss about things like most kids. If she told him to pick up his toys, he immediately obliged. If she said he had to eat all his vegetables, he nearly licked the plate clean. While many mothers might brag about such deferential obedience, Erin found it concerning. What kind of kid didn't balk, at least occasionally, about setting the table, putting away their clothes or brushing their teeth?

She glanced over her shoulder and caught Kitt watching Burke intently as his uncle made short work of his pancake stack. She frowned as her son practiced holding his fork the same way Burke did, his index finger spread along the length of the utensil's spine. He tried cutting into his pancake in an imitation of Burke and then shoveled a too-large bite into his mouth.

"Slow down, Kitt. There's plenty more here."

Kitt didn't acknowledge her, but he chewed his food with concentration. Burke cleared his throat, as if the admonishment had been directed at him.

"Sorry, I just forgot how good your pancakes are."

Erin turned back to the stove. "They used to be your favorite." She spoke the words before she thought better of them. Burke was quiet for a beat too long.

"Gavin's, too," he finally said.

Erin didn't respond. After another minute, she scooped two more pancakes onto her spatula and moved to slide them onto Burke's plate.

"Thanks," he murmured as he reached for the syrup.

The kitchen was silent for another few minutes as Erin scraped the last of the batter from the bowl and flipped the final pancakes on the griddle. When she was finished, she joined the guys at the table. Burke was already halfway through his second stack of pancakes as she began her first.

"So…" She kept her gaze lowered as she carefully drizzled a stream of golden syrup across her plate. "How are you feeling this morning? About…everything?"

He didn't speak a word, and Erin soon grew uncomfortable with the quiet. She looked up and found him staring off into the distance. His mouth was quirked downward, but he didn't appear…heartbroken. Not like she thought he would.

"I don't know. It's a lot to process, I guess." His gaze fell to Kitt. She slid a glance toward her son, following Burke's eyes. "I guess if Tessa didn't want to spend the rest of her life with me, it was better to find out now rather than later."

Erin slipped a bite of pancake into her mouth as she contemplated this outlook. The buttery flavor of fluffy dough and blueberries melted on her tongue.

"It might have been more convenient if she'd decided that just a *little* sooner," Erin said. But she didn't really intend any malice in the words. She didn't imagine Tessa Worth had a single selfish bone in her body. The younger woman was one of the nicest people she'd ever known.

Erin had found it hard to be jealous of Tessa's engagement to Burke, when they both seemed so suited to each other. After all, Tessa had done what no woman before had been able to since high school—she'd anchored Burke to one location for more than six months at a time. That in itself had proved to Erin that Burke must really love Tessa.

As a traveling photojournalist, Burke had lived in dozens of places over the years, including a few exotic destinations, as he built up a successful career. He'd been published in some of the world's bestselling publications. But he'd taken a small hiatus from his career once he moved back to town and became engaged to Tessa.

So she couldn't quite be jealous, except for deep down, where she felt the sting of resentment. Tessa had managed to keep Burke in Findlay Roads. So why would the other woman abandon the possibility of becoming his wife? Erin found it hard to understand.

She shook her head slightly, trying to shake these thoughts from her mind.

"What will you do now?" Erin asked, both anticipating and dreading the answer.

Burke paused, fork halfway to his mouth, and stared at her. She could see the question bothered him. Perhaps he hadn't given any thought to what came next.

"I—" he started, then stopped. Kitt looked up from his plate and focused on his uncle.

"I don't know," Burke admitted. "I guess… maybe I should try to talk to Tess?"

Erin frowned, uncertain about this proposed course of action. "You could try…but what if she doesn't want to talk to you?" She was ashamed the moment the words left her month. Not so much because of how they might be received but because she spoke them for selfish reasons. She didn't want Burke to speak with Tessa. And she felt horrible for experiencing a certain sort of gladness at the split in their relationship. She spoke again, trying to repair the suggestion. "Or, I don't know, maybe you should give her some time?"

Burke didn't respond. Erin poked at her pancakes, her appetite lost. There was a greater issue at hand here. Erin had invited Burke to spend the night at the B&B, at Aunt Lenora's urging. But she had assumed it would be only that—one night. It wasn't until the light of day that she remembered— Burke had sold the boat he'd kept berthed at the marina. That's where he'd been living for the last year and a half since he'd returned to Findlay Roads. The plan had been for him to move in with Tessa after the wedding, so he'd sold the boat last week and had spent the last two days before the wedding staying in a hotel suite at the Delphine. But where did he plan to live now?

As if her son had read her mind, Kitt spoke up with a suggestion. "You could stay here."

Erin raised her head sharply. From the corner of her eye, she noticed Burke did the same. She wasn't sure which stunned her more—Kitt's suggestion or the fact that he'd spoken at all. He kept so much to himself that Erin had grown used to his silence. The sound of his voice often startled her. It was changing, losing some of its baby lisp and becoming more enunciated. But the fact that Kitt might want Burke to keep staying at the inn was the most shocking thing of all.

"Kitt, I'm not sure—" Erin began and was quickly silenced by Aunt Lenora's imposing voice.

"Of course he's staying here."

For the second time in the last sixty seconds, Erin and Burke's heads swiveled in unison. Aunt Lenora stood in the doorway, a worn terrycloth robe wrapped around her thin frame.

"This is his home."

It had been, long ago. But Erin had to bite her tongue to keep from pointing out how few were the times that Burke had actually stepped through the inn's doors in the years since he'd left.

"Aunt Lenora, I can't stay," Burke said.

Erin's shoulders sagged in relief, grateful that Burke knew this was no longer his home.

Aunt Lenora waved a hand in dismissal.

"Of course you can. So you've been jilted. That's no reason to tuck your tail between your legs and run."

The old woman shuffled toward the table. Erin noted that Kitt was grinning and her jaw nearly dropped. Kitt's grins were even rarer than the sound of his voice. Overcoming her shock at her son's expression, she looked to Burke, waiting for him to shoot down Aunt Lenora's idea. To her consternation, he seemed to be considering.

"But where would he stay?" Erin asked.

Aunt Lenora began stacking pancakes on a plate. "In the Galway Room, where else? It's his old bedroom, after all."

"But what if you need that room for a booking?"

Aunt Lenora took a seat at the table, her movements slow and deliberate. She arched one gray eyebrow at Erin.

Erin dropped her head from the piercing gaze. Even without using words, Aunt Lenora made her point. The inn's business had dropped dramatically in the last year, ever since the Delphine resort had opened up nearby. While summer was usually the Moontide's busiest season, they had fewer than half the stays on the books than they normally did, and the autumn and winter months had been stagnant.

Tourism, especially in the summer months, made up a large portion of the town's economy. Last year, Findlay Roads had been busier than ever. The Delphine had been booked solid nearly all summer long, and tellingly, most of the business the Moontide had snagged had come from couples and families who were unable to get a room at the resort. This summer wasn't shaping up to be any better. It was unlikely the inn was suddenly going to have a flood of bookings, so there was no need to worry about Burke taking up one of the rooms.

"I'm not sure that's a good idea," Erin said in a desperate attempt to sway the way things were going.

Three pairs of eyes turned to stare at her, and she fought a blush of embarrassment. She didn't want to seem inhospitable, but the last thing she needed was Burke living in such close proximity, under the same roof as her.

"I—I mean, it's just that, Burke has a lot to figure out now, and I'm sure he needs his space and, well…and…" She ran out of steam, floundering.

"No, Erin's right."

She relaxed once more as Burke spoke.

"It's probably not a good idea. I can find a hotel outside of town or something. It's probably better that way. There's less chance of running into Tessa."

The table fell silent. The quiet was so deafening that Erin squirmed. Burke was staring down at his empty plate, and Erin felt sick to her stomach. She didn't want him here. But she didn't want him bunking at a hotel either.

From the corner of her eye, she noticed Kitt frowning. Aunt Lenora stood to her feet, drawing everyone's attention.

"You both are being ridiculous. Burke has nowhere to go, and we have an inn full of empty rooms. He's staying here. And that's final."

Aunt Lenora's announcement silenced any further protestations. Erin didn't like it, but while it was her home, she didn't own it and had little say about who stayed and who didn't. Aunt Lenora had raised both Gavin and Burke in their teenage years. After losing Gavin, it would make perfect sense that the old woman might want Burke to stay.

But it didn't change Erin's feelings on the matter.

She stood to her feet, picked up her half-eaten plate of pancakes and carried it to the sink.

"I better get going," she announced. "Kitt, behave for Aunt Lenora." She didn't really need to caution Kitt to behave, but she said it anyway.

Burke frowned. "Go where?"

Erin said nothing. She exited the room, pretending as though she hadn't heard, and left it to Aunt Lenora to answer him if she chose.

CHAPTER THREE

BURKE WATCHED ERIN LEAVE, disappointed by her abrupt departure. It was obvious she didn't want him here. The feeling was mutual. He'd never felt at home at the Moontide. But as much as he didn't want to remain at the B&B, he knew he didn't have the luxury of rejecting Aunt Lenora's offer. He still had a relatively steady income from royalties of his photos, as well as a series of travel books he was contributing to. Yet he was by no means wealthy, and so he needed to get back to work at some point.

He'd pushed off any jobs in order to stay in Findlay Roads and plan the wedding. He and Tessa had agreed that he could maybe start traveling again in the autumn, after their wedding and honeymoon and after they'd settled into a marital routine.

He'd sold the boat that he'd called home for the last year and a half, which left him effectively homeless. As much as he loathed being at the Moontide for more than a night or two, it looked like he'd have to accept Aunt Lenora's suggestion and remain there for a bit longer. He had to regroup and determine what to do next.

"I'm glad you've decided to stay."

Burke looked to Aunt Lenora. She'd resumed her seat and was cutting daintily into a small stack of pancakes.

Burke hesitated. As much as he appreciated her generosity and had no choice but take her up on her offer, he still hated doing so.

"Aunt Lenora, I don't want to put you out. Maybe Erin's right, what if you need the room?"

Aunt Lenora snorted. "Have you taken a look at the guest register? There haven't been any new bookings in three weeks." The old woman slid a glance at Kitt and frowned. "My feet are cold. Kitt, would you be a dear and go fetch me my slippers?"

Kitt looked from Lenora to Burke and back again. Then, without a word, he stood and left the room. Aunt Lenora waited until he was gone before she spoke again.

"Erin tries too hard," she suddenly declared.

Burke shifted uncomfortably in his chair. "What do you mean by that?"

Aunt Lenora reached for the syrup bottle. "She's been trying to drum up business. The local book club meets here once a month. They used to go to the library, but when they started complaining it was too drafty, she offered them use of the inn instead…for a nominal fee that includes scones and tea."

"That sounds like a good idea," Burke said, uneasy about where the conversation was headed.

Aunt Lenora shook her head. "She quit her job, at Callahan's."

"I know."

She continued shaking her head. "That young chef who owns it, Connor…he was sorry to see her go. Told her she was welcome back any time."

Burke didn't speak. Aunt Lenora obviously had something on her mind, and he figured he'd just have to wait for her to reach her point. He'd witnessed it a time or two in the past—when she had something to share, she rambled on with steadfast determination until she reached her conclusion.

"I worry that she spends too much of her

time here. With me and Kitt. She should go out more."

"Well, where did she go just now?"

Aunt Lenora looked sad. "To the lighthouse. She goes there to feel closer to him."

Burke leaned back in his chair. "Him?"

"Gavin."

"Oh." Burke felt the familiar tug of grief… and shame. He cleared his throat. "Why the lighthouse?"

Aunt Lenora shrugged. "You'd have to ask her."

Burke didn't reply even as the conversation faded into silence. Aunt Lenora worked her way through her pancakes while Burke sipped his coffee. He had a feeling the old woman wasn't finished, and his suspicions were confirmed a second later when she spoke up once more.

"You should talk to her."

"Me? Why? What would I say?"

"Tell her not to worry so much about me, or the inn. Tell her it's okay to go out, to be with other people, to be…happy again."

Burke wasn't exactly comfortable with this directive, but before he could formulate a response, Aunt Lenora switched topics.

"And how about you? Have you heard from Tessa?"

The reminder of his runaway bride pierced his pride. "No," he admitted. "I haven't." He'd checked his phone before heading downstairs for breakfast. There had been several texts, expressing sympathy, including one from Harper, Tessa's sister. But nothing from his fiancée. No texts of explanation. No voice-mails saying she was sorry or offering an explanation. Only silence.

"Then you'll stay."

"Aunt Lenora, I don't want to be an inconvenience."

She ignored him.

"I can pay you, if it helps, since your bookings are down—"

"You can work for your keep."

Aunt Lenora knew him too well. When he'd first come to live with her, at fourteen, he was already scarred by too many relatives who made him and Gavin feel like a burden. He didn't appreciate handouts, couldn't abide feeling indebted to others. By offering him the option to work for his room and board, she'd eliminated one of his strongest objections.

And he couldn't share the other one with her.

"I don't know," he hedged, still trying to find a way out. "Maybe it would be better if I just left town. I mean, with Tessa here and all…"

Aunt Lenora made a face. "You cannot run forever." Just then, Kitt reentered the kitchen, carrying a pair of fuzzy slippers. He took them to Aunt Lenora and without a word, placed them at her feet where she could easily slide her toes inside.

"Thank you, Kitt." She patted his hand and met Burke's gaze. "You know, there's some drywall that needs replaced in the upstairs hallway. I think your uncle Burke planned to work on that this afternoon. Perhaps you could help him?"

The little boy's gaze flitted to Burke, his eyes lighting with joy. There was no way he could say no to Aunt Lenora, or Kitt, now.

But he couldn't stay forever. His conscience would never allow it.

THE BREEZE OFF the bay whipped the flag that sat next to the lighthouse. Erin listened to the fabric snapping in the wind and imagined it was Gavin, his spirit reminding her he was nearby. She wasn't sure she believed that, but sometimes, just the thought of him watching over her was enough to get her through the day.

She shifted, settling more comfortably on the bench that offered a magnificent view of the water, and started her weekly conversation.

"So, you'll never believe what happened yesterday. Tessa stood Burke up at their wedding."

It had felt strange, at first, speaking aloud when she was all by herself. She refrained if there were others nearby, but she'd learned that during this particular time of the day, on Sunday mornings, the lighthouse grounds were usually pretty empty. So this had became her time, the time she spent with Gavin.

"Burke stayed at the inn last night. Aunt Lenora insisted." Erin bit her lip, uncertain how much of her thoughts she wanted to voice aloud. "And now she's invited him to stay for as long as he needs, until he can figure things out. I wish she hadn't. I don't want him living there. He's never liked the Moontide." She felt a ripple of guilt for such uncharitable thoughts. "I know he doesn't

have anywhere else to go, but it just seems…
wrong, somehow. To have him there when
you're…not."

She sighed and paused in her one-sided
conversation to watch a seagull swoop down
over the water.

She didn't know how to express it. Or
rather, didn't want to speak aloud the real
reasons Burke's presence made her uneasy.
She might have been talking to the air, but
on some level, a small part of her believed
Gavin could hear her. And she wasn't willing to share her secret with him. Not yet. Perhaps not ever.

"Sometimes, I think I'm a terrible person,"
she whispered into the wind. "Burke just lost
the woman he loves, and now he has nowhere
to live. It makes sense for him to stay at the
Moontide."

But his presence is a reminder of my guilt.

She cleared her throat and fell silent as she
noticed an older couple shuffling along the
brick path that wrapped around the lighthouse. They were both hunched over slightly,
their arms threaded tightly together as they
moved along.

Her heart ached. That was supposed to
have been her and Gavin, growing old to-

gether, spending Sunday mornings walking beside the lighthouse. That had been the plan. There had never been any question that Findlay Roads was where they'd make their home after Gavin was finished with the army. It was here that they both had found peace after years of moving around the country—her as a military brat before her mom had settled her in Findlay Roads while she was still in the middle of high school and Gavin being shuffled between family members after his parents' death. They'd wanted to raise Kitt there, to have him know the stability and relationships they had missed as a child.

So much for that, Erin thought bitterly. All because one person had one drink too many and decided he wasn't too drunk to drive. It was no consolation that the man responsible for taking Gavin's life was serving a five-year prison sentence for vehicular homicide.

Erin didn't want revenge for what had happened. She wanted Gavin back. And nothing in the world could make up for the ocean of tears she'd cried nor the sadness that still resided in her son's eyes.

"It should be you," she spoke aloud, now that the older couple had moved beyond earshot. "It should be you, living at the Moontide. Not Burke."

But deep down she wondered if this was fate's way of punishing her for the past.

BURKE USED A utility knife to cut carefully into the drywall surrounding the crack Aunt Lenora had pointed out in one of the upstairs bedrooms. He felt Kitt at his side, though the little boy didn't say a word. But he huddled close, and Burke sensed the child's gaze fastened on his movements. He finished cutting and pulled away the drywall paper to begin chipping at the compound underneath. Kitt leaned in so close that Burke could feel the little boy's breath on his chin.

"You want to give it a try?"

Kitt jerked back in surprise at being addressed.

"It's not hard," Burke assured. "Watch." He demonstrated how to use a drywall knife to scrape off any loose debris then held the handle toward Kitt.

The little boy took it and edged in closer, tongue tucked between his lips, as he awkwardly tackled the repair Burke had started. His attempts to scrape the loose compound free resulted in a few more nicks to the wall.

"Here, like this." Burke took the smaller hand in his and helped guide the blade along the wall, loosening a spray of debris.

"There you go." He removed his hand and let Kitt have another try.

The little boy moved slower this time but with more precision and after another minute, Burke moved away to get the drywall compound for the next step in the process. By the time he sat back down on the bedroom floor, Kitt had done a decent job of clearing the surface.

"Not bad," he declared. "Maybe we should go into business. Daniels and Daniels Drywalling. It has a nice ring to it."

Kitt didn't say anything, but the grin he flashed was the biggest Burke had seen yet from his nephew.

Burke continued the repairs and made short work of applying compound and sanding down the wall.

"There we go. All that's left is to paint."

"How'd you learn to do that?" It was the first Kitt had spoken since they'd come upstairs together.

He shrugged in response. "I don't know. I just picked it up somewhere, I guess." He cocked his head. "Did you ever help your dad around the house?"

Kitt didn't respond but lowered his head. Burke winced. Kitt had only been four years old when Gavin had died. Not old enough to have participated in too many projects around the inn. And given how Gavin had been deployed in the army for months at a time only reminded Burke just how much Kitt had been shortchanged in his relationship with his father.

"I probably picked it up from your dad, actually. He was always good at this kind of thing."

Kitt's head lifted. He followed Burke as they moved into the hall, where Aunt Lenora had mentioned there was another crack that needed to be repaired.

"He could fix anything," Burke went on. "He was like the resident handyman here at the inn when we were teens." Burke paused, remembering. "Actually, I'd forgotten that. Your dad and I both had chores when we lived here. I usually had to mow the lawn and rake leaves in the fall. But Gavin, he got all the repair jobs because he was so good at it. I mean, this house is *old*. So things were always breaking, and Gavin would fix them right up."

"How old?"

"Hmm?" Burke asked distractedly as he searched for the crack Aunt Lenora had mentioned. He found it relatively easily. She, or perhaps Erin, had positioned a small table in front of the worst part to hide it. But it was still visible if you stood a few feet back. He put down the drywall tools and lifted the table out of the way.

"How old is the Moontide?" Kitt asked.

"Oh, way old. From before the 1800s. It was built several years after the end of the Revolutionary War, I think. I remember once this guy came to stay here for a weekend, and he kept talking at breakfast about the archeology of houses like this, how they survived attacks during the War of 1812 and stuff, when the British were trying to take the Bay."

Burke turned and caught Kitt's befuddled expression. He grinned.

"Let me put it this way. This inn has been standing for well over two hundred years."

Kitt's eyes grew round at this number. "Two hundred years?" he breathed.

"Yep."

Burke examined the six-inch gash in the wall, wondering how it had happened and then decided it didn't matter. Aunt Lenora had grumbled often enough about how the more careless guests at the inn treated the house. People didn't worry about damages when they'd be gone by the end of the week. Although, with a house as old as the Moon-tide, repairs had to be expected. A building didn't get to be around this long without its fair share of aches and pains.

"It looks like this one is going to take some work. You want to help me cut out the wall?"

What little boy didn't like the chance to do a little demolition?

But Kitt hesitated.

"You're going to cut the wall?"

Burke laughed. "In this case, it's okay. It's kind of like…we have to make this part—" he pointed at the crack "—worse before we can make it better."

He tugged the utility knife free of his pocket and handed it to Kitt.

"You want to take a shot at it?"

Kitt stared at his hand for a long moment before reaching for the handle.

Burke squatted down next to him and pointed two inches left of the wall's gash.

"We're going to start here." He held Kitt's hand steady and helped him press into the wall.

And then he heard Erin's voice, shrill and sharp.

"*What* do you think you're doing?"

CHAPTER FOUR

ERIN FELT HER cheeks warm with anger at the sight of her six-year-old son holding a utility knife in his tiny hands. The sound of her voice caused Kitt to let go of the plastic handle and pull back, leaving the incriminating object in Burke's hand.

"Hey," Burke greeted her, his tone belying his confused expression. "What's up?"

"What's up?" She experienced another swell of ire and moved forward to pluck the utility knife from Burke's hand, careful to avoid the sharp end. Belatedly, she realized it had a safety mechanism that prevented the blade from remaining out. It was securely sheathed beneath a plastic guard. "Oh."

"Oh?"

She was not about to let this offense go. "What do you think you're doing, giving a knife to a child?"

Burke blinked, his lips parting in surprise.

"I was right here. Nothing was going to happen."

"He's six years old, Burke. You can't let him play with a knife."

"He wasn't playing," Burke defended. "We were patching drywall."

Erin's lips pursed. This was why it was a bad idea for Burke to live at the inn. He just didn't understand. He hadn't been around kids enough. He didn't know what was acceptable and what wasn't. He wasn't Kitt's father—

She drew this thought up short. Of course Burke wasn't Kitt's father. But he was his uncle. And in truth, Erin couldn't remember the last time she'd seen Kitt interact with anyone the way he'd been interacting with Burke a moment ago. Some of her anger deflated.

Some. But not all.

"You have to be more responsible, Burke. If you plan to live here—"

"Whoa. Hold on." Burke held up a hand. "This is temporary, Erin. I'm not planning to stay here long. Just until I can figure out what's next."

These words should have relieved her. But she experienced a pang of disappointment instead.

Kitt stood to his feet then, turned and hurried away, his tiny footfalls echoing through the upstairs hall as he headed downstairs. She sighed.

"What did I say?" Burke asked, confusion evident in his tone.

Erin didn't answer. She wasn't sure what Kitt's abrupt departure meant. Maybe her and Burke's disagreement had bothered him. He wasn't used to hearing Erin raise her voice. He rarely gave her reason to.

"I should talk to him," she said and headed toward the stairs.

"Erin, wait."

She halted, her heartbeat picking up speed as Burke came up behind her.

"Are we...good?"

She tensed at the question, too aware of how closely Burke stood. She could see every dark fleck in his eyes, and the way his lashes started out dark and then lightened toward the tips. Gavin's eyelashes had been a dark brown the whole way through. She swallowed.

"I don't know what you mean."

Burke shifted from one foot to the other, the action moving him just slightly away from her. It was all she could do to keep from leaning in his direction to bring him closer again.

He scratched the back of his head, looking uncomfortable.

"I just meant… I don't want it to be weird for you, with me staying here. I know it's where you and Gavin—"

"I don't know what you're talking about." She crossed her arms over her chest, willing Burke to drop the conversation. She didn't want to think about what his words meant. She didn't want to relive a past that needed to stay buried.

Burke stopped talking when she interrupted him, but his eyes were intent on hers. She blinked, refusing to look away. Refusing to back down. She would pretend as though his presence didn't affect her, that none of it touched her. She was a master of denying her emotions.

She'd had to be or her grief would have pulled her under a long time ago.

She stared him down until his features smoothed out, understanding darkening his eyes.

"Okay then."

She gave a short nod and made to move past him. He blocked her way for a moment longer.

"This is only temporary, Erin. I promise."

She didn't react, and after another few seconds, he stepped aside to let her pass. As she brushed by him, she schooled her features to a blank slate so he couldn't see the turmoil inside her.

AFTER HIS ENCOUNTER with Erin, Burke finished up a few more of the drywall repairs on the second floor. His chores eventually led him to the large windows overlooking the Moontide's expansive backyard. He paused to stare out the window, admiring the gazebo that had been the showcase for so many weddings over the years.

When he and Tessa had first begun planning their wedding, she had suggested the Moontide as the venue. He had been adamant in his refusal, and when Allan had proposed holding the wedding at the Delphine, Burke had pushed Tessa in that direction. She'd broached the subject of the Moontide only once, asking why he seemed to have such bitter memories of the only real home he'd known after his parents' death.

He'd been sharp in his response, snapping something about the Moontide and all it represented for him—family vacations that he'd lost, memories that had been stolen be-

fore they were made. Tessa, with her typical
sweetness, had not taken his tone to heart
but rather wrapped her arms around him and
replied, "Then we'll create new memories,
enough for two lifetimes, to make up for the
ones you never had."

Her goodness shamed him. She'd been understanding, far more than she should have
been, especially because his answer to her
was only part of the truth. The Moontide represented not only the childhood that had been
taken from him...but the woman he'd once
loved.

Even though she'd chosen his brother over
him.

He ground his teeth, conflicting emotions
assaulting him. He missed Tessa. If she were
here now, she'd find a way to lift his spirits
without pushing him to share what had soured
his mood. Tessa had a way of knowing when
he just needed her to wrap her arms around
him without speaking a word. He would miss
having that in his life.

Thinking of Tessa prompted him to pull
his phone out of his back pocket and check
the screen. No missed calls. No new texts.
A couple of email alerts but nothing urgent.

He clicked into the screen and began typing a new message.

Tess, are you...

He stopped and deleted the last two words and started again.

Tess, I'm sorry for...

He stopped a second time but continued to stare at the screen until the light dimmed and the phone went dark. He'd just lost the woman who was supposed to be his wife. Shouldn't he have something to say to her?

With a sigh, he pocketed the phone and looked out over the backyard once more. As his gaze swept the overgrown lawn, his eyes caught on a flicker of movement behind one of the white oak trees. He looked closer and noticed a small foot, moving back and forth, nearly hidden from view but just barely visible with the movement.

Even from this distance, he recognized Kitt's sneaker. His nephew must have fled outside after he'd left him and Erin earlier.

Burke stood there for another minute, waiting to see if the little boy made any moves to come inside. When he didn't, Burke decided he'd earned a break from his repairs and headed for the stairs so he could step outside and check on his nephew.

BURKE FOUND KITT in the same position he'd witnessed from the second floor windows. The little boy was hidden behind the trunk of one of the Moontide's ancient oaks, his foot moving back and forth to the silent rhythm that had betrayed his position. He had a book in his lap, but he wasn't reading. The day was warming up, with only a smattering of clouds in the sky. The rain from yesterday had dried up, and the ground was dry as Burke sat down beside his nephew.

"Hey," he greeted.

Kitt didn't respond, didn't so much as look at Burke.

"I wanted to thank you for your help this morning," Burke continued, unfazed by Kitt's silence. "Why'd you run off? We were only halfway done with the drywall repairs."

Kitt still said nothing. His silence was nearly palpable, his sadness even more so.

"Did your leaving have something to do with...your mom and me?"

Though Kitt didn't speak, he shifted noticeably.

"Sorry, little man. Your mom and I, we... well, she had a good point. I should have been more careful with that knife."

"It's not your fault. I shouldn't have touched it. Mom always tells me not to touch knives."

The words came in such a rush that Burke suspected Kitt had been holding them in ever since Erin had confronted him earlier that morning.

"I didn't mean to get you in trouble," Kitt mumbled, his voice so low that Burke had to lean in close to hear him. He smiled at Kitt's concern.

"Who, me? Don't worry about it. Your mom won't stay mad for long."

He didn't know about that last part. There was a time when Erin wouldn't have stayed mad at him. But a lot had changed since then, an ocean of silence and distance. It occurred to him, however, that maybe Erin needed him more than she let on. Not because of the friendship they'd once shared but because of what she'd lost.

What they'd all lost. Gavin.

If anyone knew what a grounding force Gavin had been, it was Burke. His older brother had held him up after the death of their parents. He'd stepped into the gap of loss and filled it as best he could. Though death had brought instability and grief, Gavin had been the one constant to see Burke through the hard times. Burke had taken that for granted, not only as a child but into adulthood. He'd been selfish in keeping his distance, assuming Gavin would always be there.

But in the end, the brother he'd idolized had been a mere mortal when death came calling. He sniffed, his eyes filling at the thought. He blinked away the tears, refusing to let Kitt see him cry. When his vision cleared, he saw his nephew was watching him.

"You think that's true? About Mom not staying mad?"

He forced a grin. "Are you kidding? How can she stay mad at two of the most handsome guys in Findlay Roads?" He nudged Kitt, trying to draw a laugh. The most he got was the ghost of a smile.

They sat in silence for another couple of minutes. Kitt didn't seem uncomfortable, but the sadness that constantly surrounded him lingered in the air between them. Burke tried to think of something else to say, words that could draw Kitt out of his shell.

"You asked me this morning about your dad, and stuff he did when we were kids."

It wasn't Burke's first choice of conversation, but he found himself desperate to lighten

Kitt's mood. If that meant talking about the past, well, then, he'd give it a try.

"He loved to make people laugh," Burke began, "and he could be a shameless prankster. For years, I thought he liked eating bugs."

Kitt's brows furrowed together. "Why?"

"Because he'd pretend to see a bug, like a fly or whatever, and he'd act like he swatted it or stomped on it to kill it, then he'd reach down, pick it up and pop it in his mouth."

Kitt's eyes went wide. "He really ate bugs?"

Burke smiled. "No. He usually had something else in his hand, like a raisin or a piece of food that just looked like a bug. And that's what he'd eat. But he was so tricky with the sleight of hand that I didn't catch on for a long time that he wasn't really eating bugs."

"What's sleight of hand?" Kitt asked.

"Like when a magician pulls a quarter from your ear, but he didn't really find it in your ear—it was in his hand all along."

Kitt narrowed his eyes. "Show me."

Burke laughed. "I don't have a quarter on me just now, but I promise I'll show you later."

Kitt seemed satisfied with this. "So, what else?"

"What else?"

"What else did my dad used to do?"

"Oh, right. Um, well, a couple of times a year, he'd wake me up early on a Saturday and tell me we had to go to school."

"But Saturday is a no-school day," Kitt pointed out.

"I know, but your dad would always try to convince me it was a special day. Once, he said it was because we have snow days sometimes so we had to go to school on Saturdays to make up for it. I bought into it, and I'd end up dressed and ready to go before my mom finally realized what was going on and told me I could go back to bed. I was usually wide awake by then, which was exactly what Gavin wanted. Then he'd rope me into playing ball or riding our bikes or whatever."

Burke fell silent, remembering how he'd felt, flying along on his bike beside his big brother. Once he was grown, he learned that most older brothers considered their siblings pests. Not Gavin. He'd always treated Burke like his best friend, even more so after their parents were gone. A painful lump lodged itself in his throat. He should have spent more time with his brother while he had the chance. Now he'd never have the opportunity again.

"Did you get mad at him?"

"Hmm?" Burke had to reorient himself to understand Kitt's question.

"Did you get mad at him? For playing tricks on you?"

Burke thought about it. "Not really," he softly admitted. "It might sound weird, but all his teasing made me feel, I don't know, special. Like he did that stuff because he wanted to make me laugh. I don't know how to explain it."

Burke tried to find the right words so he could explain to Kitt that was just how his dad was. There was no malice in Gavin's pranks. He did those things to lift people's spirits. His brother had been one of the most bighearted people he'd ever known.

"No one laughs anymore, now that he's gone," Kitt said.

The words were like an arrow, straight through Burke's heart. "It's hard, losing someone you love. Your dad and I lost both our mom and dad. We were older than you when it happened though. It takes time, but I promise, Kitt, you will learn to laugh again."

Kitt didn't look convinced. "What about my mom?"

"Your mom?"

"Yeah, will she learn to laugh again, too?"

Burke frowned. He hadn't noticed it, but now that Kitt brought it up, he realized Erin's laughter had been a rare thing in the last year and a half that he'd been back in Findlay Roads. If Gavin had been here, that would have been his top priority.

Making Erin laugh again.

"One day, she will, Kitt. I promise."

But nearly two whole years had passed since Gavin's death. How long would it take for Erin to laugh again?

BURKE WAITED UNTIL after dinner to approach Erin. He volunteered to do the dishes while Aunt Lenora took Kitt into the living room. Erin helped finish tidying up a few things and then disappeared. Burke took his time, rinsing off dishes and loading them into the dishwasher, then wiping down the counters and table. When he felt everything was sufficiently in order, he went in search of Erin.

He found her curled up in an armchair on the inn's veranda, staring out at the backyard. She didn't even look up as he took the seat next to her.

He sat in silence, listening to the chirp of crickets and the distant sounds of the nearby bay. The air was tinged with damp, and there was the faint scent of burning wood in the air, probably from someone's bonfire. He closed his eyes for a moment, remembering many evenings much like this one, with him and Erin sitting in companionable silence. But then he remembered how long gone those days were, and he opened his eyes.

"I'm sorry about earlier today, letting Kitt handle the utility knife."

She didn't speak, but he caught the faintest shift in her posture, a flicker of interest at his apology.

"You were right, I need to be more careful."

She relaxed, some of the stiffness leaving her shoulders, but she didn't look at him. "Thank you. I appreciate that."

Burke let silence fall for a few minutes before speaking again.

"You know, he said something to me today. Kitt did, I mean."

She cocked her head in his direction without shifting to face him.

"He asked me if you were ever going to laugh again," Burke said.

This statement finally drew her full attention. She turned to look at him.

"I didn't realize it until he asked me that, but he's right. You never laugh anymore."

Erin winced. "There's no timetable for grief. I can't just will myself to laugh again."

"I know, I know," Burke hastened to reassure her, noting her slightly bitter tone. "But Aunt Lenora is concerned, too. She said you don't get out enough."

"What? Am I supposed to play the part of the merry widow?"

She was even more prickly than usual tonight. He wondered what had put her in such a foul mood. Maybe it was him. He knew she wasn't comfortable with him staying here.

"Erin, I'm not trying to be critical. You've lost a lot, and no one expects you to just shake that off and be happy again. But for Kitt's sake—" It was the wrong thing to say, and he knew it the instant the words left his mouth.

She stood to her feet with sharp, abrupt movements and stepped past where he was sitting. "Don't tell me how to raise my son. You barely know him."

"But I'd like to know him."

That brought her up short. She froze, halfway to the inn's back door, but she didn't turn around.

"I know I wasn't around much, after he was born, but now that I'm here—"

She whirled on her heel, eyes sparking. "And why are you here?"

He blinked. "Excuse me?"

"Why are you here, Burke?"

He felt a prickle of irritation. Did she want him to relive the humiliation of his failed wedding from the day before?

"You know why. I had nowhere to go, after Tessa…left."

She made a quick, impatient gesture with her hand, dismissing this explanation. "Not now. Why did you come back to Findlay Roads at all? You missed Gavin's funeral. You sent an impersonal card to us and wrote only one sentence. One. *So sorry for your loss.* And then, six months later, you show up here, as if nothing had changed."

"That is not fair," he snapped, rising to his feet. "Everything had changed."

"Not for you! You'd barely been home in years—"

"I lost my brother!" he cut her off. "I lost my best friend! You think you're the only one who has grief to manage? You're not alone in this, Erin. You're not the only one who misses him."

He could see her jaw working, teeth grinding beneath the skin. He couldn't tell if she was searching for words or simply trying to contain her emotions.

"But don't you see?" she murmured, her voice raspy. "You'd left years ago, you had all this time and distance already. How can you possibly know what it felt like to lose him, without a choice?"

Burke's tone turned cool, the words low but hard. "But I do know. You forget that I lost both my parents without a choice. And then my brother, too. Without a choice."

Erin's jaw clenched tight, and he could tell she was holding back the things she wanted to say. He knew the expression well. It had haunted him for a long time. It was the same countenance she'd worn over the years, during the handful of times he'd come back to town. It was part of the reason he visited so little—it was a look he hated because it only emphasized the distance that had grown between them when they had once been so close.

When she finally spoke, she said nothing more about Gavin but rather warned, "Just don't get so close to Kitt that you break his heart when you leave."

With that, she turned on her heel and headed back inside, leaving him to wonder just whose heart she was really worried about him breaking.

CHAPTER FIVE

THE FIGHT WITH Burke stayed with Erin for days. She spent Sunday night tossing and turning, following their heated exchange, and after running a few errands the next morning, she spent the entire drive back to the B&B voicing her frustration to her car's empty interior. She cleaned the inn's bedrooms with unnecessary force, carefully checking the hall before moving on to another room so she didn't run into Burke as he emerged from the Galway Room.

When she was finally forced to face him as they all sat down to dinner on Monday evening, she kept her tone polite but cool and didn't engage him in conversation. Aunt Lenora carried the dinnertime dialogue anyway, chattering more than she had in months, about the weather, the influx of summer tourists, local news and the repairs Burke had undertaken on the inn. She praised her great-nephew for the work he'd done, and while

Erin knew she should have added her appreciation, she couldn't bring herself to speak up. She was too busy fuming.

It bothered her that she was still so angry, especially by Wednesday when she didn't understand why she couldn't let go of her frustration with her brother-in-law. Why did she care what Burke thought? True, they had once been friends...more perhaps...but those days were long past, and she had convinced herself years ago that none of it had mattered.

Then why did Burke's presence unnerve her so? And why was she reliving their argument, at least a dozen times a day?

The Moontide had guests arriving on Thursday, and Erin was putting final touches on the upstairs bedrooms when she ran into Burke in the hall.

He'd been working tirelessly all week, doing minor repairs and updates to the house. The Moontide had been around for a long time, and while it had undergone extensive renovations over the years, it had been too long since some necessary upkeep had been done. Erin was impressed with how much Burke had accomplished over the last five days since he'd come to stay. She suspected he was keeping busy to take his mind off his failed wedding, but a small part of her wondered if he was working to avoid her as much as she was trying to avoid him.

When they stumbled across each other in the hall—quite literally, since Erin tripped over the edge of a loose piece of carpet—she fell right into his arms, as he tried to keep her from falling.

"Hey, sorry, I was just getting ready to fix that carpet."

She was too aware of his arms around her, one hand on her back, the heat of his palm seeping through her shirt and into her skin. She pulled away and righted herself.

"It's fine."

She turned to go, and she might have pretended not to hear him calling her name, if his voice hadn't taken on such a pleading tone.

"Erin."

She paused, willing herself to keep moving forward. She didn't want to hear what he had to say. And yet…she did.

"Can we talk?"

She should have told him no. She should have said they had nothing to talk about. He would move on soon enough—there was no point in putting her faith in Burke. He'd already proven it was a lost cause.

But no matter the reasons, she couldn't convince herself to walk away from him. She turned.

"Okay. What do you want to talk about?"

Her agreement must have surprised him because he looked unexpectedly flustered. A small smile stole its way onto her mouth. It was gratifying to put Burke off his guard. Her tiny grin must have soothed his uneasiness because his shoulders relaxed.

"I thought we could talk about what happened on Sunday night."

"All right," she agreed. "So talk."

He drew a deep breath, some of the tension stealing back into his shoulders.

"I'm sorry I wasn't here," he said, "for the funeral. And I'm sorry for how long it took me to come back, after Gavin died. It was self-serving and wrong and..." He sighed. "I just couldn't deal. I couldn't come back here. As long as I stayed away, nothing had changed. Gavin was still alive. I knew that the minute I set foot in Findlay Roads, I'd know he was really gone. I'd sense it. And then, I'd have to learn to accept it."

Her eyes filled with tears. "It took you six months. Six months. I needed you here."

Saying those words triggered some sort of

release. Months of pent-up emotion suddenly found their way to the surface, and she began to weep.

"I was alone, Burke. You were the only one—" her breath hitched on a sob "—who could have understood what losing him did to me."

He didn't say anything, and she feared she'd pushed him too far. But she couldn't see through the blur of her own tears. She wouldn't blame him if he thought her selfish. It had been nearly two years since Gavin's death, while it had been less than a week since Tessa had left him at the altar. Not the same in terms of grief, but she knew he still had to be smarting from the rejection.

Before she could open her mouth to apologize, she found herself back in his arms. He wrapped them so tightly around her that for a minute, she lost her concentration and couldn't remember what had set her crying in the first place.

Within seconds, it came back to her and the stability of Burke's embrace released another flood of tears. This was what she had needed, two years ago. Someone to hold her, to remind her she was not as alone in the world as she felt. She needed some essence of Gavin, some small thread to cling to. It was why she had often gone into Kitt's room at night, long after he'd fallen into a restless sleep, and wrapped her arms tightly around him. Kitt was a piece of Gavin, an anchor to keep her tethered to this life, no matter how much she might want to drift away.

On some level, she had known it was wrong to wish for Burke during those dark days. Her emotions had been a torment of guilt for wanting him there and anger that he hadn't come back.

Even now, the sharp claws of shame dug into her, but she couldn't pull away. His hand stroked her back in slow, soothing movements, and she felt some tension drain out of her. It felt good to be held like this, to feel so safe and secure. She let her head rest against his chest, counting the steady beats of his heart as the crown of her head brushed against his jaw.

She didn't know how long they stood like that. Far longer than what was appropriate, she knew, but she didn't want him to let her go. She finally shifted, trying to turn her head to look at him, and her lips came in perilously close contact to his. He froze, and so did she, only a breath apart.

She wanted him to kiss her. She wanted to remember what it was like to be loved, wanted. Her eyes slid closed, and she willed herself to walk away from him. But she couldn't.

"Erin?"

The sound of Aunt Lenora's voice broke the spell. Erin and Burke jumped apart at the same time.

"Erin, where did you put the welcome packets for the guests?"

She couldn't look at Burke. "They're in the bottom right desk drawer in the foyer," she called down the stairs.

Aunt Lenora didn't respond, and Erin presumed she'd shuffled off to search the desk for the preassembled packets Erin kept on hand for new arrivals.

"Thank you," she finally managed.

Burke's tone was puzzled. "For what?"

She finally looked at him. He was stone-cold serious, his blue eyes almost gray. His T-shirt was damp with her tears, dark smudges marring the pale blue color. He had Gavin's lips. When she realized that's where her gaze had wandered, she jerked her eyes away from his mouth.

"For being here."

"You don't think I'm too late?" he asked, his voice soft.

She wasn't entirely sure what he meant. Too late for what? To say goodbye to Gavin? To be here for her, Aunt Lenora and Kitt? Or was there something even deeper to his question?

"You're here now. That's what counts."

She was torn between wanting to hear what he might say next and avoiding questions that she couldn't answer. She turned to go and then stopped.

"Gavin would be glad."

And then she hurried down the stairs to see if Aunt Lenora needed any help.

ERIN WAS KNEE-DEEP in a stack of invoices and receipts that needed filing but had been unable to maintain her focus that entire Friday morning. After the roller coaster of emotions from the last week, she had yet to regain her equilibrium. First, her fight with Burke, her outrage over the next several days and then yesterday, his apology where she'd ended up in his arms…

She shook her head, realizing she'd been staring at the same sheet of paper for…six minutes, a quick glance at the clock confirmed. She had tried to make excuses to herself, reasons why she had experienced the insane desire to be kissed by Burke the day before. It was just a reflex, a reminder of the past, a call to her youth.

She and Burke had been so close that summer Gavin had been away, and they'd shared one unbelievable kiss. Her body had reacted in similar fashion to what she had experienced back then. That was all. She was not attracted to Burke.

She could not be attracted to Burke. He was recovering from a failed wedding, a lost fiancée. And she was—or had been—married to his brother. It didn't matter that she was a widow now. Falling for Burke felt like a betrayal of Gavin.

She was simply thankful, she decided, relieved that she and Burke had made some sort of amends and grateful for how he'd managed to draw Kitt out over the last week. As a result of her gratitude, she'd felt…something. That was only natural…wasn't it?

She forced herself to file a few invoices, making a conscious effort to clear her mind from thoughts of Burke. But within minutes, she was staring blankly at her desk once more, remembering the feel of his hand stroking her back as she'd cried. When was the last time she'd been held by someone, been comforted? For so long now, she'd tried to be the strong one—for Aunt Lenora, for Kitt, trying to keep the inn afloat and stick to routines. Kitt's counselor had said routines were important.

But since Burke had come to stay at the inn, their routines had been shattered, and Kitt was happier than she'd seen him in a very long time. Maybe routines weren't all they were cracked up to be. Maybe she needed to shake things up once in a while.

Or maybe it wasn't the routines or lack thereof. Maybe it was just Burke. She'd missed him, all these years, she realized. She'd missed having him as her friend, the person she'd always been able to share her deepest, darkest secrets with. She'd missed that. She'd missed *him*.

"Trying to stare a hole through that desk?"

She jumped at the sound of his voice, turning her attention from the paperwork to see him leaning against the doorframe to the inn's office. His hair fell across his forehead, and her heart gave a little jerk in response. There was nothing particularly inappropriate in the way he grinned at her, but the feel of his eyes on her caused her to flame in embarrassment just the same. With a considerable amount of effort, she forced her gaze away from Burke and down to the paperwork in front of her.

"Just trying to make ends meet," she said and then immediately regretted her choice of words. The inn's struggle wasn't something she wanted to burden him with. He'd made it clear, in the years of his absence, that he wanted nothing to do with the inn. A part of her feared that if she troubled him with the inn's situation, it would cause him to flee. Which was strange because she had told herself repeatedly that she didn't care whether Burke stayed in Findlay Roads or left again.

"You spend too much time scowling over those accounts," he said, stepping fully into the room.

Her frown only deepened at his words. When had Burke noticed the amount of time she spent reviewing the inn's financial statements? The idea that he'd been observing her made her feel a little uneasy but mostly, secretly thrilled. She quashed the emotion.

"Well, you know what they say—it's a dirty job and all that."

Burke arched an eyebrow. "But why are you the one doing it?"

The tone of his voice, somehow disapproving, made her raise her head.

"What do you mean? Who else is going to do it?"

Again, she'd voiced more than she intended. Burke didn't need to know just how much of the inn's responsibilities she'd taken on in the last few years, nor did she want him aware of just how deeply the business was sinking into the red.

"Well, can't you hire someone to take care of the office stuff?"

She snorted, a gut reaction she failed to check in time. "Um, no." She looked back at her desk and straightened her spine. "I mean, it's fine. I don't mind doing it."

Not entirely the truth—the details of office work had never been her thing, but she loved the inn and was determined to bring things back on an even keel. With Aunt Lenora getting older and Gavin gone, it was up to her to keep the business afloat. It had been her and Gavin's dream—to run the B&B, make it their home, raise their children there together and grow old surrounded by its walls.

The inn had a rich history of families who had lived in it—from the time it was first built after the Revolutionary War, surviving the attack by the British on Findlay Roads during the War of 1812, serving as a spot on the Underground Railroad before the Civil War and sheltering generations of families up until the present day. The inn was old, but it was still alive with voices from the past.

Erin ran a hand across the worn, wooden surface of her desk. She couldn't remember its provenance, but she knew Gavin had told her it had belonged to a great-great-great-someone-or-other. Erin might have preferred to be in the kitchen of the B&B instead of the office, but she loved every square inch of this place.

Her attention shifted from the desk's surface to its edge as Burke came over and leaned against it.

"It's past lunchtime. When was the last time you took a break?"

She glanced at the clock and felt a stab of shock. How had it gotten so late? She swept a glance across her desk. And how had she gotten so little accomplished in that amount of time?

"I ate this morning, after the guests did."

Burke arched an eyebrow. "Wasn't that at like seven or eight o'clock?"

As if in reply, Erin's stomach issued an audible growl. Burke laughed.

"I guess that answers that. Come on. It's time you ate something."

Erin hesitated. "I have too much to do. I'll just make a sandwich and eat at my desk."

"I don't think so." His tone was playful but also firm. "You need a break."

"I'll be fine," she hedged.

Burke shook his head. "Erin, you do know you're not good to any of us if you don't take care of yourself first, don't you?"

The words warmed her, a feeling of belonging settling on her spirit. She couldn't remember the last time anyone had tried to take care of her. In the months after Gavin's death, there had been plenty of phone calls, cards, flowers and visits... But it had been almost two long years since his passing. In that time, everyone else had moved on, even if she still felt stuck in limbo. For so much of her marriage, Gavin had been deployed overseas. There were still some days when she woke up and started her day, not even thinking about the fact that Gavin wasn't just away—that he was never coming back.

"It's a beautiful day," Burke pressed. "Kitt

and I packed a picnic lunch, but it's way too much food for just the two of us."

She felt the tug of temptation. "What about Aunt Lenora?"

"Kitt and I took her to the community center for the afternoon. Then we ran errands, picked up some stuff for the picnic."

Erin checked the clock again. Maybe if she stepped away she could clear her head. Although that seemed unlikely given that Burke was a large part of her mental distraction, and here she was, thinking of joining him for a picnic.

"Come on," Burke coaxed. "I promise it'll be worth your while."

She pretended to narrow her eyes with suspicion. "I'm not sure what your game is, Daniels, but I'll play along." She pushed back from the desk and ignored a stab of guilt. She was only taking a quick lunch break. She'd make up the hours later tonight, after she put Kitt to bed and prepped the morning's breakfast.

Besides, she was starving, and she remembered that Burke always packed the most creative picnic baskets. A surge of giddiness swept away any lingering doubts. It had been years since she'd been on a picnic. What could an hour away from the inn hurt?

CHAPTER SIX

WHEN THEY ARRIVED at the park, Burke led the way, carrying the inn's battered picnic basket in one hand and a worn, blue-checkered blanket in the other. The weather had provided the perfect excuse to lure Erin outside—the day was mild for June, with the temperature hovering in the mid-seventies, the sun shining brightly and a faint breeze coming in off the Bay to keep things comfortable, even in direct sunlight. The park was busy, but not nearly as hectic as it would be over the weekend if the weather stayed this nice.

It was one of those days that almost made him forget why he ever left Findlay Roads. Though he'd traveled the world, on a day like today, it felt like the best place on earth was right here by the Chesapeake.

Kitt kept pace beside him, and though his nephew didn't speak, Burke sensed their outing excited the little boy. Burke stopped walking when they reached the lighthouse and then felt a twinge of hesitation when he saw the expression on Erin's face. She paled and tucked her lower lip between her teeth.

"Is everything okay?"

"Um...yeah. Sure. Of course." It was too many reassurances, and he thought about calling her out on it. But then she grabbed the blanket out of his hands and began spreading it on the grass, and he decided to let it go.

Even though they weren't the only ones with the idea to take advantage of the beautiful day by heading to the park, there was no one in their immediate vicinity. A couple of guys were throwing a Frisbee back and forth nearby, a family was circling the lighthouse (likely visitors doing the town's walking tour) and a couple was spread out on the grass a few hundred yards away.

He helped Erin straighten the blanket and then placed the picnic basket on the fabric's edge. Kitt was busy studying an ant mound he'd found in the grass as Erin settled herself on the blanket. She reached for the picnic basket, but Burke grabbed her wrist before she could make contact. He was suddenly in tune with her pulse, jumping erratically beneath her skin, and felt her skin warm beneath his touch. He released her as though burned and cleared his throat.

"Sorry, but not yet."

Erin pulled her hand back into her lap and kept her head lowered. He saw the telltale hint of a blush staining her cheeks and was embarrassed that he'd gotten things off to such an awkward start. He decided the only way to break the rising tension was to push forward with his plan.

"So, do you remember how, on your eighteenth birthday, you were all bummed because Gavin was deployed, and you thought everyone else had forgotten it?"

Her head lifted, her cheeks returning to a normal hue. "Yeah." A faint smile ghosted her lips. "My mom was out of town visiting friends, and Dad never called from wherever he was stationed. I was pretty grumpy that whole weekend."

He nodded. "You wouldn't tell me what was wrong, and I practically had to drag you out your front door for a picnic."

The smile grew, and with it, so did Burke's confidence.

"So I told you—"

"That we were running away to join the circus," she finished, her smile turning into a soft giggle that set Burke's heart to an elevated rhythm.

"And you told me I was ridiculous, that we weren't going anywhere."

"But you finally convinced me to at least trust you enough to see what you had up your sleeve."

"So you agreed to sneak out with me, and—"

"You had it all planned," she said. "You blindfolded me, and we pretended to walk the tightrope."

"You did cartwheels on the shore."

"You had cotton candy and peanuts, popcorn and hot dogs for us to eat."

"And the ring toss, don't forget that."

She burst into laughter. "You could not catch a break with that game."

"You destroyed me," he admitted. "I couldn't believe I lost so completely to you."

"And you had that stuffed elephant hidden in the picnic basket, and you pulled it out as my prize."

"Oh, yeah. I'd actually forgotten about that part."

"Are you kidding? I loved that thing. I still have it."

Burke was unable to suppress the ripple of

pleasure he experienced at her words. "Seriously?"

She nodded. "I kept it on my bed, slept with it every night until Gavin—well." She broke off, and he wished she had finished the thought. Until…what? Until Gavin had returned? Until he'd asked her to marry him? Until Burke had left Findlay Roads? It shouldn't matter. What was past was past. And yet, he couldn't resist torturing himself. He never could. He had given his heart too quickly and too fully to Erin as a teenager, and he'd never quite shaken her hold on him.

"So, what's in the basket?" she asked, changing the direction of the conversation, somewhat to Burke's dismay. "Don't tell me you've got a pony in there."

"Not quite. And it's not a circus theme, either. Kitt and I did, however, manage to pull together a few of your favorites."

Her eyes widened. "Really? Such as?"

Kitt gave up on the ants to join them on the blanket. "Let me show her!" he demanded.

Burke let him reach into the blanket.

"We got baby oranges." He held up the fruit.

"Tangerines," Burke corrected him as he grabbed another one of the fruits and tossed it in Erin's direction. She caught it with one hand and sniffed the citrus skin. "Mmm." She began peeling it before they moved on to the next item.

"Hummus and pita bread," Burke announced, pulling the items from the basket.

She narrowed her eyes. "Roasted red pepper?"

"Do you eat any other kind?"

She beamed as he handed her the container and bag of pita bread.

"I made a trip to that farm stand by the marina and picked up a few things like bruschetta, halloumi cheese, olives." He pulled the containers out, one by one, and spread them across the blanket.

"I got to pick dessert," Kitt informed her.

"Because that's the most important decision when going on a picnic," Burke said with a wink at his nephew.

"Oh, that's true," Erin agreed. "There's a lot of responsibility that goes with that. So, what did you choose?"

Kitt fished around in the basket for a second before withdrawing a plastic container and holding it high.

"Cookies with peanut butter chocolate chips."

"I knew I raised you right." Erin reached

out to draw Kitt onto her lap and dropped a few kisses on his sandy brown hair. Kitt pretended to squirm, but Burke could tell he enjoyed the attention. He wondered just how much time Erin had to spend with her son these days, given how much she juggled at the inn.

Burke watched them for a minute, overcome by a swell of affection for them. They were his family. Erin, Kitt and Aunt Lenora were really the only family he had left that mattered. He had no contact with the distant relatives who had shuffled him and Gavin around in their youth, following their parents' death. His parents were long gone. His brother had passed. He needed to appreciate the few loved ones he had left.

Although it was obvious Kitt enjoyed his mom's attention, he could only sit still for so long. He squirmed out of Erin's lap to dig through the picnic basket once more.

"Uncle Burke said we had to get this to drink." He withdrew a couple of glass bottles, and Erin laughed.

"Snapple?"

She took one from Kitt. "Kiwi strawberry! I haven't had that in forever!"

Her little exclamations of pleasure brought

him more joy than they should have. "It was always your favorite."

"I practically drank it by the gallon when I was a teenager." She twisted off the cap and took a long swig. "Just as delicious as I remember."

"And the final touch..." He moved closer to the basket and pulled out a Styrofoam container. "Crème brûlée, specially made for you, from Callahan's."

She stared. "You even went to Callahan's and asked for it?"

He shrugged. "As soon as I told Connor who it was for, he agreed to make some. Even gave it to me on the house. He said to tell you they all miss working with you."

She dropped her head again and fiddled with the peel of her tangerine, tearing off little flakes and tossing it onto the blanket like confetti. Burke knew to tread lightly.

None of them said much for a time, filling the silence by snacking on the picnic contents. After consuming several cookies, Kitt had energy to burn off, and he wandered off to look for more ant mounds. Burke and Erin kept a close eye on him, but once they were alone again, Burke worked up the nerve to ask Erin a few questions.

"So, what happened that you quit working for Connor?"

He reached for the bag of grapes and fished out a few, popping them into his mouth and chewing while the silence stretched between them.

Erin picked at another tangerine but didn't taste it. He waited until she finally opened the box of bruschetta before he dared to speak again.

"So what happened there?"

"Hmm?" She didn't look at him but pulled out a piece of bruschetta and began nibbling on it.

"Why did you leave Callahan's? I thought you loved working there."

"I did." She shrugged. "But I don't know. Life took over."

He tossed aside the bag of grapes and reached for the hummus. "Like how?"

She fished a napkin out of the basket and put the slice of bruschetta on it. He felt a pang of disappointment that she was losing her appetite because of their conversation. And yet, he was curious to know why Erin had made the choices she had.

"You used to say you were going to be one of those fancy pastry chefs," he reminded her when she didn't answer his question. "I thought working at Callahan's was part of your plan to gain experience with how a kitchen works and then eventually go on to pastry school."

She made a face. "Life doesn't always go the way you want it to."

He couldn't argue with her there. "That doesn't mean you had to give up on your dreams."

She didn't respond, and he chafed at the silence. They munched on the picnic goodies for a few minutes, distracting themselves from the awkwardness by observing the park's other inhabitants.

Burke watched as the family by the lighthouse made their way toward the promenade that circled the Bay before he shifted his attention to the other couple relaxing on the grass. They were obviously comfortable with one another, their postures slack with ease. The same could not be said for him and Erin…but he remembered a time when it had been. When their relationship had been innocent, a friendship born of loneliness and shared interests. She made him laugh, and he'd given her confidence.

Or so he'd once believed. Where was that

girl now? Because he knew the girl he'd come to love still lived within the woman across from him.

"I come here every Sunday."

The words were so unexpected that it took him a second to realize she was speaking to him.

"Oh. To the park?"

She gestured toward the lighthouse.

"To the lighthouse. I come here to talk to Gavin."

He swallowed, remembering how Aunt Lenora had told him that Erin usually spent part of her Sundays here. That's why she'd looked so unsettled when they first arrived at the park. He gave himself an internal kick. Why had he chosen the lighthouse for their picnic? It was a beautiful day, they could have picked a dozen spots in town.

But he also knew the answer to that question. The park was likely to afford him a little more privacy, the chance for some quality time with Erin. That's why he'd picked it. He hadn't realized the park would only make her think of Gavin.

"The first time he kissed me, we were standing by the lighthouse." She drew a deep breath. "And that's where he proposed to me. It's always been our spot."

"I'm sorry," he automatically apologized.

She looked puzzled. "Why?"

"For infringing on your sacred space."

Her posture relaxed. "It's okay, Burke." She looked away. "I guess…maybe it's time to make some new memories."

He could only hope she intended for some of those memories to include him.

ERIN DIDN'T KNOW what had come over her. Maybe it was the June sunshine coupled with the cool breeze blowing off the bay or maybe it was just getting away from her responsibilities for a couple of hours, but as Burke drove them back to the inn following the picnic, she felt light and lethargic in the best possible way. For the first time in a long time, the weight of loss didn't feel so heavy on her shoulders.

The day was beautiful. The future still held promise. She didn't know what sort of adventures awaited her, but she thought it might be worth finding out.

She slid a surreptitious glance in Burke's direction and caught him sliding a similar look her way. She stifled a giggle as he quickly turned his gaze straight ahead. But she noticed the curve of his mouth, amusement curling along his lips.

It had been a good afternoon. She had needed a break from the pressures and disappointments at home. And it was nice to be able to spend some uninterrupted time with her son. It was obvious that Burke cared about his nephew. Gavin had rarely been home enough to just take an afternoon to spend with her and Kitt. It was a strange but pleasant experience to have Burke take the two of them on a picnic.

But then came a little swell of guilt. It wasn't right, was it? To be comparing Burke and Gavin like this. Gavin had done the best he could, given how much time he'd spent away. She just wished...that he'd retired from the army sooner. That they hadn't lost so much time together. That Kitt had had more days like this with his dad. But she didn't want to tarnish Gavin's memory with the what-ifs of their life together.

And today, for this moment, she decided none of it mattered. She wanted to be content to be here, to be in Burke's company, to treasure the friendship they'd once had... and hopefully could have again. Burke made her feel as if she could do anything. That's how it had been when they were teens. He'd made her believe that anything was possible, even her far-reaching dream of becoming a pastry chef.

It was funny he'd brought that up again. She hadn't thought about pastry school in what felt like forever. Her life had become consumed with Gavin, their wedding, then their first years apart as she settled in at the inn, then her pregnancy, and by the time Kitt had come along, becoming a pastry chef had seemed a distant dream. Having Burke question her about it brought it to the forefront of her mind...along with every other youthful dream she'd once possessed.

Such as Burke himself. It had been a dangerous friendship they'd established that summer so long ago. She hadn't quite been thinking straight. It was Gavin she'd loved, but Gavin was so very far away. And Burke had proved himself to be a steadfast friend in her hour of loneliness.

Kitt was dozing in the back seat as she glanced in Burke's direction once more, admiring the cut of his clean-shaven jaw, the edge of his chin. All these years later and she still remembered the feel of that chin beneath her fingers, the almost-invisible scar on its underside. She remembered the way he'd shivered slightly beneath her touch and could still hear the catch of her own breath before their lips met.

As if her memories had touched him, he turned to look at her, his eyes dark with a reflection she knew all too well. She felt herself begin to warm in response. Did he remember?

He turned his attention back to the road, and she jerked her eyes away, feeling...

Not embarrassed, as she'd expected. Just... uncertain. But also a tiny spring of desire that would not be quenched. And followed by that, a familiar rise of guilt.

A few moments later, they pulled into the inn's private drive, and Erin felt her heart drop. The emotions of a moment before dissipated. She wanted to look at Burke's face, to judge his reaction, but she couldn't bring herself to do it.

And then, she couldn't bear not to. She had to know what he was thinking. When she turned, the jaw she had so admired a moment ago was clenched tight. His hands gripped the steering wheel with unnecessary strength, especially since he had already put the car in

Park. He didn't seem to feel her eyes on him. His own were riveted on the slender, blonde figure standing on the inn's veranda.

Tessa Worth had finally come to see him.

CHAPTER SEVEN

BURKE COULD ONLY sit there, his emotions in a tangle.

Tessa was here.

What did that mean? For him? Had she come to reconcile? Or to end things? His jaw tightened. Things had already ended. Skipping out on their wedding had pretty much decided that. So why had she come? And why did she have to show up now, after he'd had had such a wonderful afternoon with Erin and Kitt? He could already feel his mood souring.

"Burke?" Erin's voice soothed his ravaged spirit. "What do you want to do?"

He didn't know how to answer that question. "I guess I should talk to her."

Erin didn't say anything. He turned to look at her, but her expression was void of emotion.

"Okay." Her eyes flicked to the clock. "Kitt and I should probably head over to the community center to pick up Aunt Lenora anyway. There are some leftover banana walnut muffins in the kitchen, if you want to offer Tessa something to eat."

Erin, ever the proper hostess. But he didn't think it was going to be the kind of visit where they had coffee and pastries and talked about old times.

He tugged on the car's door handle and began to exit the vehicle.

"Burke—"

He paused at the sound of his name, waiting for Erin to finish whatever she'd started to say. He looked at her.

"Just...good luck."

He nodded but didn't say anything more. Once he climbed out of the car, he headed in Tessa's direction. He was only dimly aware of Erin switching seats in the car and then backing out of the driveway. He didn't hear her drive off right away, and when he neared the porch, he tossed a glance over his shoulder. Erin was still positioned at the end of the drive, watching. When she met his gaze, she shifted her attention and pulled away and back into the street.

Burke approached the porch and looked up into the face of the woman he'd intended to marry. Tessa stared down at him, her expression somber.

"I'm sorry."

They were the first words out of her mouth, and he had to admit, they soothed him a bit.

"Are you okay?" he asked.

She didn't answer right away, and that bugged him a little.

"Where did you go, Tessa? Where have you been all this time?"

She licked her lips and lowered her face. Her blond hair was plaited into a braid that fell just past her hunched shoulders. Several strands of hair had come loose in the breeze and fluttered around her face. She looked... defeated.

"Why don't we go around back? We can sit in the gazebo and talk. Erin made banana walnut muffins this morning. I'll grab some from the kitchen and meet you out there."

Tessa didn't argue. With a slight nod, she brushed by him and headed around the side of the inn. Burke watched until she rounded the corner and disappeared from view. Then he headed inside the house.

KITT HAD FALLEN into a deep sleep in the back seat on the drive back from the park, which was just as well since Erin didn't want to answer any questions about Burke and Tessa. She drove slower than necessary on the way to the community center, distracted by her curiosity over what was taking place at home and needing some time to sort through her emotions.

Had Tessa come to reclaim Burke? And why should it matter if she had? Erin had no claim on him. They were friends, nothing more. And despite a wayward daydream or two, Erin knew they'd never be anything else.

Tessa was great. Erin had always liked her, long before she and Burke had started dating. She was kind and conscientious, the peacemaker in her family and among her friends. Erin couldn't imagine anyone nicer for her brother-in-law…and yet…

The truth was, she'd been torn for a very long time, stifling her jealousy when she saw Burke and Tessa together. Though she admired Tessa, she didn't like seeing the other woman with Burke. If she was being completely honest with herself, she never had.

She had behaved appropriately. She'd welcomed Tessa to the occasional family dinner, gushed over Tessa's engagement ring and even gave a little speech at the engagement party, about soul mates and how much Gavin would have loved having Tessa as a sister-in-law. Yet somewhere, deep inside, she'd been suffocating on her strangled longing.

She'd wanted Burke for herself. Whatever flame had sparked between them in their youth had cooled to embers during their time apart. But it was still there, banked underneath resentment and uncertainty but still glowing, even if buried. When he'd moved back to town, she'd tried avoiding him, still mired in grief and angry that he'd stayed away so long. She'd kept him at a distance. She'd been polite but cool. But it was impossible to ignore him completely. He was family. And having him at the inn this past week had melted whatever defenses she'd tried to employ. Burke was her friend.

And in her heart of hearts, in the place she wouldn't reveal to another living soul, she knew she wanted him to be more. Just the acknowledgment of this traitorous thought, however, caused her cheeks to flame. She gave herself a quick glance in the rearview mirror and saw Kitt. He was still sleeping soundly, oblivious to her disloyal thoughts.

He's not for you, she reminded herself. Whether he and Tessa ended up together again or not, it didn't matter. He was not meant to be with her. She'd loved Gavin. She would remain true to Gavin.

And besides, how could she even know if Burke had feelings for her beyond that of a brother? Sure, he'd taken extra care with their picnic, and he'd done his best to support her while he'd been staying at the B&B. But he'd kept his own kind of distance over the last two years—first by staying away in the six months following Gavin's death and then by treating her with respect but also a certain detachment after he'd returned to town.

He'd been doing his duty, that was all. He'd come back to watch over her and Kitt in Gavin's absence. It was a way to honor his brother, nothing more. And then he'd started dating Tessa, and Erin had used that as an excuse to bury her feelings even deeper. She continually reminded herself that Burke stayed in Findlay Roads for Tessa. Not for her.

But since his failed wedding and his days at the inn, Erin had begun to reconsider. She'd allowed those feelings to rise once more, toyed with hope and the idea of her and Burke together, even while she knew it was wrong. And now she faced the crushing possibility that Tessa had come to her senses and returned to reclaim her fiancée.

Erin was so mired in these thoughts that when the car behind her honked, she jerked back to reality. She'd been stopped at a red light and had no idea just how long it had been since it had turned green. She quickly pressed the gas and moved through the intersection, offering a wave of apology to the vehicle behind her.

The noise had already woken Kitt, however. She glanced in the rearview mirror again and saw him blinking owlishly.

"Are we home yet?"

"Not yet," Erin said. "We're on our way to pick up Aunt Lenora at the community center."

"Where's Uncle Burke?"

"He's back at the Moontide. He had a visitor."

"What kind of a visitor?"

This was exactly the question on Erin's mind. Had Tessa come as a friend...or with the intent of becoming Burke's fiancée once more?

"So...how are you?"

Tessa's question felt awkward, but then, it

only matched his own discomfort. The easiness he'd once felt around her was gone, replaced with doubt and hesitation.

"I'm...okay." He wasn't sure how else to respond.

They sat in silence for the span of several, painful seconds. Tessa picked at the muffin he'd given her, pulling off the walnuts and piling them on the plate she balanced in her lap. She pinched off an end of the pastry and nibbled at it while he took a swig from the iced tea he'd carried, along with the muffins, to the gazebo.

She finally set the plate aside and shifted toward him.

"I'm so sorry, Burke."

"Yeah, you said that already." He wasn't angry, but his ego was still smarting.

Even though he'd tried to keep any malice from his tone, Tessa recoiled.

"I didn't mean..." He stopped with a sigh. "It's okay, Tess. Really. If you didn't want to be with me, it was better for you to back out *before* we were actually married."

"It wasn't that I didn't want to be with you. I do—" She stopped and he cocked his head.

"You...do?"

Her head remained lowered, and she didn't

speak for a long time. He sensed mixed signals from her, as though she was holding something back. When she looked up again, her eyes were awash in tears, and he felt the urge to offer comfort. But something kept him from reaching out to her. Things had changed between them. And he wasn't sure he could, or even wanted, things to return to the way they'd been.

"Tessa, just tell me what happened. You're not that girl. The one that leads a guy on or gets overdramatic or just...bails the way that you did. If you stood me up at our wedding, I know you had a good reason. And the only one that makes sense is that you just didn't want to marry me. Either that or you were kidnapped or something, but that seems a little far-fetched."

His lame attempt at humor elicited the ghost of a smile.

"That's about the only reason I can think of that would keep a girl from marrying you." This statement was at complete odds with her actions. It almost sounded as if she still wanted to marry him. She offered him a sad smile, and again, he was struck by the feeling she was holding something back.

"Tessa...are you okay?"

Her lower lip trembled. "Don't worry about me." She suddenly stood to her feet. "I just came to apologize. For leaving the way that I did. You deserved better."

He frowned as he rose to his feet. If there had been any resentment or anger left in him, it had disappeared. Whatever had kept Tessa from marrying him, it still weighed on her. If she thought she'd made a mistake in accepting his proposal, it was evident that she still carried the burden of her choice. It puzzled him. But he also knew that her decision was final. He didn't sense she'd returned to reclaim him. Only to offer him closure.

"I hope..." He trailed off. A breeze kicked up, and Tessa shivered, drawing her arms tightly around herself despite the warmth of the day. She seemed to be holding herself together, or holding something back. Maybe both. "I hope we can stay friends."

"I hope so, too," she admitted. "And for what it's worth, it wasn't you or anything you did."

This statement only raised more questions, and he couldn't help pressing for more information.

"Then...why? Why did you give up on me, on us?"

Tessa looked down, obviously unable to meet his eye. "It's complicated, but…things changed."

Her voice wavered with emotion, and Burke could sense her heartache.

"I realized that I can't be the person you want me to be, Burke."

This statement struck him hard. Who did Tessa think he wanted her to be? Erin? He cleared his throat.

"Tess." He reached out and tried to tip her chin up to look at him, but she jerked away as though his touch burned.

"Don't," she said.

They stood there awkwardly for a minute until Tessa finally drew a breath and looked at him.

"I don't want to talk about it. Just believe me when I tell you that you didn't do anything wrong." She swallowed, hard. "It's only that I realized we're not r-right for each other. That's all."

It was his turn to look down. Her words echoed something he'd known for a long time, even if he hadn't wanted to admit it. While he cared for Tessa, he perhaps didn't love her as much as he should have for a woman he'd intended to spend the rest of his life with.

"In that case, it was brave of you to walk away," he said. "And to come here and apologize. I guess I owe you an apology, too."

She shook her head. "No, you don't."

He would have argued this point with her, but she seemed somewhat fragile, and he didn't want to push her more than he already had.

In the silence that followed, a peace settled between them. The mood didn't feel nearly as awkward as it had a moment before.

"Are you seriously doing okay?" Tessa asked. "I mean, I'm glad you have a place to stay. I know you were supposed to…um… move in to the cottage, after the…"

He tried to spare her the discomfort of bringing up their honeymoon and terminated living situation. "It's worked out all right. I don't mind it as much as I thought I would, being back at the inn."

"I'm glad. I know your feelings about this place are complicated."

He gave a short nod to acknowledge this statement. And in that moment, he let go of whatever life he had envisioned with Tessa. It disappeared as if it had been a dream, and he'd finally woken.

"I hope you find your happily-ever-after, Tessa."

Her lower lip began to tremble, and she quickly tucked it beneath her teeth. She drew a deep, shuddering breath before she managed a weak, "Thank you. I wish... I hope the same for you."

She stood up. "I should get going. I return to work on Monday, and I need to run a few errands."

He rose with her. "Sure, and... Tess, if you ever need to talk... I'm still here."

She sniffed and looked away, wrapping her arms around herself once again. "Thanks, Burke. I appreciate that."

He believed in her gratitude, but he didn't think she'd take him up on the offer. There was a finality to this conversation. Despite all their words of friendship, he didn't think he and Tessa would talk much in the future.

"Can I...give you a hug?"

She blinked rapidly. "I'd like that."

He opened his arms, and she slid into them, molding against him as she had so many times before. He felt her tremble in his embrace, and he experienced a swell of affection, more brother than boyfriend.

"Take care of yourself, Tessa." He dropped

a kiss onto the crown of her head, and he felt the tension in her, as though she was holding back a sob.

"You, too." She pulled away with a sniffle and turned to go.

He watched as she headed back around the side of the inn, feeling a strange mixture of relief and regret. He'd meant what he said. He only wished good things for Tessa.

But she was no longer part of his life.

CHAPTER EIGHT

ERIN HAD HOPED Burke might say something over dinner about his conversation with Tessa. By the time she returned from the community center with Kitt and Aunt Lenora, Tessa was gone, and Burke was in the attic, checking the ventilation. Erin had swallowed her disappointment, and while Aunt Lenora and Kitt went outside to do some gardening, she returned to the office.

But what little concentration she'd possessed before Burke had lured her away for a picnic had utterly evaporated in the wake of the day's events. She soon gave up and headed to the kitchen to get a jump on dinner and prep the morning's breakfast.

Over the course of the following hour, she attempted to lose herself in the details of preparing a lemon meringue pie—a dessert she chose because she knew its complexity would require her to concentrate on the creation... and also because she knew Burke liked it.

Once she had the meringue in the oven, she decided to take a break and check on Kitt… secretly hoping she'd run into Burke when she did. Her idea was rewarded when she found the two of them in the downstairs library.

Guests often gravitated to this room after dinner. It was paneled in cherry wood, and the furniture and decorations were all antiques. There was an extensive book collection lining the built-in shelves, including a few sacred titles that were published as far back as 1801, though Aunt Lenora kept those in a locked cabinet with a glass front. The room was cozy, even though it was rather masculine, and it was one of Kitt's favorite spots, provided there were no guests about.

It was only Burke and Kitt there at the moment, and Erin's heart caught at the sight of them, bent together over a book. Burke was talking to Kitt in a low voice, its gentle timbre soothing her spirit. Now wasn't the time to ask about his conversation with Tessa. She lingered in the doorway as long as she dared, marveling at the sight of Burke and her son before she eased out of the room and returned to the kitchen.

There was no other opportunity to talk to Burke until dinner, and she wasn't going to bring up Tessa in front of Aunt Lenora, much less Kitt. It wasn't really any of Erin's business anyway. But she was itching to know how things had gone. Was Burke leaving because he and Tessa were getting back together? She managed to keep her mouth shut during the meal and when she and Burke were alone finishing up the dishes.

Burke had been quiet throughout dinner—except to comment on how much he enjoyed the lemon meringue—and had remained so even now as they stood side by side at the kitchen sink.

She didn't sense any unhappiness from him, just a subdued thoughtfulness. And as much as she wanted to know what Tessa had said, she rather enjoyed the comfortable quiet between them. It was one of the things she had appreciated most about their friendship when they were younger—they could just sit together, sometimes for hours, and never utter a word. It made her feel safe, somehow, and settled, as though she was so obviously a part of Burke's life that he could just *be* when he was around her, without the need to fill the gaps in conversation.

So she savored the silence and didn't approach Burke until later that night, after the dinner dishes had been washed, loaded in the dishwasher and she'd finished up the last of the breakfast prep for the morning. Only then did she check on Kitt, making sure he'd bathed and brushed his teeth and was curled up with a book, and then she headed outside, drawn by the light of the back porch that told her Burke was probably outside looking up at the stars.

She stepped onto the veranda and nearly gasped at how much the temperature had dropped since the sun had gone down. It was downright chilly for a June evening. A quick scan of the backyard, illuminated by the porch lights, showed Burke spread out on the lawn, hands behind his head, staring up at the stars.

She stepped back into the house long enough to grab a lightweight blanket from the mudroom closet and then headed down the steps. She tossed the blanket to Burke as she sat beside him. "It's kind of chilly tonight."

He didn't reply, but he took the blanket and sat up to spread it across his torso, making sure it stretched enough to cover part of her lap, too. The gesture warmed her more than the blanket did.

She looked up at the night sky, still hesitating to speak. Burke nudged her.

"If you're cold, you can lie down beside me."

She wasn't quite that cold, but the invitation was too tempting. Burke stretched his arm out, and Erin lay back, using it as a headrest. He drew her in closer, and without meaning to, she released a sigh. Burke radiated warmth, which was just as well since the ground beneath them was hard and cool.

Perhaps their posture was too intimate, but at the moment, she didn't much care. Besides, she had too many other things on her mind, and she thought he likely had Tessa on his. This thought finally prompted her to speak up.

"So…how did it go today? With Tessa?"

She tried to keep her tone casual but knew she had failed miserably. Her body was tense with interest, and unless he thought it was because she was cold, Burke could surely feel her stiffness.

He didn't answer her immediately, and her tension only grew. He finally expelled a breath.

"It was good. I think."

She furrowed her brow. "You think?"

He shifted slightly, likely considering the question.

"I don't know. Tessa just wasn't herself."

Erin's heart was thumping out of time. "But you didn't, um, get back together?"

He jerked a little, moving to try to see her face. "No."

She experienced a wave of relief and was glad she wasn't standing since his answer made her feel light-headed. In a good way.

"Why would you think Tessa and I would be getting back together?" Burke asked.

She tried to lift her shoulders in a shrug, but it was impossible from her position on the ground. "It's just that you were really quiet at dinner, as if you had a lot on your mind."

"That doesn't mean Tessa and I reconciled. Only that I have a lot to consider now."

Erin wanted to express her happiness, but at the same time, it felt wildly inappropriate. She shouldn't be so thrilled that Tessa and Burke were finished. But she was. She couldn't imagine why any woman would turn down Burke, but then, hadn't she done the same when she was younger? Of course, she'd had a very good reason. Gavin. She assumed Tessa had her reasons, as well.

"It couldn't have been easy for her to come

here." Erin bit her lip, thinking how awkward she would have felt were she in Tessa's position. It had been brave of her to seek Burke out, although Erin also felt Tessa owed him an explanation. "Did she say…why?"

"Why she left me standing at the altar?" he supplied, seemingly not in the least disturbed by the inquiry. "No, not really. I think she came to offer her apologies in person. And to say goodbye."

"Oh."

"Yeah."

They fell into a comfortable silence once more. Erin closed her eyes and breathed deeply, inhaling the cool smell of the summer night, the fresh earthiness of the ground beneath them and Burke's own spicy, woody scent. She grew drowsy and content until his earlier statement made her curious.

"What did you mean when you said you have a lot to consider now?"

Burke didn't answer immediately, and she felt herself growing more rigid with each second that ticked by.

"I guess it's just that I had this entire future mapped out. Marry Tessa. Settle down. Restructure my career so I didn't have to be away so much. Have a few kids," he whispered. "That was what I was looking forward to most. Becoming a dad."

This came as a surprise to Erin.

"I didn't know you wanted kids," she whispered.

"Oh yeah," he answered, his voice equally as soft. "Tessa and I talked about it all the time. She wanted a bunch of kids and so did I. I think that's one thing that really helped us click—when we found out how much we both love children."

Erin felt the stirrings of jealousy once more. Even though his relationship with Tessa was finished, she couldn't help but feel resentful of the other woman and the fact that she'd almost been the mother of Burke's children.

The emotion frightened her. She was becoming entirely too possessive of Burke. Emotions that she'd kept in check for years were rising to the surface. Burke was not hers. And she had no right to the jealousy she felt. But now that the danger had passed, just the thought of Burke being married to Tessa left a deep and hollow place in her stomach. She shuddered.

"You're still cold?" Burke questioned and tugged her even closer so that her cheek now rested on his shoulder, her lips a mere inch from his jaw. He used his free arm, the one that didn't hold her against him, to rearrange the blanket that covered him.

Erin could have spoken up, told him she wasn't really that cold, but her voice refused to speak the words. She felt a ripple of shame as she burrowed closer into Burke's side but not guilty enough to pull back.

Erin wasn't sure how long they lay together like that. The night was peaceful, the sky clear, though she wasn't looking at it. She would have had to turn her head away from Burke, and she was far too content resting her head on his shoulder, her arms pressed against his side.

Finally, after an indeterminate amount of time had passed, she said, "I'm sorry."

"I'll be all right," he replied, his voice a soft rumble in her ear. "I'm glad Tessa didn't go through with it, if it's not what she wanted."

"No, I don't mean that. I mean, I do." She forced herself to move, rolling over and shifting her arms beneath her so that she could lean on them as she looked down into Burke's face. "I mean, yes, I'm sorry about you and Tessa. But more than that... I'm sorry for the way things happened between us, fifteen years ago."

His eyes widened, and even in the dusky light, the blue in them was bright and clear. He watched her intently, hanging on her every word. It nearly made her blush.

"When Gavin came back from his army training and asked me to marry him, I couldn't say no."

"You loved him," Burke stated, his voice low and sad with finality.

"I did," Erin agreed, "I loved him very much. But that's not to say that I didn't love you, too."

"Just not as much," Burke said, and she could see that he was misinterpreting what she was trying to tell him.

"Not less," she said. "Just differently. Gavin had been my world for a year already at that point. I never expected for you and I to become as close as we did while he was gone. If I had known how things would happen, I probably wouldn't have hung out with you at all during those months he was away. But I wouldn't trade that time for anything."

Now the color in his eyes darkened to match the night sky, the blue deep and fathomless. She stared into them, feeling herself fall.

"Erin," he said her name, the sound of it

rough and yet gentle on his tongue. Her eyes closed, and she leaned lower.

There was a part of her that resisted, crying out in protest that she had to pull back before it was too late, but the greater part urged her on. And she felt Burke arch his neck to meet her, their lips brushing softly at first and then fiercely.

Fifteen years of curiosity and longing finally found its way to the surface, and the next thing Erin knew, Burke was sitting up and sweeping her into his arms. Perhaps to be sure she couldn't pull back. Not that she had any intention of doing so. Burke cradled her so that she could push back at any moment but tightly enough that she knew he didn't want to stop kissing her. She had never felt so secure, so protected…not even with Gavin.

The thought of her deceased husband caused her to hesitate, and she pulled her lips from Burke's briefly. She met his eyes and felt a shock of pleasure at how he was looking at her right now. She licked her lips, swollen and bruised from Burke's attention, the taste of him lingering in her mouth. And then she pressed her mouth to his once more, abandoning all sense of what was appropriate.

She wanted him to hold her, she wanted to

remember what it was to be cherished. And Burke filled that need, running a hand along her back as they kissed until they were both out of breath.

When they finally broke apart, he placed his palm on her cheek. "Don't freak out on me."

She allowed him a small smile. "I'm not freaking out."

His shoulders sagged in relief. "Good."

To show him she meant it, she burrowed into his side once more, and when his arm came around her, she moved to press a kiss onto his jaw. Erin didn't know how long they sat like that, silent but content as they held each other and watched the stars twinkle and shine.

ERIN COULDN'T STOP SMILING. She knew the book club ladies probably wondered about her cheery disposition. If only they knew that it had nothing to do with the beautiful summer morning and everything to do with Burke's kiss the night before.

She bit her lip as she remembered, nudging away the ripple of guilt that accompanied the memory. She would not feel badly about it, she'd decided in the wee hours of the morning. Besides, she'd promised Burke she wouldn't "freak out." And she wouldn't. There was nothing wrong with kissing Burke. Not really. And besides, he was an even better kisser now than he had been when they were eighteen.

"Is everything all right, dear?"

Erin realized she'd been grinning at the pot of tea she held in her hand for far too long. She'd already refilled each of the china teacups for the book club attendees and only had dregs left in the pot.

"Everything's fine, Mrs. Cleary. Would you like me to brew another pot of tea?"

"In a bit. First let's finish our discussion on the motives behind Gerald leaving Sophia."

Erin finished distributing shortbread cookies around the table and resumed her seat. It wasn't necessary for her to sit in on the book discussion, but it seemed to tickle Mrs. Cleary and her friends when she did. And if it meant they'd continue visiting the inn each month, it seemed a small price to pay in the greater scheme of a paying gig.

She grabbed a nearby copy of *Love's Light* and perused the cover. Each member of the group was allowed to choose a book on a rotating schedule. This month's selection had been made by Mrs. Huber. It was a Regency romance featuring a rakish-looking hero and a swooning damsel in distress. Erin flipped through a few pages and found herself engrossed by several passages.

When was the last time she'd picked up a book and read for pleasure? It felt like years. She missed that kind of little luxury. Before Kitt was born, when Gavin had been deployed, she read books voraciously. Now, though, she couldn't even remember the last title she'd finished. She began reading through the first chapter as she let the conversation concerning Gerald and Sophia flow around her. It wasn't until she'd reached the end of chapter two that Mrs. Cleary cleared her throat, and Erin realized the room had gone silent. She placed the book aside.

"Sorry, what was that?"

The little old ladies exchanged a glance, and Erin felt a ripple of uneasiness. Were they getting ready to tell her they'd decided to meet elsewhere for their book club? She hoped not. They were the perfect guests, and even if the income from their monthly book club was small, at least it was consistent.

"Well, dear, as we said, we don't want to pry…"

Erin put the book down.

"Pry about what?"

They each exchanged a look again, and Erin swallowed. "About your brother-in-law. Burke. It's only that we heard what happened, at the wedding, and how he's come to live here at the inn."

"It's only temporary," Erin declared, inwardly cringing at the defensiveness in her tone. "He sold his boat. Before the wedding. He was going to move in with Tessa, but obviously that's not happening. So he's just here until he figures things out."

She bit her lip to force herself to stop talking. The more she said, the closer the group leaned in.

"We haven't seen him about," Mrs. Johnson commented, rolling her eyes around the room as if expecting Burke to be hiding behind the china cabinet.

"Um, well, he's often busy doing repairs around the inn." She picked up the paperback again, hoping they'd take the hint to drop the subject. "Tell me about this Captain Harris. Is he really Sophia's long-lost brother?"

"Not by a long stretch," Mrs. Dennis put in, but apparently not to be deterred, "I can't imagine it's easy having him around."

"Who? Captain Harris?"

The old ladies chuckled.

"No, dear," Mrs. Whitaker corrected. "We meant Burke. Having a man in the house again, after Gavin…" She trailed off.

Erin felt herself stiffen. "Gavin was gone so much of the time, due to the army, that I never really thought about it."

The ladies clucked their tongues in sympathy.

"He was such a selfless, charming man."

Erin said nothing. She had heard this sort of remark many times over the last couple of years.

Gavin had been beloved in this town and rightfully so. But sometimes, she secretly had to admit that she grew slightly weary of hearing others sing his praises. She'd loved Gavin, body and soul. But he'd been human, just like any other man. He had habits that annoyed her. They'd argued, especially about how much time he spent away from home. He wasn't perfect and neither was she, and their marriage had been filled with the same challenges any other couple faced.

But she nodded politely and smiled vacantly as the ladies sighed their sympathies.

"And how is Kitt?" Mrs. Whitaker asked.

Erin relaxed but only marginally. Kitt was

a safer subject, but given how much he'd turned inward since his father's death, even he wasn't her first choice of topic.

"He's all right," she answered warily.

"And how does he feel about having his uncle here?" This, from Mrs. Cleary.

Erin frowned, starting to get the vibe that this was an inquisition. "They get along fine," she replied and decided to leave it at that. She knew the old ladies meant well, but she wasn't comfortable offering up the details of her life for gossip fodder.

"And you?"

Erin felt a flutter of discomfort. "Me?"

"How do you feel about Burke being here?"

Erin pushed back her chair and stood. "I—I think I'll just check on the…mmm…tea. I'll brew you another pot."

"But, dear, we don't need—"

Erin didn't wait to hear the ending of that sentence. She hightailed it from the room without even grabbing the teapot.

As soon as Erin reached the kitchen, some of the tightness in her chest eased. She leaned her back against the kitchen door and drew a deep breath. Why had Mrs. Cleary's question made her so uncomfortable? She didn't mind them asking after Kitt and how he felt about Burke. So why should it be any different for her?

She swallowed. She knew why. And she'd always feared that others knew it, too. That was the problem.

"Erin, dear?"

She heard Mrs. Cleary's voice on the other side of the door. Clearing her throat, she stepped away from the door and turned to open it.

"Yes, Mrs. Cleary? Did you need something?"

The older lady appeared concerned. "No, it's not that. We were only worried that you were all right. You seemed flustered in there."

She forced a smile. "I'm fine. Really. But I appreciate your concern. I was just getting ready to brew another pot of tea."

"Oh, that won't be necessary. Our discussion is winding down. We thought perhaps you'd like to join us as we finish up."

In some ways, it was tempting. Erin liked the group of elderly ladies. Sometimes they gossiped too much, but they were also funny and warm. Yet, given the topic of conversation a moment before, she thought it was better to avoid them at the moment.

"I appreciate that, Mrs. Cleary, but I should really tidy up the kitchen. We have guests at the inn this weekend, and I'll have to prep for tomorrow's breakfast before too long."

It was only an excuse. She could spare a little time. But too many more questions about Burke, and she'd likely say something she shouldn't.

Mrs. Cleary didn't take this cue to depart, however. Instead, she followed Erin as she moved toward the sink. She was a little uncertain as Mrs. Cleary shuffled up behind her.

"If I may, dear, I thought I might speak with you."

Mrs. Cleary moved toward the kitchen table without waiting for Erin to respond. She pulled out a chair and settled herself into it. Erin had little choice but to follow her lead.

"The ladies and I have been talking, and we're concerned about you."

Erin frowned. "Um…how so?"

Mrs. Cleary leaned forward as if she had something significant to impart.

"We're worried about Burke's presence here at the inn."

Erin flinched, feeling an immediate stab

of shame. "As I said, Burke's presence here is only temporary."

"Yes, of course." Mrs. Cleary waved a hand in dismissal. "But surely you see how it looks to the rest of the community."

A spark of anger flared. "What do you mean, the rest of the community?"

"Oh, Erin, I'm not trying to upset you. It's only that it's a strange situation. You are living with your husband's brother."

Stating it so baldly heightened the sense of shame Erin had experienced a moment before.

"But it's not, we're not together—" She stopped. But they were working their way to that point, weren't they? After last night, after their kiss, hadn't that been the direction her thoughts had gone? Her and Burke. Together. She felt her cheeks flaming and turned her face down, embarrassed.

Mrs. Cleary's words had made her feel as though Gavin was still alive and had witnessed their kiss from the night before. She would never have kissed Burke if Gavin were still living. She had been a faithful wife, had buried any feelings she'd ever had for Burke. They'd seen relatively little of each other dur-

ing her marriage to Gavin. She had nothing
to feel ashamed for...until now.

What if falling for Burke was wrong, no
matter whether Gavin was living or not?
Given their past, the feelings that had blossomed in their youth, perhaps that meant she
could never atone for those emotions. If she
loved Burke now, maybe it was no different
than if she'd loved him during her marriage,
whether she'd acted on it or not.

"Burke is a very handsome man. Just like
his brother."

"Yes," she whispered, unable to find the
words to speak further.

"Surely you can see where people would
talk."

Surely, she could. But it didn't make the
pain any less.

"And I worry about you. And Kitt."

Kitt. How had she not put more consideration into Kitt and his feelings on this subject? Sure, he adored Burke. But admiring his
uncle was very different from Burke replac-
ing Gavin, something she didn't really want.
Gavin was Kitt's father. Was it fair to Gavin's
memory to place Burke in the role that rightfully belonged to his brother?

How stupid could she be? She should have

known better, but she'd allowed the emotions of a moment to propel her in a direction that wasn't appropriate.

"Burke will only be staying here until he gets back on his feet," Erin said. Her tone sounded distant, detached. "He's Kitt's uncle, after all. It's good for him to have the opportunity to get to know him better. But I can promise you, Burke is my brother-in-law. Nothing more."

He can never be anything more.

"I'm relieved to hear it," Mrs. Cleary admitted. "And I'm sorry, if I've disappointed you. But better to hear it now before any damage is done between the two of you. For Kitt's sake."

Erin's chest ached, but she was unable to tell the older woman that it was already too late for that—the damage was irreparable. To taste hope, to believe in love again, only to have it shattered.

She and Burke were not meant to be. Ever. It had been a futile fantasy, a brief reliving of her teenage self. She wiped at her eyes and realized they were dry. No tears then. She'd learned to control them well.

"Yes, you're right," she said, again in that same removed tone.

Mrs. Cleary patted her arm, and it was all Erin could do to keep from jerking away. She didn't resent Mrs. Cleary's interference but neither did she welcome her expressions of sympathy.

She stood to her feet.

"Thank you for your concern, Mrs. Cleary. If you don't mind, I'm just going to tidy up a few things here in the kitchen. Please let me know if you or the ladies need anything else."

"Of course, dear. You are such a treasure. It's a shame..." She trailed off, shaking her head. "Such a shame."

Erin didn't respond and waited until Mrs. Cleary had departed before she turned back to study the kitchen, looking for items to tidy up. The photo of Gavin still hung in its honorary place in the center of the refrigerator. She turned her back on it, unable to meet her husband's eye.

CHAPTER NINE

BURKE WAS GRINNING before he even opened his eyes. His dreams had been filled with the scent and feel of Erin in his arms. For a moment, his smile slipped, wondering whether his memory of the night before had been merely a dream. But he quickly dismissed that idea, and his grin returned.

He knew it had been real, every sweet second. He was suddenly grateful to Tessa, for what she had done and for coming to visit him the day before. Without that closure, he'd be feeling very differently this morning. If Tessa hadn't ended things as she had, he'd be married now…and he could see that his heart hadn't been where it should have been. It would have been wrong to marry Tessa. Whatever her reasons, he blessed her for having the foresight to call things off. A part of his heart was still tender toward her, but he could see now, by his reaction to last night's kiss, that a part of him had always loved Erin, all these years.

The question now was what came next. The two of them hadn't spoken of logistics. They hadn't spoken much at all, in fact, had just savored holding each other under the stars. But Burke knew they had a lot to talk about. He hoped after last night, there was the possibility they could begin...well, as old-fashioned as it sounded, a courtship.

There'd never been anyone for him other than Erin, not really. Tessa was the first woman he'd dated more than a handful of times in the last few years. His job kept him on the move so much that there'd never been much chance to establish long-term relationships.

And he'd liked it that way. He'd experienced a lot as a traveling photojournalist, but love wasn't on the list. He'd always figured he'd done that already, with Erin, and though he'd eventually shelved those memories with her, he had never been very keen on experiencing those emotions again with someone else.

Perhaps that's why Tessa had seemed so right for him. He liked her, enjoyed her company and found her attractive. They got along well. In fact, they'd never had a fight. Not once in the year and a half they'd dated and not even while planning their wedding. He'd felt great affection for Tessa, even love…but there hadn't been that spark, the fire he'd once—and still—experienced with Erin.

He pushed off the covers and sat up, his mind still reliving the evening before as he went through the motions of taking a shower in the bathroom attached to his room and getting dressed for the day.

By the time he headed downstairs, the sun had been up for a couple of hours. He'd overslept, and now he was more than eager to see Erin.

He found Kitt at the bottom of the stairs. His nephew beamed at the sight of him, a reaction that never failed to warm Burke's heart. Kitt was a great kid. He was still rather quiet and a little bit subdued, but that was getting better with each passing day. Burke hoped that by Christmas his nephew would be as well-adjusted as any child his age could be for having lost their father so young.

Burke knew it had taken him years to adapt to being parentless. And the loss of his parents still affected him, but he'd had Gavin—and eventually Aunt Lenora—to see him through. Now perhaps it was his chance to pay things forward by giving Kitt a reason to smile again. He was more than happy to do it, even if Erin had not been a consideration. But after last night, he was filled with all sorts of warm and wishful thoughts about what the future might look like—for the two of them...for the three of them.

He tousled Kitt's hair and then looked up to find Erin watching him from the doorway to the foyer. He felt a jolt of awareness, his skin tingling at the sight of her. He wanted nothing more than to go over and draw her into his arms as he placed a long and lingering kiss on her mouth, but he restrained himself. They hadn't discussed anything—having a relationship, revealing it to others and especially not how they'd tell Kitt. He had to play it cool no matter how much he was itching to touch her. But if he couldn't kiss her, he at least offered her what he hoped was a smile that conveyed everything he was feeling.

To his dismay, she didn't return the gesture. He frowned, realizing her eyes were bloodshot, as though she hadn't gotten much sleep.

Oh no. No.

"Have fun at the library with Aunt Lenora," she spoke toward Kitt. "Don't get any more than three books this time, okay? Aunt Lenora will take you again next week."

"Can Uncle Burke come?" Kitt asked.

Burke barely spared a glance in Kitt's direction. He was too focused on Erin, trying to figure out what had gone wrong.

"Not right now, buddy. Maybe we can do something together this afternoon," Burke said.

"Okay," Kitt agreed and trotted off, presumably in search of Aunt Lenora.

"Erin—"

But she had already turned and headed in the direction of the kitchen. He followed, all his earlier happiness dissipating.

Erin stepped into the kitchen ahead of him, and he stood in the doorway for a moment, watching her, the tense line of her back and the way her glossy brown hair fell past her shoulders. More than anything he wanted to wrap his arms around her, draw her into him and plant kisses along the back of her neck. But the stiffness in her posture kept him away, a wordless warning to stay back.

"You said you wouldn't freak out," he said, the words sounding loud in the kitchen's stillness.

She tensed even more at this, frozen for

the length of several heartbeats before she
began to scrub furiously at a serving platter
that looked clean already.

"I'm not freaking out," she replied, but
she didn't look at him. Burke felt as though
a bag of rocks filled his stomach, weighing
him down.

"Then come here and kiss me."

That snapped her out of the coldness she
was radiating. She whirled, eyes wild.

"Stop it!" She sounded almost... desperate.
He took two steps forward, and she shifted,
backing up against the counter as if afraid he
would do her harm. He stopped, brow furrowed.

"Erin, what's going on?"

She was shaking her head, and he had the
sense she was fighting to remain under control. When he saw a tear fall, he moved toward her and wrapped her in his arms before
she could protest.

She clung to him for a moment, her grip
fierce and sure. But it only lasted for a breath
before she pushed him away and held out a
hand to keep him at arm's length.

"I'm sorry for kissing you last night," she
said, but she wouldn't meet his eyes.

"I'm not," he replied, his voice firm with conviction.

"It was a mistake," she went on, "I never should have…"

"Erin, what happened?"

She finally looked at him directly. "Nothing happened," she answered, but her tone said otherwise.

"Erin."

She shifted toward the sink, turning her back on him once more. "You and me, it's not right."

He tightened his jaw, trying to keep his temper in check. "Why?"

"Because you're Gavin's brother—"

"Gavin's dead."

Even he was appalled at the harsh finality of that statement. Erin's head shot up, but she didn't turn, just stared straight ahead. Her back was tighter than ever, a rigid line of disapproval.

Burke knew he should stop talking, but he couldn't. Resentment welled and bubbled over.

"I loved my brother. More than anyone, with the exception of you and Kitt. But he is gone, Erin. He's *gone*. You can stay married to his memory, but it won't bring him back.

It will keep you, and Kitt, trapped in the past when you need to find a way to move forward with your life."

She took several long, deep breaths before she turned, grabbing a dishtowel to wipe her hands as she met his eyes. "You can't love me, Burke. It's not possible."

"Not possible? Or not allowed?"

Her lips settled into a thin line, and he knew he had to tread gently.

"Erin...you said—" He stopped, choosing his words carefully. "I thought, from what you said last night, that maybe you had, or have...feelings for me."

She swallowed, her gaze faltering as she glanced at the floor.

"Were you lying?"

Her eyes flew back to his. "No. I wouldn't lie about something like that." She looked appalled but also extremely uncomfortable with this conversation.

"Then help me understand." She had feelings for him, he was sure of it. But how deep did those emotions run?

"If you and I were to..." She trailed off, her face growing red. "It just wouldn't be right," she finished.

"Why? Because of Gavin?"

She flinched but didn't hesitate to answer, "Yes. Because what will people think, if you and I were to...you know."

He made a face. "I don't really care what people would think. Especially when my happiness—and yours—is at stake."

"It's not that simple, Burke. It's never been that simple."

"But it is that simple. Either you love me or you don't. Either you choose me or you don't. But if we're going on record, I choose *you*, Erin." His feelings for her welled up after fifteen years of being suppressed. "It's always been you," he whispered. "Every single day."

"Tessa?" she questioned, her voice catching.

He gave a nod of acknowledgment. "I cared for Tessa deeply—I still do. But it's different. I have fun with her, and we get along well. But there's no...fire. Not like there's always been with you. Tessa is my past." He drew a deep breath, daring himself to say the words. "You're my future." And then, knowing it was a risk, he said, "Just like Gavin will always be a part of your past."

He left the rest of the thought unsaid for her to finish herself.

Let me be your future.

He watched her struggle with the words, battling whatever had put her wall back in place. Her eyes slid closed, her posture still rigid. Her fists clenched and unclenched at her sides.

Come on, Erin. Choose me. Be with me.

"Excuse me?"

A voice sounded at the kitchen's second door, the one that led from the guest's dining room. Burke's eyes slid closed in frustration.

"Excuse me, I don't mean to interrupt, but I have to tell you how much my husband enjoyed those gluten-free muffins you served at our breakfast this morning. It can be so difficult to find pastries without wheat that are as delicious as the real thing."

Erin smiled, but it looked strained to Burke. "Of course, Mrs. Atwell. I'm so glad you enjoyed them."

"I wondered if you'd mind sharing the recipe with me? It's my husband's birthday next month, and I know he'd love it if I served them."

"Sure, I'll type up a copy and leave it outside your room."

"Oh, that would be lovely, thank you! George will be so surprised."

Burke gritted his teeth. It wasn't the guest's

fault, he knew that. But it was also why he had never loved living at the inn. It felt like everyone else was the first priority. It had to be that way, he knew, but it didn't mean he had to like it.

By the time Mrs. Atwell had finished offering her thanks and left them alone again, he knew that whatever slim chance he'd had of Erin choosing him was gone. He could see it in her eyes as they shifted their focus back to him.

Her expression held a combination of sympathy and regret, and he held up a hand to forestall whatever she might say next.

"It's okay. I get it. I can't compete with a ghost—especially not Gavin's. He was always the better brother."

"Burke—"

"Don't." He hadn't said it to earn her sympathy—he had no patience for pity. It was simply the truth.

Everyone loved Gavin. He'd always had a way of making people laugh, helping them feel better about themselves. Burke counted himself lucky to have had him for an older brother. And he didn't blame Erin for loving Gavin more than him—he never had. It was only that, even with his older brother gone, he was still competing with him.

And he knew he could never quite measure up to Gavin, especially in death.

BURKE FOUND HE couldn't stay in the house after his conversation with Erin. He grabbed his camera from his room and headed out on foot, just to walk around, distract himself, burn off some creative energy. He hadn't touched his camera since coming to the Moontide, but as soon as he had it in his hands, he felt marginally better.

Photography was more than just a hobby or livelihood; it was his coping mechanism. He'd started playing around with it after his parents died, when he and Gavin were being shuffled among relatives. It provided stability. Photos didn't change. They preserved certain moments in time forever. He could hold onto a place, even if he had to leave it. He still had a piece of someone he loved, even after they were gone.

Unfortunately, he didn't have many photos from before his teenage years. They'd been lost in the fire that had destroyed his childhood home, as well as taken his parents' lives.

He and Gavin had been away at a sleepover that night. People said it was a mercy.

Burke had never quite seen it that way. Not that he would have wanted to die with his parents. But neither did anything seem merciful about that tragic loss of life and home and memories stolen far too soon.

He headed right out of the inn's driveway for no reason other than the park was in the opposite direction, and he didn't want to run into Aunt Lenora and Kitt. He needed some time to compose himself, to readjust his thoughts, particularly before he saw Kitt again.

Nothing that happened between him and Erin would change how he felt about Kitt, how much he loved his nephew. But it did mean he'd have to be more careful with his expressions. He didn't want Kitt to guess how deeply he felt about Erin. There was no point confusing the kid. He needed as much stability as he could find, and Burke's feelings for Erin were anything but steady.

It was a fair walk to Fallon Point overlooking the town, but despite the distance, Burke headed in that direction. His thoughts were a mire of uncertainty. He couldn't believe he'd lost Erin a second time, just like he had years before. It made his presence at the Moontide all the more complicated. He wasn't sure how much longer he could stay there. The painful memories of his teenage years at the inn, combined with Erin's rejection, would make it even harder to be within its walls.

So he faced the question he'd been avoiding ever since he'd realized Tessa wasn't walking down the aisle: Where did he go now?

Financially, he was doing fine. He'd kept up with his photography, but his direction had shifted to subjects within a hundred-mile radius rather than exotic locales. The market for these wasn't quite as lucrative as international photos, but he'd been in the business long enough and had established enough of a reputation that he did all right. Plus, he was under contract for a series of travel guides with an international publisher. He continued to receive steady royalties from his photos that had been used in travel brochures, advertisements and campaigns, as well as other well-known publications, and his savings account was healthy thanks to the years he'd spent traveling, when the largest expenses he'd incurred had been camera equipment and accessories.

But the question remained—what did he

do now? If he stayed in Findlay Roads, he couldn't continue living at the inn. The inn had never quite been home to him, and now, with Erin...

He didn't know if he could bear to see her, day in and day out, living some sort of detached existence together. Especially not after last night's kiss.

He forcefully steered his thoughts away from that encounter. Kissing Erin had been the single best experience of his life, not once but now twice. If he dwelt too long on it, knowing how she felt about him, he'd sink into depression.

He paused to take a few photographs, losing himself in capturing several frames. By the time he'd finished and begun walking once more, he felt at least slightly re-centered.

The most looming question he faced right now was whether he should even stay in Findlay Roads.

He'd returned a year and a half ago because he'd been worried about Erin and Kitt. And because he'd never come back to say goodbye to Gavin. He hadn't been sure how long he'd stay in town, but after he met Tessa and they began dating, it seemed like maybe this was where he was meant to be after all.

Now, though, he wasn't so sure. He'd been rejected, not just by one woman but two. And while he was grateful to Tessa for having the courage to break things off, he was sad about Erin. And what did this say about him? Maybe he shouldn't be here. This town represented too much heartbreak and disappointment for him.

But even if Erin didn't want him around, what about Kitt? Could he really just abandon his nephew, especially after he'd managed to draw Kitt out a little more? He wasn't sure he could. If not for Kitt, then for himself. He'd grown attached to the kid, and he couldn't imagine not getting to see him every day.

But seeing Kitt would mean seeing Erin, and he wasn't sure if his wounded heart could take that on a daily basis. Then again, he'd managed to convince himself for fifteen years that he was no longer in love with her. Was there a chance he could bury those feelings again?

He didn't think so. He was older now, more sure of what he wanted. And what he wanted was Erin. Now that Gavin was gone...was it so wrong to admit how he felt about her?

He reached Fallon Point and stopped to take a few breaths. He wished he had thought to bring along some water. It had been quite the hike from the Moontide to here. But it was worth it. The view was magnificent. It overlooked the entire harbor and town, including the lighthouse.

He began taking photos as he wandered the area until he ended up heading down a lane with a For Sale sign. When he reached the end of the drive, he came upon a cute, though slightly rundown, Cape Cod house with a wraparound porch. He took a few photographs of the building since it had a quaint, charming feel to it.

After a few clicks, he lowered his camera. The house really was a hidden jewel. It was slightly out of the way, given the overgrown lane behind him, and it needed some work. But it overlooked one of the best views he'd ever seen in Findlay Roads.

He walked around the side of the house. Clearly, it had been uninhabited for some time. It wasn't in severe shape, but it was definitely in need of a little TLC. The longer he looked at it, the more he felt drawn to it. Without meaning to, the thought entered his mind—*Erin would love this place.*

She could even look out over the lighthouse. If things had worked out differently, maybe the two of them could have shared a life in a house like this one. The reminder of Erin's rejection struck him anew.

He turned and started back down the lane, leaving the charming little house behind him.

When would he ever learn to stop hoping for things that were not meant to be?

THOUGH SHE TOLD herself it wasn't because of Burke, Erin couldn't stop herself from looking outside every ten minutes. He'd left the inn, camera in hand, shortly after their exchange, and he'd been gone for almost three hours now. Where was he? The thought of him just up and leaving left her with a strange sort of dread.

Of course, he'd be coming back. Though he didn't have a lot in the way of possessions, his luggage and clothes were still here. Most of his stuff remained at Tessa's, as far as Erin knew, but he wouldn't just leave without saying goodbye.

Would he?

Maybe to her. She deserved to be snubbed after rejecting him. But Burke would never just up and leave without saying goodbye to Aunt Lenora and Kitt. Erin was sure of it.

So even though she pretended she was

just checking the weather, she consistently stepped to the window to see if she could catch Burke returning. Aunt Lenora and Kitt came home from the library, and Erin fixed lunch for the three of them...and still, Burke didn't come back.

Aunt Lenora asked after him, and Erin replied that he'd gone out with his camera. If the older woman had any questions about this, she kept them to herself, much to Erin's relief. After lunch, Kitt asked if he could play outside. Aunt Lenora offered to keep an eye on him from the back porch, so Erin agreed.

Another painstaking half hour passed with no sign of Burke. Erin was moving from room to room, tidying up because it gave her better access to peer out the windows, when she heard Aunt Lenora calling her name. Erin was on the first floor, dusting shelves in the library, when she heard it.

Puzzled, she set aside her polish and dust rag and moved toward the window to see what the other woman needed. She had a limited view of the backyard and couldn't see the porch where Aunt Lenora was seated. She heard her name called again, and something in Aunt Lenora's tone elicited a sense of urgency.

She moved swiftly toward the doors that led to the veranda and opened them to find Aunt Lenora partway down the steps toward the lawn, her gaze focused on something several yards away.

Erin followed her gaze and felt her heart catch in her chest. Kitt stood in the yard, several steps away from the gazebo, and faced a large, scruffy-looking dog.

"Kitt!"

But her son ignored her, his attention focused solely on the animal. Erin moved across the porch and past Aunt Lenora down the steps, heading toward Kitt automatically. The dog saw her coming and reacted with a low, warning growl.

Erin stopped, her heart hammering in her chest.

"Kitt, come here," she pleaded.

"It's okay, Mom," he replied. "He's hurt."

Erin didn't bother looking for any wounds on the dog. All she wanted was for Kitt to be safe in her arms.

"Kitt," Aunt Lenora spoke from behind her, "go to your mother."

She knew Aunt Lenora was thinking the same thoughts as her. A little over a year ago, a stray dog had attacked a child in the town nearest Findlay Roads. The boy had been a few years older than Kitt, and he'd required several surgeries to correct the damage the dog's bites had inflicted. Erin shuddered at the memory, remembering how she'd ached for the boy's mother, thinking how traumatized she'd have been if that had happened to Kitt. And now, a similar nightmare faced her.

She tried to calm herself and look at the situation logically. Even if Kitt came to her, there was a chance the dog would lunge at him before he made it to her side. She tried taking another step forward, but the dog shifted his eyes in her direction. She froze, even though the dog didn't react.

Where had he come from? His coat was shabby, a tangle of fur and thorns. She could see what Kitt meant about it him being hurt. He held his front left leg up off the ground, balancing his weight on his other three limbs. She couldn't be sure, but it looked as though there was blood matted into his fur, though it could be mud. Even if the dog was injured, didn't that just make it more of a threat?

"Aunt Lenora," she spoke without turning. "Call animal control."

Before she could turn to see if Aunt Lenora

was doing as she asked, Kitt took a step toward the dog. Erin's breath caught, and her stomach dropped.

"Kitt! Don't!"

CHAPTER TEN

BURKE'S HAND WAS on the front door of the inn, preparing to head inside, when he heard Erin yell out Kitt's name. He moved into action immediately, leaping over the porch railing and running around the side of the house toward the backyard.

He raced onto the scene in time to see Erin grabbing Kitt from behind, tugging him toward her and away from the mangy animal he recognized as the perceived threat. It took him a matter of seconds to make it to their side, placing himself between Kitt and Erin and the dog. The animal backed up with a snarl and tensed, as though ready to spring.

"Take Kitt inside," Burke commanded and was surprised to hear his nephew protest.

"No! He's hurt!"

"Kitt, come on," Erin entreated.

Kitt must have been struggling against his mom, but Burke didn't take the time to turn and look at them. He kept his eyes on the dog, assessing, and realized Kitt was right.

"Aunt Lenora! Did you call animal control?" Erin asked. From the range of her voice, Burke realized she'd managed to pull Kitt a couple of yards back.

He spared a glance behind him and saw that Aunt Lenora was still on the porch steps, her hand grasping the railing for support. As he suspected, Erin was closer to the porch now than to him and the dog.

"Wait," he called over his shoulder. "Hold off on that, Aunt Lenora."

"What do you mean, 'wait'?" Erin said. "He could be rabid for all we know!"

"I don't think so. I think he's frightened."

"That makes two of us," she retorted.

Burke kept his movements slow and deliberate as he moved toward the wounded dog. He couldn't quite tell how badly the animal was hurt. His fur was matted with mud… maybe blood, too…and he suspected that leg might be broken from the way he avoided putting weight on it.

"Hey there, buddy…"

"What are you doing?" she demanded.

"Having a look. I want to see how badly he's hurt."

"Burke—" She stopped, and when she spoke again, her voice was softer. "Please be careful."

Her tone pained him. It sounded almost as if she cared what happened to him. Well, maybe she did. She didn't have to be in love with him to worry about his well-being.

He gave a short nod to acknowledge that he'd heard her and then approached the dog. The animal growled again, softer this time, and tried to take a step back. He nearly stumbled and then righted himself, trotting awkwardly a couple feet away. Burke looked for some form of identification, but he didn't see a collar. He wondered what had happened, whether the dog had been hit by a car and how long he'd been wandering around like this.

Burke crouched down, trying to appear as harmless as possible.

"What happened, huh? Looks like you got yourself into some trouble. You on your own?"

The dog didn't come any closer, but at the sound of Burke's friendly tone, his tail gave a couple of swishes.

"When was the last time you ate, fella? You hungry?"

The dog whined and took two small steps in Burke's direction. Burke considered this positive progress, but he heard Erin's gasp even from a distance.

"Burke," she hissed loudly. "Let's just call animal control."

Burke raised a hand to hold her off. The dog limped around in a circle and whimpered.

"She's right, you know," he said. "Calling animal control would probably be the best thing."

The dog looked forlornly at Burke, silently begging.

"But if no one claims you, in the end, they're likely to put you down." He sighed. "I'd hate to see that happen. But you're not really helping me out here." He gestured behind him, keeping his voice low and gentle. "See that lady there? Her name's Erin. And she's a pretty kindhearted soul but not when there's a risk to her son. That's him there. His name's Kitt."

The dog looked over Burke's shoulder and then back at him. It was uncanny, but the way the dog stared at him so intently, Burke could almost believe he understood.

"So, here's the thing. If you think you can win Erin over, we could maybe take you inside and get you fed. But if you're going to play it all shy-like, we'll have to get animal control out here to claim you."

Burke stayed kneeling, eyes focused on the dog. Beneath the layers of mud and tangled fur, he had a feeling the animal was a credit to his breed. Chesapeake Bay retriever, if Burke had to make a guess. Or maybe just a golden retriever, once all the dirt was washed off of him.

Burke held out a hand, expecting the dog to bolt, but to his surprise, the retriever hobbled one step closer to him.

"Don't let him get away, Uncle Burke!" Kitt cried.

The retriever heard the command and gave a soft, gentle woof in response.

"That's my nephew, Kitt. He's a good kid. I bet you'd like him." Burke still had his arm extended. "What do you say? How about you let me take a look at that leg?"

The dog huffed, as if in acceptance, and then took a few stumbling steps toward him, nudging Burke's finger with his nose.

"Well, hey there." Burke ran his palm over the retriever's head and scratched behind his ears. He moved slowly, bringing his other hand around to feel for a collar buried in the fur or some other form of identification. But there was nothing. The dog's tail wagged furiously, but he had to occasionally do a little skip to keep himself balanced on only three legs.

Erin called out, "Burke Daniels, don't you even think about it. We are not taking that dog inside."

"Of course not," Burke agreed and then looked over his shoulder at her. Her back posture was rigid with determination, her jaw tight. She was beautiful when she was irritated.

The unbidden thought caused him to look back down.

"I'm taking him to the animal clinic on Highland Avenue."

"What? No. That's going to cost a fortune."

Now that the dog had given in and decided Burke was trustworthy, he was much friendlier. He kept pushing his head against Burke's palm, demanding he keep scratching his ears. Erin had moved a little closer to speak to him, but she was still holding on to Kitt to keep him from going near the dog.

"I'll cover it. Don't worry."

"You can't."

"Why not?"

"You just…can't."

He steeled himself before looking up at her this time. She was frowning.

"Kitt, go to Aunt Lenora."

Kitt didn't, but he backed away, looking wistfully at the dog. Erin waited until he was out of earshot to speak again.

"I don't want Kitt getting attached if…if this dog already has an owner or he needs put down or something."

Burke understood her reasoning, but he didn't feel right about letting the dog go to a shelter, especially not in his current condition. "We're just driving him to the animal clinic, we're not picking out names and buying him toys or anything."

Erin's lips flattened to a thin line, and she folded her arms across her torso. He didn't need to be a body language expert to know that her posture screamed anger.

"Come on, Erin. Don't you remember the time we found that stray cat with all those kittens? You insisted that rather than turning them over to the SPCA or somewhere, that we find homes for them. We spent the better part of a weekend going door to door, trying to give away cats. It convinced me you could have had a job in sales if you wanted one."

Her lip twitched, but it was barely discernible. "That was different."

"Not that much different."

"Mom!" Kitt's voice came to them from the porch where he stood at Aunt Lenora's side. "Are we going to keep him?"

Erin's exasperation was obvious. "Fine. But it's up to you, Burke, to get him in the car. In the very back, away from Kitt."

"You don't have to go along. I can handle it myself."

"I don't want to see Kitt moping around here while you're off playing animal rescue. And if Kitt's going, then I'm going."

She stomped off with steam practically puffing out of her ears. Burke looked back at the dog.

"Don't worry. Her bark is worse than her bite."

THE WAITING ROOM at the animal emergency clinic wasn't too busy, which Erin was grateful for. She didn't relish the idea of spending hours waiting to hear an update on the retriever, especially with Kitt asking so many questions. Although, in truth, every time he spoke up, her heart gave a little tug of joy. She hadn't seen him this animated since before his dad's death. It was a relief to consider he might finally be emerging from his grief.

Her eyes wandered from her son to Burke, who was leaning down, answering Kitt's question about whether the dog would have to get any shots. Burke's brown hair fell over his forehead, threads of burnished gold shining in the strands from hours spent in the sunshine.

Her fingers itched to reach out and brush the hair back. Gavin's hair had always been trimmed short, thanks to his army career, but Burke had always worn his just a little bit longer. She privately preferred the way Burke's hair framed his features, but it was a minor detail. Both Daniels brothers had been able to turn heads in high school, and looking at Burke now, Erin imagined Burke had continued to do plenty of head-turning over the last fifteen years.

He'd been in contact so rarely, and mostly with Gavin, that she had no idea what sort of relationships he'd had since high school. There was Tessa, of course, but beyond that, Erin didn't know if he'd fallen in love at any point while he'd been gone. The idea was like a vise around her chest, squeezing the air from her lungs. It shouldn't matter how many relationships Burke had had over the years.

It *didn't* matter, she reminded herself. That was his business, a part of his life she was not privy to. Her fingers began to tremble, as though they might reach out and touch him of their own free will. Erin clenched them tightly in her lap.

"Mr... Daniels?"

All three of them turned at the sound of Burke's name. A middle-aged woman in a white lab coat stood in the doorway of the waiting room. "I'm Dr. Harris. Why don't you come on back?"

As soon as they entered the examination room and the retriever got sight of them, his tail began to wag, creating a swishing sound as it slid over the stainless steel table he laid on.

"Hey, buddy," Burke greeted, and the dog's tail moved even faster. "Feeling better?"

Kitt edged forward as Burke went up to the dog and gave him a scratch behind the ears. Erin stubbornly held her ground but didn't reach out to pull Kitt back—the dog didn't appear in the least bit dangerous now. It was clear it had been frightened earlier. Besides, she was curious to see just how far her son's bravery extended. She still marveled at how far he'd come since Burke had started living at the Moontide.

"Good news. Our films confirmed the leg isn't broken," Dr. Harris said as she flicked off the lights and moved to stand before a light board that displayed a set of radiography films.

"You can see that the bone is entirely intact with no fractures." She pointed a pen along a glowing line of bone. "But there is evidence of previous breaks, as you can see here…and here."

Erin frowned. "Is that why he's limping? Was there permanent damage?"

Dr. Harris turned the lights back on as she shook her head. "No, he was limping due to an issue with his paw. All of his paws are cut up pretty badly, but especially the left front one—it's scraped raw. It's difficult to tell how long he's been out on his own, but it appears as though it's been some time. He's undernourished and dehydrated."

Erin felt a tug of sympathy and a touch of guilt for how she'd reacted to the animal earlier. Under Burke's watchful eye, Kitt had edged his way closer to the dog and was now cautiously running his hand along the animal's side. The retriever shifted a little to give Kitt better access to his belly.

Dr. Harris checked her clipboard. "It's my understanding that you've agreed to assume all medical costs for the dog, Mr. Daniels, is that correct?"

Burke nodded. "I already gave my credit card information to your office staff."

"Well, we'd like to keep the dog here overnight in the clinic for observation, but then there's also the matter of ownership. The dog isn't chipped, and you found no identification on him, as I understand."

"That's correct."

"There's a three-day holding period while we attempt to find the owners, but as it stands, I think this poor guy was probably abandoned. I doubt there will be anyone to claim him. Still, the law requires us to try."

"Of course. I understand."

"Then am I correct to assume you and your wife—" she glanced in Erin's direction "—will be adopting this dog, provided no one steps forward to assume ownership?"

Erin froze at the vet's assumption, her eyes sliding toward Burke. Other than a slight stiffening of his shoulders, he didn't appear in the least disturbed by Dr. Harris's mistake. But he didn't correct her either.

"We'll need to discuss it."

"We're not married," she put in, irritated by the thrill she experienced just at the thought of her and Burke as husband and wife. That was ridiculous. Hadn't she already realized how wrong that would be? She had to stop reacting like a lovesick teenager.

"Oh." Dr. Harris looked from Burke to her, eyebrows raised. "I apologize. I shouldn't have assumed."

"It's okay." Burke tried to brush away the awkwardness, but inside, Erin fumed.

Why did she have to step in and be the one to make things awkward? Why couldn't Burke have just told the vet they weren't a couple? She knew some of her irritation was irrational, but she couldn't help herself. She took out her frustration by snapping, "We're not keeping the dog."

He looked at her. "As I said, we'll need to discuss it." His voice was calm, but his eyes had narrowed slightly.

"We're getting a dog!" Kitt crowed.

Dr. Harris cleared her throat. "Well, there's still the matter of whether an owner claims him."

It was a gentle reminder to Kitt, but her son wasn't deterred.

"They won't," he assured. "He's going to be ours."

"See?" Erin's focus shifted to Burke, her anger flaring. "This is what I meant when I said we should let animal control handle it."

"Erin—"

"I told you." She felt tears of resentment and frustration rise. "I told you, but you wouldn't listen."

She shook her head, embarrassed to be losing her cool in front of a stranger but more worried about Kitt. He'd experienced enough loss for one so young. And now he'd already laid claim to an animal that she absolutely could not let him keep.

"Maybe I'll give you a minute," Dr. Harris suggested as she edged toward the door.

"That won't be necessary," Erin said. "Kitt and I will wait in the car."

She reached for her son's hand, but he jerked back. "Not yet! I need to say goodbye to Scout."

Scout? He'd already attached a name to the creature, and to make it all the worse, it was a name she recognized. Scout was the dog in a book that Gavin used to read to Kitt, during their intermittent Skype sessions while he was deployed. A hollow ache ballooned in her stomach.

"Kitt," she breathed, but her son was nuzzling the dog, who was cheerfully licking his cheek, any doubts about them obviously having vanished.

"See ya later, Scout. I hope you feel better real soon so we can take you home!"

Erin couldn't bear any more. She grabbed Kitt's hand and tugged him toward the door. The action didn't seem to faze him. He went willingly but used his free hand to wave goodbye to his newfound friend.

Before she exited the room, she cast one final, dark look in Burke's direction.

THE FOLLOWING MORNING, Erin woke even earlier than usual to prepare the breakfast items for the inn's guests. She sliced strawberries and layered them along with blueberries and her homemade vanilla cream into parfait glasses before putting them in the fridge to chill. Next she started on the bacon and gruyere quiche with rosemary oven-roasted potatoes.

Typically, she would serve these with her standard assortment of baked goods, such as raspberry muffins, chocolate chip scones and sourdough toast. But with Mr. Atwell's condition, she swapped out the usual pastries for gluten-free almond coffee cake and peach streusel. There would also be sausage links and sliced ham, along with a variety beverages: coffee, tea and juices. Whether she was serving two or twenty, Erin always tried to provide quality breakfasts.

She focused on her work, using it as a means to ignore everything that had occurred in the past forty-eight hours, from Burke's kiss to Mrs. Cleary's subtle disapproval to the incident with Scout. Or rather, *that dog*, she mentally corrected, not ready to adopt a name for the animal as easily as Kitt had.

The inn's current guests had informed her they'd be rising early in order to get a head start on their last day in town, so Erin made sure the table was laid and breakfast was served by 7:00 a.m. After explaining the breakfast offerings, she left them to enjoy their meal in private, checking in occasionally to see if anything was needed and spending the interim fiddling in the kitchen and trying not to grow impatient for them to finish up. As soon as they were done (and with another request for recipes from Mrs. Atwell),

Erin made short work of clearing the table and storing the leftovers. She left the dishes in the sink with plans to wash them later, wrote a note on the chalkboard by the fridge for the rest of the household as to where to find breakfast and then hurried out the door in order to visit the lighthouse.

She was particularly eager to talk to Gavin this week, which is why she'd been determined to leave the house earlier than usual for her Sunday conversation with him. She was rewarded with utter solitude—there wasn't another soul in sight as she took her seat on the bench within view of the lighthouse and savored the morning air, blessedly mild since the sun hadn't been up for more than a few hours. This Sunday morning at the lighthouse, her feelings were even more conflicted than the last time she'd sat here.

"It's been strange," she spoke aloud. "with Burke living at the Moontide." She shook her head. "You wouldn't believe the difference in Kitt, having Burke there. Maybe no one else would even see it, Gavin, but I do. I've been so worried about him for so long that every little smile or laugh is something I cherish." She quirked her lips. "He's started to mimic

Burke in these tiny ways. Like the way Burke cuts his food or how he scratches his temple when he starts to get tired. And he has this way of—"

She suddenly stopped, feeling a flood of guilt. Just how much attention had she been paying to Burke to have recognized all his little tics? She cleared her throat. It was because of Kitt. She wouldn't have picked up on any of this if she hadn't been so aware of how Kitt imitated his uncle.

Still, she didn't feel quite comfortable detailing the rest of her observations to Gavin, especially after what had occurred Friday night. So she shifted the direction of the one-way conversation.

"I hope it means he's finally turning the corner of his grief and coming out of his shell. He's had a hard time, Gavin, without you." This truth caused her to blink back tears. "He didn't get enough time with you before you were gone. I wish you had quit before your last deployment. At least he would have a few more months, a few more memories. So much of what he remembers about you comes from what I or Aunt Lenora have told him or from home videos or photos. I'm not sure

how much of his grief is from what he remembers of you or what he *thinks* he remembers of you."

She expelled a breath. "But I guess it doesn't
matter. His grief is real, no matter how many
of his memories are." She clenched her jaw.
"I know you were working toward a better
life for us, but I would give just about anything to trade every second you spent away
and have had all that time with you, me and
Kitt together."

For the first time, she allowed a little bit of
anger to leak through her sadness.

"You should have quit sooner, like we
talked about. You should have been here,
Gavin, to see your son growing up. If you'd
been *here* instead of heading back to the base,
then maybe you'd *still* be here...and our son
wouldn't be forced to consider his uncle as a
replacement for his dad."

She bit her lip then as the shame flooded
in. Was it really Kitt that was thinking that
way, putting Burke in the place that should
have been filled by Gavin?

Or was she the one viewing Burke in that
light?

She swallowed. "I miss you. But you were

gone so much of the time that it's hard to separate my grief from my regret. We spent so much of our marriage apart, and I don't know who to blame for that. Should I have begged you to stay? Or would that only have driven a wedge between us?" She released a sigh. She didn't like dwelling on these questions. It made her feel disloyal somehow. But somehow, death had made it easier to be angry at Gavin, and at times, that anger was all that kept her from breaking down in tears.

"So Burke rescued this dog." She latched on to the first topic at hand, even if it was a sore subject. "It scared me to death, at first. It just stumbled into the backyard, and Kitt—" She broke off, not wanting to relive the terror of those moments when she feared her son was in danger.

"Burke came in like some kind of knight in shining armor. He put himself between us and the dog. And it turns out, the poor thing was just scared. But Burke didn't know that, not at first." She grew thoughtful. "He put himself in harm's way for us."

The realization made her heart ache anew. She couldn't speak the words aloud, couldn't unload her guilt and longing while she was hampered by the idea of being disloyal to her husband. But the awareness stayed with her—that Burke had protected them without a second thought. By reflex. It might have been something he'd have done for anyone...but it hadn't been just anyone. He'd done it for them, for her and Kitt.

"Well, anyway. Now I think he plans to adopt the dog, even though I made it clear it's probably a bad idea. I'm afraid Kitt will get attached, and what happens if we can't keep it?"

She saw another couple approaching the lighthouse, her solitude about to be interrupted. She was suddenly overcome with the urge to tell Gavin everything—her and Burke's kiss, Mrs. Cleary's comments and her own fears that she had somehow failed him. But the other couple had drawn near enough that they would now hear any words she spoke aloud.

By the time they'd moved on, she'd lost her nerve. "Anyway, I better get back." She stood up. "But I'll come again next week."

She'd been coming to the lighthouse for so long, she couldn't remember the last time she'd failed to visit. Maybe Gavin didn't need her to come, maybe he wasn't even listening. But she couldn't shake the feeling that his spirit, his soul, whatever part of him still existed, met her here each Sunday.

And as long as she believed that, she'd never stop coming.

CHAPTER ELEVEN

BURKE RECEIVED A call from the animal clinic on Monday morning to let him know that Scout was much improved. The dog was eating and drinking well and had even begun moving around, putting more weight on his front left leg. They'd found no matches in their systems for a missing dog of Scout's description, and if no one claimed him within the next twenty-four hours, he could be released into the adoption program or into Burke's care.

Burke didn't hesitate. He told them he'd come for Scout as soon as they would let him. It was only after he hung up the phone that he considered how he was going to broach the subject with Erin. He'd already mentioned adopting the dog to Aunt Lenora over the weekend. She'd been skeptical but was willing to let him bring the dog home and give things a try.

He hadn't even tried to bring up the topic

with Erin, already knowing how she felt. Plus, it wasn't as if they'd been chatting a lot since Friday night…and their kiss. But he couldn't put it off any longer. He steeled himself for the confrontation ahead and sought Erin out in the inn's office to ask if he could have a word with her.

She frowned at this request, and he could practically see the wheels of her mind turning, wondering if this was somehow about their kiss from a few nights ago. As immature as it was, he didn't immediately come to the point but rather sat in the chair she gestured to and waited, as if uncertain how to begin, in order to build the suspense. It amused him to see how she fidgeted, her nerves obviously ratcheting up. It was a petty revenge, perhaps, but he found it gratifying that he made her uneasy. It meant he was able to have an effect on her, even if it wasn't exactly the one he wanted.

Finally, he sighed and announced, "The animal clinic called. No one has claimed Scout." He let that hang in the air, giving her the opportunity to shift her expectations for where this conversation was headed.

"I plan to adopt him," he said.

She began shaking her head. "I told you, that is a bad idea."

"Why? Because you're afraid you'll fall in love?" It was a low blow, but the words were out before he could consider the wisdom of them.

Erin's lips flattened to a straight line, and he felt a ripple of shame.

"Sorry, that was uncalled for. But I think you're wrong. It would be good to have a dog around."

She made a face. "How do you figure? The fur piling up everywhere, making the housekeeping even harder? The inconvenience of taking him out every two hours? What if we have guests with allergies? It's going to affect business."

"Or it might be a plus," he offered. "A pet-friendly B&B. That might be a good thing."

Her jaw hardened. "You've lived here for just over one week. I wouldn't get ahead of yourself. You don't know what works and what doesn't around here."

"It doesn't seem like much of anything works around here," he commented sarcastically, beneath his breath.

It seemed that all he'd done since arriving at the inn was repair and patch. Not that he minded helping out, in fact, he liked feeling as if he was contributing. But Erin's remark chafed a little. It wasn't as if it was entirely undeserved, though. He hadn't been very involved with the inn over the years. But he also knew she only used this as a defense to keep him from bringing a dog into the house.

In any case, she ignored his comment as she said, "I don't want Kitt getting attached. He's lost enough in his life. What happens if the dog gets sick or needs to be put down or something?"

He stared. "Erin, you're getting way ahead of yourself here. Scout can't be more than two or three years old. Hopefully, it will be years before anything happens to him. And even so, don't you think the good a dog would do for Kitt would outweigh the loss he'd experience in the future?"

"I won't invite more grief into his life."

"You can't prevent that, any more than you could prevent Gavin dying." She winced, but he pressed on. "Life is filled with grief, Erin, it doesn't mean you stop living it."

She ignored him and turned her attention to some papers in front of her. He didn't think she was really looking at them, but it was a handy excuse to avoid meeting his eyes.

"After my parents died, I'd have given anything for a dog like Scout. I think it would have been good for me, something to invest my emotions in outside of my grief. And technically, it wouldn't be your dog or your concern. I'd be the one adopting Scout, but I'd let Kitt help take care of him. It would teach him responsibility, give him a sense of importance."

She still wouldn't look at him. He tapped a foot impatiently on the rug. He hated to play this card, but she wasn't budging.

"It was something Gavin wanted for him."

Her head shot up. "Gavin? What are you talking about?"

"One of the last times I spoke to him, he mentioned how he wanted to get Kitt a dog. He was waiting until his deployment was up and he was living here permanently. We had a dog when we were young. But she was old, and she died in the fire. She'd actually been really sick for months, so we were a little more mentally prepared, I guess, than we were with our parents."

"Daisy, I remember. Gavin told me."

He dipped his head. Of course Gavin would have told her about Daisy. He sighed. "Erin, please. Let's do this. You don't have to be responsible, I'll take care of everything. Besides, it's not just for Kitt. I'd really like to give this dog a home. I don't exactly know why except that, on some level, I think it reminds me of how I felt growing up. Unwanted. Unloved."

Her face softened, revealing the Erin he knew and loved.

"It's not really up to me, you know. The inn doesn't belong to me."

"Aunt Lenora already said it was okay. I just wanted to get your blessing first."

Her lips parted in surprise. "I...you didn't... thank you. I appreciate that. But if Aunt Lenora's fine with it, then you have your answer."

It wasn't exactly approval, but he'd take it.

"Thank you. I'll probably be picking him up tomorrow. Do you mind if I tell Kitt and take him along with me?"

"That would be fine."

"Thanks." He stood, planning to let her get back to her work.

"Burke?"

He waited.

"Maybe I should be the one thanking you. For considering Kitt."

There was more he wanted to say, more

he wanted to offer. But that door was closed. He tipped his head and said nothing more as he left the office to tell his nephew the news.

BURKE DECIDED TO wait to share the news about Scout with Kitt until the next day when the animal clinic called to confirm no one had claimed ownership of the dog. When he asked Kitt if he was up for a drive, his nephew had shrugged, as if he had nothing better to do, and then followed Burke to the car.

It wasn't until they pulled into the parking lot that he caught on to the plan. His brows furrowed in confusion, and then his eyes grew wide.

"Are we here to see Scout?"

"Actually, we're here to pick him up. He's coming home with us."

Kitt gasped with happiness, but on the heels of that, he frowned. "Wait...did you tell Mom?"

Burke couldn't help chuckling. "I already talked to her. Scout is going to be my dog, technically, but you can spend time with him whenever you want. In fact, I was hoping you'd help me take care of him. He's still a pretty young dog so he'll need lots of exercise and care. It's a big responsibility. You think you're up for it?"

Kitt considered this question with a thoughtfulness that was endearing. "Will I have to take him on walks?"

"Not by yourself. I'd go with you."

"And feed him?"

"Maybe. But he'd be my responsibility, too. I might need you to help play with him sometimes, and maybe train him to behave. I'm not sure how much work he'll need."

Burke didn't add that Kitt's assistance with these tasks were also dependent on how long he'd be living at the Moontide. Once Burke found a place of his own, Scout would most likely have to go with him. Of course, Burke was still planning to spend plenty of time with Kitt in that case.

"I can do it," Kitt decided. He looked so determined that Burke laughed.

"Thanks, buddy. I think you'll do a great job."

They exited the car together and headed into the clinic. It took forty-five minutes before they emerged, with Scout on a leash the vet had provided since Burke didn't have one of his own.

"We'll have to stop at the pet store for supplies," he said. "We don't have dog food or bedding or anything for this guy."

Scout woofed softly.

"That's right, or treats."

Kitt looked impressed that his uncle must have understood Scout's communication.

They climbed back into the car with Scout in the back seat and drove the short distance to the pet shop where Burke loaded a cart with everything he thought a new pet might need. Kitt helped by choosing an assortment of toys for Scout, asking the dog's input at every juncture.

"This one lights up." He presented it to Scout who only cocked his head as if uncertain what the point of said toy was. Kitt put it back on the shelf. He picked up a plush hedgehog instead. It gave a vibrating squeak as Kitt squeezed it. Scout barked, so Kitt added it to the cart. Burke watched in amusement as his nephew continued talking to the dog, filling him in on what to expect as a member of the family.

"Lenny is really old, but she doesn't act like it. Well, maybe sometimes she does, like when she asks me to bring her slippers to her because her knees hurt too much to try and stand up."

Burke ducked his head to hide a smile. He'd seen Aunt Lenora make this request of Kitt more than once.

"But she tells the best stories, and she's funny, and she smells like peppermint." He frowned. "But don't lick her. I don't think she'd like that. Maybe not until you know her better."

Burke cleared his throat to keep from laughing as they continued to stroll the aisles. Scout followed along beside them, his head inclined toward Kitt, as if hanging on the little boy's every word.

"You'll like Mom. She's extra nice, and she smells like cinnamon. She won't care if you lick her, I don't think," he added, as an aside. "But she gets sad a lot, so when that happens, you just need to try and cheer her up by being extra good so she doesn't get more upset."

Kitt sighed, and Burke marveled that he was talking so much. He hadn't heard this many words out of Kitt...well, ever. Something about the dog had allowed him to open up.

"It's because of my dad," he went on explaining. "He died. He was extra nice, too, just like my mom. He didn't get to be home a lot because he was in the army. I don't remember lots about him, but I liked when we'd hang out. He'd buy me a doughnut, and he'd tell me it was our secret. You'd have liked him." Kitt grew quiet, and Burke had to swallow hard to keep his emotion in check.

"I wish he didn't die. But I'm lucky he was my dad."

Burke stopped in the aisle and pretended to study the different types of dog shampoo so Kitt couldn't see the tears in his eyes.

"You're lucky, too," Kitt went on, "because Uncle Burke is going to be your dad now. He's pretty cool. He'll take good care of you, just like he's been taking care of me and Mom and Lenny since he moved into the Moontide. The Moontide is our home. Only, it's not just a house, it's also a place where people can come and stay and eat breakfast and stuff. I like it there, even though it's weird sometimes because Mom and Lenny have all these other people to worry about."

Burke picked a bottle of shampoo at random, unable to really focus on the different brands as he listened to Kitt, and tossed it onto the growing pile. He wondered if Gavin had known, on some supernatural level, that his son would do well with a pet. Because it was obvious Scout had already been able to draw Kitt out of his shell in a way the rest of them hadn't.

They turned the corner of the final aisle and headed for the checkout. The cashier smiled as they approached.

"Hi, did you find everything you needed?"

Burke gestured to the cart. "I think we have half of aisle nine in here."

She laughed and began unloading the goods to scan them. Kitt had drawn back into himself, but he kept a protective hand on Scout's back.

"What's your dog's name?" she asked him.

"Scout," he softly replied.

"He's a cutie," she said and winked. "Just like you."

Kitt looked at Burke.

"It runs in the family," Burke teased him.

"Is this your son? I can see the family resemblance."

"Um…"

"He's my uncle," Kitt announced. "But he's kind of like a dad, too. Not my real dad, though."

"Oh." It was obvious she didn't want to pry about this curious statement.

But for Burke, Kitt's claim gave him a warm sense of belonging. It was a shame he hadn't made the effort to be more involved in Kitt's life sooner. Because the affection he felt for Kitt was growing beyond just the obligatory family bond. The more he got to know his nephew, the more he loved him. He was such a perfect mix of Erin's fierce will and Gavin's acute observation along with a certain candidness that was all his own.

The rest of the transaction proceeded with a discussion about the weather, and then they loaded everything into the car for the drive home. Kitt began his commentary to Scout again when they were alone once more, telling him about the town and pointing out different stops along their route. Some of it was so comically entertaining that Burke burst out in laughter a time or two, which didn't seem to bother Kitt in the least.

But as soon as they pulled up to the inn, Burke's humor faded. He put the car in park and sat there for a minute, staring at the vehicle in the front drive. He considered it for so long that Kitt eventually asked, "Uncle Burke? Why aren't we getting out of the car?"

Burke turned off the ignition in response to Kitt's question, but he was still puzzled.

What was Allan Worth doing at the Moontide?

CHAPTER TWELVE

BURKE COULDN'T SAY WHY, but his stomach churned with uneasiness as he and Kitt stepped inside the inn's front door. He had Scout on a leash, grateful the dog was on his best behavior. He didn't strain or wander, just followed patiently as Burke stepped from the foyer and toward the parlor area.

The parlor was where Aunt Lenora often greeted guests, and he made the assumption that's where Allan Worth would be. His guess was proved correct as he entered the room and saw Tessa's father seated on the edge of the couch, a glass of iced tea in his hand.

"Burke, it's good to see you."

The older man placed his glass on the side table and stood to extend a hand. Burke moved forward to take it, trying to curb his impatience and keep from demanding why Allan had shown up here now. He hadn't heard a word from Allan Worth since the day of his aborted wedding.

"And what is this?" He leaned down to take a look at the dog. "I don't remember you owning a dog."

Scout had taken a few steps back, as much as he could manage with the restraint of the leash. Kitt was hovering at Burke's side, and Burke was surprised when his nephew spoke up.

"This is Scout. Uncle Burke adopted him."

"Ah." Allan was wise enough not to try to touch the dog. Burke knew Scout was friendly enough but given this new environment and whatever past experiences had traumatized him, it was likely best if a stranger didn't attempt to pet him too soon. "Well, that's nice."

"Kitt?"

Burke turned his head to see Erin enter the room. She looked as uncertain as he felt, but Kitt lit up at the sight of her.

"Mom, look! We got Scout!"

"I see that." She forced a smile for her son's sake and knelt down instead of approaching the dog. Scout took the cue as his invitation to greet her and moved toward her, tail wagging furiously. Burke released the leash to Kitt so Scout could get closer to Erin. Obviously, the dog did well enough with people. Or maybe Erin just had that soothing effect. She scratched behind the dog's ears and sighed, as if resigning herself to falling for him.

"And we went to the pet store, and Uncle Burke spent over a hundred dollars, and we almost couldn't fit everything in the car!"

Burke might have found this commentary amusing if he wasn't so distracted. He shifted his attention back to the man before him. Why was Allan here? He couldn't imagine Tessa had sent her father. It wasn't her style. Besides, they were no longer a part of each other's lives, at least not like they had been. Still, he couldn't refrain from asking about her.

"Is everything all right, I mean, with Tessa?"

He sensed Erin's gaze on his back.

Allan appeared troubled. "She's...well enough. Rather subdued of late, actually. But I suppose that can be expected?" Allan looked a little distressed, and Burke couldn't help feeling sympathy seeing his concern for his daughter.

"Kitt, why don't we start unloading the car and get Scout something to drink?" Erin suggested.

Burke didn't turn, but he sensed Erin leave the room with Kitt in tow.

"She said she…spoke to you," Allan went on. "I'm sorry that things had to end the way they did." He reached out to give Burke's arm a squeeze. The gesture seemed unnatural. He had never sensed Allan disapproved of him exactly, but he had always believed that Tessa's parents found him a somewhat lackluster choice for their youngest daughter. But he detected genuine sympathy from Allan for how Tessa had left him at the altar.

"And how about you? Are you doing all right?" He continued before Burke had a chance to respond, sweeping his gaze around the room and saying, "I can't imagine a better safe haven after an experience such as yours. This place…it's a treasure."

Burke slid a glance at Aunt Lenora, who was still seated silently on the settee. Her expression gave away nothing of the conversation that had been taking place before he entered the room.

"Thanks." He felt uncomfortable with Allan's words, especially given his feelings about the old house. It was true, it had been a safe haven—twice now, in his life—but it also had served to remind him of things he had lost. Burke shifted uneasily from one foot to the other. He looked at Aunt Lenora, hoping she would give him some sort of cue. She still hadn't voiced a word.

He didn't want to appear rude, but he was also confused.

"Well, I didn't mean to interrupt whatever it was you were discussing," he said and paused, hoping one of them would fill him in. But neither spoke up. Allan stood there, with a pleased smile on his face, while Aunt Lenora remained quiet, her brow furrowed as though in contemplation. "Um, can I get you anything else, Allan? Aunt Lenora, did you need me to make more tea?"

Allan spoke before she could respond. "Oh, that's all right. I think I've taken up enough of your aunt's time." He turned to her. "Lenora, you have my number. I'll check in with you in a few days, if that suits?"

She gave a short nod and moved as if to stand, but Allan held up a hand.

"No, don't trouble yourself. I'll show myself out. Please thank Erin for the iced tea." He nodded at Burke and smiled before he turned and made his way from the room. Burke thought about following him, but he was more concerned with Aunt Lenora.

He waited until he heard the front door click closed before he turned to his great-aunt.

"What was that about?"

To his consternation, she still didn't respond. Instead, she struggled to stand, her movements awkward. Her joints were obviously stiff from sitting...for how long?

"How long was he here? And why?"

Aunt Lenora didn't answer, and he had to will himself to patience. He stepped forward though and helped the old woman get to her feet. She hobbled toward the doorway that led to the office. She wasn't quite there yet when Erin appeared in the opposite entry.

"I just saw Allan leave." She looked at Burke in question. "Is everything all right? What was he doing here?"

"I don't know," Burke admitted. He looked back to Aunt Lenora, who was just passing through the door that entered into the office.

"Aunt Lenora, what's going on? Where are you going?"

"For some peace and quiet, to give a body time to think!"

Burke's jaw dropped. He looked to Erin. Her eyes were wide with surprise. Aunt Lenora had, on an occasion or two over the years, raised her voice but such a vehement reaction from her was rare.

Worried, he began to follow her from the room, but Erin's voice held him.

"Burke. Let her go."

He stopped in his tracks and looked over his shoulder. Her expression was pained.

"Just give her time to deal with it. Whatever it is. She'll tell us when she's ready."

Burke didn't like it. But he took Erin's advice and didn't pursue Aunt Lenora even as he heard the office door close.

AUNT LENORA DIDN'T join them for dinner. She stayed holed up in the inn's office and didn't emerge even as they finished cleaning up and loading the dishwasher. Kitt didn't seem to notice the tension in the house, nor Aunt Lenora's absence. He was too busy playing with Scout. Even at dinner, Erin had to prompt him to continue eating since he kept looking in the direction of the mudroom where Scout was penned up while they had their meal.

It wasn't until Erin and Burke had wordlessly finished their after-dinner tasks that Kitt seemed to remember Aunt Lenora. He appeared in the doorway of the kitchen with Scout in tow.

"Where's Lenny?" he asked. "She hasn't met Scout yet."

Burke could sense the tension in Erin as she finished wiping down the counter. He straightened after pressing the wash cycle on the dishwasher.

"Aunt Lenora is busy right now," Erin said. It was obvious she was distracted. She didn't even look at Kitt as she spoke. Allan's visit was weighing on her every bit as much as it was on him. What business did he have with Aunt Lenora?

"Where is she? I'll take Scout to her."

"Not now," Erin replied, still preoccupied. "I told you, Aunt Lenora's busy."

"No, she's not," he argued. "She says she's never too busy for me."

Burke thought about intervening, but truthfully, he wanted to see how this played out. He sensed a bit of defiance in Kitt, something he had not seen before. The kid was the most well-behaved child he'd ever met. This was the first time Kitt had gotten belligerent with Erin, and he was curious how she'd handle it.

But for Erin's part, she didn't seem to realize that Kitt was pushing back for the first time in who knew how long.

"I'm sure that's true, Kitt, but Aunt Lenora made it clear she didn't want to be disturbed." Erin's back was turned, and she was still wiping down the counters. She didn't see the way Kitt set his lips, and the expression made Burke smile. It was the same look that Erin got when she decided to dig in on something. He nearly applauded at the sight of it.

"But she hasn't met Scout yet," he protested.

"She can meet Scout tomorrow," Erin countered.

"No! I want to see Lenny *now*!"

Burke watched silently. Scout's tail was swishing like a pendulum, and his head was swinging from Erin to Kitt, as interested in this conversation as Burke was.

"Well, that's just too bad because Aunt Lenora doesn't have time right now."

Kitt's temper finally got the better of him, and Burke blinked as his nephew threw the plastic chew toy he'd been holding onto the floor. It hit the kitchen tile with a loud *thwap*!

Erin turned, nearly as surprised as Burke was by this reaction, took one look at the toy and then at Kitt. She blinked, and Burke saw it dawn on her that Kitt was actually fighting back about something. Her eyes widened, her lips parted, and then he saw the faintest twitch of a smile flit across her lips.

"Kitt Daniels, we *do not* behave like that when we don't get our way."

But there was no real reprimand behind the words. In fact, if Kitt was really listening, her tone sounded suspiciously like approval. He watched Kitt hesitate. His shoulders remained set in defiance, but his brow furrowed, as though contemplating his next course of action.

Though he shouldn't encourage disobedience, a part of Burke was rooting for Kitt to keep pushing the issue. He wanted to see his nephew get a little fired up, just like any typical six-year-old would if they didn't get their own way.

But he would never know just how far Kitt was willing to take his argument because Aunt Lenora appeared in the doorway at that moment and took charge of the situation.

"Kitt, let me see this dog."

Kitt's eyes lit up. Scout was already crossing the room, tail wagging even faster as he gave Aunt Lenora a good sniff. She patted the dog's head and then rubbed a gnarled hand against his ears. Scout bent his head into the palm of her hand, his back leg thumping happily.

"Good dog," Aunt Lenora said.

Burke and Erin met each other's eyes over the heads of the rest of the family. Was Aunt

Lenora going to tell them what had occurred
between her and Allan?

"Now, Kitt, I want you to go upstairs with
Scout. I'll come up later and read to you before bed. Right now, I need to talk to your
mother and Burke."

"Can't I be part of the talk, too?"

Aunt Lenora moved her hand from Scout
to Kitt, resting it on his head and then moving it down to cup his cheek. "Not this time.
Go upstairs and get ready for bed. Take the
dog with you."

Kitt nodded, and Burke felt a tug of dismay in seeing the familiar benign acceptance come over his features. He picked up
the chew toy off the floor.

"Sorry I got mad, Mom."

Burke felt a swell of disappointment.
He wondered just how far Kitt would have
pushed things if Aunt Lenora hadn't entered
the room.

"It's all right," Erin assured. She bent to
drop a kiss on his forehead. "Go get ready
for bed. You can play on your Nintendo DS
until Aunt Lenora comes up."

He shuffled from the room without further
argument. Aunt Lenora waited until he was
gone and then turned to face them once more.

"Let's go to the office. I have something I need to share with the both of you."

"ALLAN WORTH HAS made me an offer."

Aunt Lenora's opening statement did nothing to calm the bees of uneasiness stinging around Erin's stomach. Being in the office didn't help either. Though the room was cozy, and Erin spent many hours of each week in here, it had an air of formality that didn't exist elsewhere in the inn. This was where business was done. And clearly, whatever Aunt Lenora had to share, she meant business.

She let the silence drag on, as if building impact to her words. Erin kept her fingers locked tightly in her lap and spared only a brief glance toward Burke. His brow was furrowed—she imagined she probably looked much the same way.

"He would like to purchase the Moontide."

When Aunt Lenora finally dropped this announcement, Erin actually snickered.

"Allan Worth wants the Moontide?" She found it ridiculous. "Obviously, that man is used to getting whatever he wants. I hope you made it clear the inn is not for sale."

Aunt Lenora didn't share in her outrage, and Erin felt her uneasiness return tenfold.

"He wants to renovate it into some sort of resort clubhouse. And he'd use the land to build a golf course."

Erin could only stare as shock settled in. "A clubhouse? A golf course? But…why?"

"He feels it would attract more tourists to the area and increase our local economy. And more tourism is better for everyone."

"Except you," Erin pointed out, her tone defensive. "What good has tourism done for us so far? The Delphine has stolen half of our B&B business. And now he wants to just take the inn and make it his own?"

"Not take," Aunt Lenora patiently corrected. "He's made a rather generous offer."

"I don't care how generous his offer is. The Moontide is not for sale."

Aunt Lenora didn't seem in the least perturbed. Her expression was placid, as calm as the summer sky.

"Why the Moontide?" Erin asked, feeling slightly prickly by Aunt Lenora's serenity. How did she not find this offensive? Allan Worth had leveraged his wealth and position to build the sprawling resort that had helped Findlay Roads evolve from a growing tourist destination to the next Hamptons. And with that move, he had put a bullet in the heart of the Moontide's viability. For Burke and Tessa's sake, she had never voiced her opinion about Allan aloud before, but perhaps now was the time to speak her mind.

"He has his resort. Isn't that enough? Why does he think he's entitled to more?"

"It's a free country, Erin. If the man wants to expand his business, that's his right."

She turned, appalled at Burke's words. It was the first he'd spoken since they'd sat down.

"You're defending him?"

Burke shifted, obviously uncomfortable, but he didn't back down. "I'm just saying that we can't blame him for being successful."

Though outwardly she maintained her poise, inwardly, she flinched. Why was Burke on Allan's side? Was it because of Tessa? She swallowed, trying to control her emotions. Of course, it was Tessa. Less than two weeks ago, he'd walked down the aisle, prepared to marry her. It wasn't as if his heart could have healed so quickly. She was naive to think otherwise. All the picnics and stolen kisses in the world didn't mean Burke had so quickly forgotten the woman he'd wanted for his wife.

Just thinking those words turned her stomach. Burke still loved Tessa. And that should not matter to her as much as it did.

"He has land beside the Delphine. Let him use that for his stupid golf course. But if he moves so much as one inch over the property line—"

"He says it's not enough. He needs more land to build the golf course. This property is adjacent to the Delphine's acreage, and the Moontide has a nice bit of land attached to it. It only makes sense he'd want this property to build upon his own."

Erin didn't like the sound of this. "Aunt Lenora, you can't tell us you're seriously considering this."

She didn't reply. Erin felt as if the world had tilted.

"Aunt Lenora? Please tell me you are not considering this."

The older woman sighed. "Not without getting your opinions. But you must know, I've spent the last couple of hours reviewing the inn's financials."

Erin blinked. That's what she'd been doing in the office? Looking over the bookkeeping? Erin swept a glance around the room and noticed things that had escaped her attention when she first came in. Several old sets of ledgers, from the days when Aunt Lenora ran the inn without the aid of a computer, had been moved from their usual spot gathering dust on a shelf and now lay on a chair as if they'd been dropped there recently. The folder that contained last year's tax return was on top of the desk.

Erin shifted to see what was on the computer screen. Aunt Lenora knew the bare minimum of using a computer. She knew how to check email and visit a few websites. But had part of her time in this room been taken up with figuring out how to view the records Erin stored online? The computer was cycling an array of images of her and Gavin over the years as part of the screensaver. So she couldn't tell what Aunt Lenora had seen there. But she knew the B&B's numbers were bad. Very bad.

She flushed, feeling as if this was her responsibility. Since she'd taken over the everyday running of the inn, things had sunk deeper and deeper into the red. She blamed the Delphine, but what if she was also at fault? Was there something more she should be doing?

She'd convinced Aunt Lenora to create a website years ago, and more recently, she'd spruced up the look of it with the help of on-line tutorials. She'd also created a Facebook page (they had a modest forty-one likes) and had registered the inn with several reputable B&B registries. In addition to increasing their online presence, she'd begun advertising with the local community, looking to boost their revenue via outlets closer to home, such as Mrs. Cleary's book club.

But for every strategy she employed the Delphine had ten more, and they were bigger, more impressive, better financed, with personnel devoted entirely to marketing and publicity. Erin felt her chest tighten at the idea of trying to do more. She wanted to...but she was one person. And so far, none of her ideas had paid off in any significantly notable way.

"We've been in a bit of a dry spell," Erin began, but Aunt Lenora cut her off.

"I don't believe it's a spell. I've looked at the records over a ten-year span. Things have been steadily declining for some time."

Erin felt the bite of desperation.

"The area has been in flux for the last few years. There have been a lot of changes to the community, new businesses have sprung up—some by outsiders, even celebrities."

She thought of her best friend, Rory, and

her husband, Sawyer. They'd begun funding a charity organization last year to help underprivileged families. As a famous country music star, Sawyer had the wealth and influence to do plenty of good in the world, and he used his position to benefit others. Perhaps because of his own uncertain future with the possibility of Early Onset Alzheimer's. But his interest in the town had caught the attention of several high-profile celebs, and the area had grown even more as Sawyer's fame and philanthropy did.

"And many businesses and families have benefited," Aunt Lenora agreed. "But not, it seems, the Moontide."

"But…where would we go, if you sold it? This is our home."

"We could rent a place for a time, until something suitably permanent could be found. I intend to make sure you and Kitt are well-provided for. You have no need to worry about that."

That wasn't Erin's main concern at the moment. The loss of the Moontide and all it represented was the focal point of her fears. Erin shivered, feeling unnaturally cold, perhaps in light of the view Aunt Lenora held. The older woman turned to Burke, who had remained silent throughout most of this exchange.

"Burke? What are your feelings?"

Erin shifted her gaze to him, feeling a swell of uncertainty. His head was lowered, as though in contemplation. She could count on Burke to back her up…couldn't she? After all, this place had been his home for most of his teenage years. She knew he had a few negative emotions concerning the inn but surely not enough to want to see it close in place of a golf course?

But as the silence dragged on, her anxiety increased. When he finally lifted his head, he didn't look at her but rather kept his focus on Aunt Lenora. And when he gave his answer, her heart jerked with dismay.

"I think you should sell."

CHAPTER THIRTEEN

Burke waited until Aunt Lenora had gone to bed before he sought out Erin. It was late, and he feared she might have gone to bed already. But he found her in the library, curled up in an armchair with a photo album in her lap. He recognized it as the wedding album, a collection of some of the weddings that had taken place at the inn over the years. The oldest photo in the book, he seemed to recall, was from 1870. He knew Gavin and Erin's photo was in there, as well, and he felt a pang at the thought.

"Hey," he said from the doorway. Though she didn't acknowledge his presence, he stepped further into the room anyway.

"Erin… I'm sorry."

She flipped a page and didn't raise her head. He sighed.

"I know my opinion on the Moontide wasn't what you wanted to hear."

She flipped to another page. He wondered

if she was really looking at the photos now or just using the album as a way to shut him out.

"I don't…feel the same way about it that you do. I'm sorry," he repeated. He wished he could feel differently about the inn. But he didn't. It wasn't a bad place. He was sure it held many wonderful memories for a lot of people. Erin included. But for him, it represented everything life had taken away from him. His parents. Family vacations.

Even Erin. Because here was where her life with Gavin had begun. This was where they had lived and loved. He didn't begrudge her that. But neither did he share her fondness for the place. For him, it didn't matter if the inn was sold or not. All that mattered was that Erin and Kitt were provided for, going into the future. And selling the inn might accomplish that.

He took a tentative step forward and sat down on the edge of the settee. Erin didn't move away, but she didn't acknowledge him either.

"Erin, please try to see it from Aunt Lenora's point of view."

Erin's head came up then, and he could see she'd been crying. Her eyes were puffy and bloodshot. Belatedly, he noticed the edge of a tissue peeking from her balled-up hand.

"What about my point of view?" she demanded, her voice hoarse with frustration. "This place has been my home for almost fifteen years. My memories are here. Gavin—" She stopped suddenly and looked away, sniffing and struggling to regain her composure.

Burke tried to phrase his next words as gently as he could. "Gavin is not here, Erin," he said, his tone soft.

Her face crumpled. "I know that. Of course I know that." She drew a shuddering breath. "But this place is where we planned to spend the rest of our lives together. Losing it…would be like losing him all over again."

Her words shouldn't have hurt him so much. But they did. She still loved Gavin. She still grieved him. Why couldn't he be sympathetic? But all he felt was a jealousy that had festered for too long. Even in death, Erin's heart belonged only to Gavin.

"But Aunt Lenora is right," he argued. "This is no way for you and Kitt to live."

"I have Gavin's life insurance, money from the army that I could use to fund this place until we get back on our feet."

"You need to use that for *you*. To secure a

future for you and Kitt, to send him to college one day. You shouldn't pour resources into a black hole."

She cringed. "Don't call it that."

He bit his tongue and tried again.

"Is this really what you want? To live out the rest of your days in this inn, struggling to make a go of it by yourself?" He knew he had to tread carefully. "Think of Kitt. Is this what you want for him?"

Her eyes narrowed. "Kitt isn't you. He's not bitter about this place."

Burke remained patient. "I'm not…bitter, exactly. I just don't have any great love for the inn. I think it's outdated and it's not providing for you or Kitt or Aunt Lenora anymore. In which case, I can see the merit in Allan's offer."

Her jaw tightened, and she looked back at the photo album in front of her. "Don't pretend you're not biased. Maybe you think that selling the inn will gain you some sort of ground with Tessa."

He blinked, stunned. "What? What does Tessa have to do with this?"

Erin pushed the album off her lap and stood to her feet. "Burke, less than two weeks ago, you were prepared to marry her. And now her father shows up, wanting something, and you're all in. Don't tell me that you're not just a little bit swayed by how that will look to your former fiancée."

He was indignant. "Of course I'm not swayed by that. Why should I be? Tessa has never been involved in any of her father's enterprises."

"That doesn't mean she wouldn't look at you differently if you backed him up."

Burke stood to his feet and looked down at her. She seemed small and vulnerable, ready to burst into tears. But her words were inexplicable.

"What's gotten into you? I think Tessa ditching me at our wedding was a pretty good indication of how she felt about me."

She stood to her feet and faced off with him. "Then why are you taking Allan's side?"

"I'm not. I'm on your side." *I always have been. From the moment I fell for you as a lost and lovesick boy.* "But you're not thinking rationally. You're allowing your judgment to be clouded by grief and sentimentality."

He didn't see it coming when she lifted her arms and pushed him. He stumbled a little but caught himself. "Don't you dare treat me like some crazy widow," she said, her voice thick with anger. "Just because I lost my husband and I love this place does not mean my judgment is clouded."

He held up his hands. "You're right. That wasn't fair. I'm sorry."

His apology seemed to soothe her, at least a little. She crossed her arms over her chest and took a ragged breath. "I'm sorry, too. I shouldn't have pushed you like that."

"It's no big deal. You're upset. You're afraid someone is going to take your home away from you."

She looked at him with such wide-eyed, hopefulness that it made the next words he had to say all the more painful.

"But Erin…at least think about what Allan is offering."

The hope in her expression withered. "This inn has stood for well over two centuries. It has always been a place for families, a refuge. No matter how you feel about it, would you really be okay with Allan turning it into some kind of resort clubhouse?"

She made a good point. That wasn't necessarily something he was on board with. The Moontide was more than just a resort lounging area. But at the same time, Allan was offering Erin a way out—a chance to secure her future and the opportunity for Aunt Lenora to live out her twilight years without the burden of the inn or worrying over Erin and Kitt's future.

"It's a solution to a problem. I never said it was the perfect one."

Erin's features hardened. "Fine, if that's how you feel. But there's no way I'm letting Aunt Lenora give up on this place without a fight."

And to his disappointment, Burke knew she meant it.

"THERE HAS TO be a way." Erin sipped the latte her friend and former employer, Connor Callahan, had made for her. Connor's wife, Harper, also a friend of Erin's, gathered dessert plates while Connor finished rinsing the last of their lunch dishes in the sink. Erin was seated at the kitchen counter in their home.

Harper and Connor had a rare afternoon off from the restaurant, and they'd invited Erin over for lunch. The timing couldn't have been better, given Aunt Lenora's announcement the day before. Or more likely, Harper, as one of Allan's daughters, had heard about her father's plans and decided to invite Erin over to check up on her. However it had come about, Erin was grateful. She needed the support of her friends right now, especially after Burke's betrayal.

"Do you think you can do it?" Harper asked as she cut a peach pie into wedges for their dessert. "I mean, do you really see yourself running the inn by yourself one day, after Aunt Lenora is gone?"

"That was always Gavin's and my plan. After he retired from the army, he would get some sort of job in town, and we'd keep the inn going once Aunt Lenora was too old to keep up with it. And besides, I've been taking care of most of the day-to-day running of it myself for the last few years. Aunt Lenora can't get around like she once did, and with Gavin gone..." She trailed off as Harper handed her a plate.

"But that was before the Delphine opened," Connor pointed out. Erin noticed he didn't attach Allan's name when mentioning the resort. She wondered what he thought of his father-in-law. It wasn't a subject that had ever come up. "I'm sure that's affected the Moontide's business."

Erin poked at her pie. "Of course it has. But...it's new. And fancy. The inn just needs a few renovations, some updates to make it more appealing. Besides, I'm sure eventually people will realize that the Moontide is a much better choice for a more intimate stay. We just need to ride things out until that happens."

She raised her head just in time to see Harper and Connor share a look. Erin couldn't read what passed between them, but she felt a pang at the sight. She and Gavin had been able to do that. Communicate without words. She missed having that connection with someone. She pushed her plate of uneaten pie aside.

"You think I'm being sentimental, too."

"Who called you sentimental?" Harper asked.

"Burke. He said I wasn't looking at this rationally."

"I'm sure he just wants the best for you. And for Kitt."

Harper could be very diplomatic when she had to be. But Erin didn't want diplomacy. She wanted her friends' untainted opinion. But maybe that wasn't possible given all the connections—Harper as Allan's daughter and Tessa's sister, Connor as Erin's former boss and friend.

"What if you expanded your services?" Connor suggested.

Erin sat up straighter. "What do you mean?"

Connor wiped his hands on a dishtowel. "Well, you have that book club that meets at the inn once a month, yeah?" Connor's Irish accent was more pronounced when he got excited, and he was clearly warming to his subject. "Build on that sort of thing. Offer more options to the locals."

Erin nodded. "That's always been part of my plan. But I don't know where to begin."

"Hmm." Connor tossed the dishtowel onto the counter as he considered. But it was Harper who spoke up next.

"What about weddings?"

"The Moontide already offers weddings."

"Well, yeah, sometimes. But the last wedding that took place there was Connor's and mine, wasn't it? And that's been two years. You have all that beautiful lawn space and the gazebo…it's such a cozy venue. What if you did something like, I don't know, a wedding venue open house?"

"You mean, promote the Moontide as a venue option?"

Harper cocked her head thoughtfully. "You could hold it outside, decorate the backyard just like you did when Connor and I got married."

The room fell silent following this suggestion, and then Connor and Erin began speaking at the same time.

"Callahan's can do the catering, and you can invite a couple of local bakeries to offer samples of their wedding cakes."

"I can invite local musicians to come and play. Maybe Rory can make some suggestions since she used to play around town?"

Connor stepped to a kitchen cupboard and opened it. "And what if you had the bridal boutique participate somehow?" He pulled out a mug. "They could showcase a few dresses, put them on display or something."

"Maybe even create some sort of package promotion," Harper said, "where the bride and groom can also spend their honeymoon night at the Moontide."

"Good idea!" Erin felt the thrill of hope. Harper was right, the Moontide hadn't hosted a wedding in a very long time, having lost any wedding business to the Delphine. The resort was able to offer so much more than the inn. Even Tessa and Burke had chosen to have their ceremony there…even if Tessa hadn't gone through with it in the end.

Connor obviously liked his wife's suggestion. He went to Harper and wrapped his arms around her, planting a kiss on her forehead.

"You are absolutely brilliant, love."

Harper made a face. "Just do me a favor and don't tell my dad it was my idea."

"What will he do, if Aunt Lenora doesn't sell?" Erin asked.

Harper sighed. "He'll find some other way to build the golf course. He's not one to give up if things don't go his way."

Though it was probably her imagination, Erin thought Harper's words sounded almost like a warning.

BURKE HAD TO give her credit, Erin had meant it when she said she wasn't giving up the Moontide without a fight.

"An open house?" Aunt Lenora's brow was furrowed, adding more lines to her wrinkled forehead. "You mean invite anyone and everyone to come tramping through here, just for curiosity's sake?"

They were seated at the kitchen table. Erin had asked him and Aunt Lenora to stay after dinner while Kitt went outside with Scout. The dishes weren't even cleared away. Erin had been too eager to talk with them.

"First of all, we'd hold it outside, in the backyard. So not everyone would be tramping through the house, as you put it. And second, the payoff would be worth the hassle. We might even be able to book a few weddings on the spot!"

Erin was obviously excited about the idea, though Burke thought it sounded a little too optimistic. Sure, the Moontide had been a venue for weddings many times in the past, but it couldn't offer the kind of luxury and detail that a larger business, such as the Delphine, could. At least, not without more money for renovations and a lot more work for Erin.

"What's your long-term goal here?" Burke asked. "The Moontide isn't really set up to accommodate multiple weddings over a year. They always take extra work and coordination with caterers, florists and all the dozens of other people who are involved in pulling a wedding off. Not to mention, do you really want to be dealing with bridezillas all the time?"

Erin turned to him with a scowl, her eyes blazing anger at his interference. He should have just kept his mouth shut.

"Just because *you* don't think it's a good idea doesn't mean it's not worth a try."

"I'm just saying, is all the effort you're going to put into an open house worth the trouble?" He drew a breath and steeled himself for her anger. "Erin, do you really think something like this is going to be enough to bring this old place back to life? Are you just putting off the inevitable?"

Erin's jaw clenched, and he prepared for the argument he knew was coming. But then, Aunt Lenora spoke up, turning Erin's attention away from him.

"What all would this open house entail?"

Erin's face lit up, and Burke felt his breath catch. He wished there was some way to make her look this happy every day. Was it possible? He'd dedicate his life to trying, if it were up to him. And if the idea of the open house meant that much to her, should he really be trying to shoot it down?

He watched her expression as she went over all the details of her proposed event. The sight of her enthusiasm made his chest ache. He feared she'd be disappointed. The Moontide had the potential to be something great, but it would take far more time and money than any of them had to offer. And even then, he worried that Erin was holding onto this place mostly for Gavin's sake—for a future that had already been stolen from her.

"And Connor and Harper offered for Callahan's to cater the event with finger foods and hors d'oeuvres . Though I'd also invite a couple of local bakeries to showcase their cakes."

"Ah, so you've been scheming with Harper," Aunt Lenora commented. "I might have known."

Burke raised an eyebrow. "Harper's in on this?" As Allan's daughter, that was an interesting twist.

Erin ignored his question and forged ahead. "Maybe all the inn needs is a chance, Aunt Lenora. It's been in your family for generations. You can't let it go without some sort of fight."

"Hmm." Aunt Lenora didn't speak, but he could tell by the gleam in her eyes that she was considering.

"I'm not sure this is the solution you think it is." He didn't like being the one to deflate her optimism, but he worried she was getting her hopes up too much.

"How would you know?" she countered. "You haven't been around for years. You don't know what it takes to run a B&B."

The accusation stung, but she wasn't wrong. "I don't," he admitted, "not entirely. But I do know a few things. The Moontide is ancient, and it's going to require extensive—

and expensive—renovations to keep it operating efficiently. I've spent the last few weeks repairing some of the more minor issues, but you'll have to hire a competent contractor at some point to keep this house in working order. In addition, I've done some research. B&Bs are still a hot market, it's true, but the income isn't consistent. As a single mom with a small child, is this really how you want to live? With such a precarious and uncertain livelihood?"

"I have Gavin's life insurance money plus his army pay, as his widow."

Burke nodded, trying to remain diplomatic. "Okay. That puts you in a better financial position than most maybe. But what about Kitt's future? How are you going to pay for college? Or any other issues that arise? What if you find something seriously wrong with the Moontide, and you need to dip into that money to fix it?" He hesitated to voice his next argument, but if ever there was a time to address these issues, it was now. "And what about Aunt Lenora? How are you going to take care of her *and* run a B&B as she gets older?"

Aunt Lenora didn't comment on this consideration, but Erin wasn't deterred.

"That's why we need to make the inn viable again."

"Erin, with all due respect, I'm not sure that you can."

She blinked several times in rapid succession and looked away. He wondered if she was holding back tears and felt the bite of guilt. He didn't want to make her feel badly. That was the last thing he wanted. But he also didn't want her chasing a dream that wasn't meant to be or clinging to something when it was time to let go.

"Why are you doing this?" she asked him, her voice a near-whisper of desperation. "Why do you even care? You haven't taken an interest in the Moontide for years…maybe never. So why now?"

Her anger was warranted. He'd wanted nothing to do with the inn before this, so he didn't have a right to offer input on its future. But it wasn't really the inn he cared about. It was Erin, Kitt and Aunt Lenora and their future. He didn't want to see Erin tied to a sinking ship. The Moontide needed more than she could give it, no matter how many open houses she held.

"It's not the Moontide that I'm worried about. It's you."

Her expression hardened at this. "Well, don't be. I'm fine."

His jaw clenched. "Are you, Erin? Or are you holding on to a past that can never be your future?"

"The Moontide's future is my decision," Aunt Lenora said. "But Burke is right, Erin. You might not be able to save the inn, and you shouldn't try to if you're trying to keep something alive that is no longer here." The warning in her words was unmistakable.

"Aunt Lenora, this is my *home*. It has been for nearly fifteen years."

Aunt Lenora held up a hand. "If you believe you can do something to help the Moontide, then you have my blessing."

Erin smiled in triumph.

"When would you like to hold this event?"

Erin drew a deep breath and expelled it quickly as she said, "In two weeks."

"Two weeks?" Aunt Lenora blinked. "My, that's soon."

"Well, the inn had a cancellation for that weekend, and we don't have any other bookings, so I thought it might be a good time."

Burke didn't bother pointing out how telling this statement was. They were in the midst of the busiest tourist season, and the inn had no stays on the books? That was bad. Very bad.

"Erin, you have my blessing to hold your fundraiser, but that does not mean I'm not still considering Allan Worth's offer." She pushed back her chair and stood to her feet. "Now, if you'll excuse me, I'm going to check on Kitt and that rascal of a dog."

An indent of worry appeared in between Erin's brows as Aunt Lenora left the kitchen. Burke longed to touch the spot and soothe it away. She worried far too much. Wouldn't selling the Moontide cure some of that?

"I'll help however I can," Burke offered. "I just don't want you to get your hopes up."

Erin made a face. "No, thanks. I think I'll do better without your help."

CHAPTER FOURTEEN

OVER THE COURSE of the next two weeks, Burke did his best to stay out of Erin's way. She was a whirlwind of activity, making plans for the open house. Despite her insistence that she didn't need his help, he made a few observations and took care of things without her asking.

When he saw her frowning down at a loose board on the veranda steps, he waited until she was in the office and then went to work repairing it. When he overheard her asking Aunt Lenora about giving the gazebo a fresh coat of paint, he took it upon himself to go to the local hardware store, pick up a couple gallons of paint and do the job himself.

She didn't remark on these details—he wasn't even sure she noticed—but he felt better for helping her out in these small ways.

She kept herself so busy, coordinating with local businesses and arranging for advertising, that he sensed Kitt was feeling neglected.

His suspicions were confirmed the afternoon before the open house was set to take place when he stepped outside with the intent of mowing the lawn and found Kitt seated in front of the shed door with Scout at his side. The retriever's tongue was lolling dramatically in the summer heat, and Kitt was plucking at the tufts of grass he sat on.

Burke immediately recognized Kitt's mood based on his expression. He knew he'd worn the same face himself many times growing up, after he'd lost his parents.

Burke figured the lawn could wait. He hurried back into the house, long enough to locate a Frisbee from the box of assorted outdoor games, and then returned to the shed.

"Hey, there you are," he greeted Kitt as he approached. The little boy looked up, seemingly startled that someone had thought of him in the midst of all the open house chaos. Scout stood, tail twitching, and greeted Burke with a lick on the hand. The dog still took care not to put too much weight on his front left leg, but Burke thought it might be habit more than any lingering injuries.

"I thought we could head to the park and toss this Frisbee around. Scout probably would appreciate the exercise."

Kitt hesitated. "Don't you have to help Mom?"

"Nah, she's got things under control. Besides, she wouldn't want you to feel like we've forgotten about you."

This seemed to cheer his nephew a bit. He scrambled to his feet, and Scout let out a woof of approval. The three of them headed to the park, and Burke kept up a steady stream of conversation about the weather and stuff he and Gavin had done during the summers when they lived in Findlay Roads. Kitt didn't say much, but he listened attentively. Scout trotted along beside them, never once straying from Kitt's side.

When they reached the park, they threw the Frisbee around for a half hour or more, though a lot of the time was spent wrestling the piece of plastic from Scout's mouth. The dog seemed to think it was his job to intercept the disc before it reached Kitt, and both Burke and Kitt found the animal's attempts hilarious. After they were both winded, and Scout obviously felt he'd conquered the game, they collapsed onto the grass and let the breeze from the bay cool the sweat on their skin.

Kitt fell quiet again, and Burke sensed he was deep in thought, much as he had been back at the inn. Burke decided to feel him out about everything that was happening.

"Do you know what all is going on right now? At the inn?"

"You mean the wedding house?"

Burke smiled. "There's that. But do you know why your mom is having the open house?"

"To help the inn." Kitt fidgeted. "Lenny might sell it. And I guess it means we wouldn't live there anymore."

Burke nodded and paused to scratch Scout's belly. The dog was sprawled out on his side, panting happily. "How do you feel about that?"

Kitt was silent as he considered the question. "I don't know. I guess I'd miss it." He paused. "Where would we live?"

"I don't know, buddy. But that's not something you need to worry about. Your mom will take care of that."

He frowned. "But who will take care of Mom?"

"I will," he answered automatically, not even realizing what he'd said until it was too late.

Kitt thought about this. "Would you be like...my dad?"

The question struck Burke hard. Because the truth was, there's nothing he'd like better. But Erin didn't want him in that way, and he didn't want to edge aside his brother's memory to fill that role. Burke couldn't be his brother, and he wouldn't compete with his ghost.

"No one can replace your dad, Kitt."

"I know. But you're my uncle. You spend time with me, and you take care of Mom and Aunt Lenora. And you got me a dog. So you're kind of like my dad. My Uncle Dad."

Burke grinned. "Uncle Dad? I kind of like the sound of that."

They sat in silence for a minute as Kitt absently stroked Scout's head. The dog sighed blissfully.

"I wish I remembered him more," Kitt suddenly spoke. "Mom is sad, so I feel like I should be sad, too."

Burke frowned. "Are you really sad? Or are you just…pretending?"

Kitt looked at him. "I'm kind of sad," he said. "I'm sad for Mom. She still cries sometimes, at night, when she thinks I'm sleeping."

Burke's stomach twisted at this insight.

"I'm sad for Mom. Because she's alone."

Burke tried to steady his emotions before replying. "She's not alone, Kitt. She has plenty of people who love and care about her. She has friends and me and Aunt Lenora. Most important, she has *you*."

Kitt didn't respond at first, and Burke didn't press him. He began to pluck at the grass as he'd been doing back at the inn when Burke stumbled upon him.

"I think maybe Mom is afraid to be happy. She thinks she's not allowed."

"Why wouldn't she be allowed?" Burke asked, his voice soft.

Kitt shrugged. "Maybe it means she'll forget my dad, that he'll think she doesn't love him anymore. But… Dad's dead. So how would he know? Unless he's looking down from heaven, like Aunt Lenora says."

Burke drew in a deep breath. Kitt's questions weren't easy ones to answer, but he understood their source. He'd lost his own parents at a young age, and he'd been hounded by so many doubts and questions concerning the hereafter. He still didn't have all the answers to those uncertainties, but he responded to Kitt as best he could.

"There's one thing I know about your dad," he said. "He liked to see people happy. In fact, he'd do whatever he had to in order to make someone smile. So, if he's looking down from heaven, I know that more than anything he'd want your mom and you to be happy again. I bet he misses you. But he'd know that you can't be sad forever. You can miss him. I know I'll always miss him. But he'd tell you that it's okay to smile again."

Kitt looked at Burke, his expression sober. "I wish my mom would smile again. If she can smile, then I'm allowed, too."

And that's when it made sense to him. Kitt couldn't move on until his mom did. All this time, Erin had been worried about Kitt, when really she was the one who was still stuck in a state of grieving.

Burke couldn't help it. Despite the warmth of the day, he pulled Kitt onto his lap and hugged his nephew tightly.

"Kitt, I want you to know that no matter what, if you ever need anything, you just tell me. It doesn't matter where I am or what I'm doing. I'll be here for you. Okay?"

Kitt's voice grew worried. "Are you leaving? Dad left a lot. And then one day, he didn't come back."

And that's when Burke realized something else. He'd never be able to stray far from Erin and Kitt. Even if he wasn't meant to be in her life the way that he wanted, she mattered to him, and Kitt was his nephew. If he had to leave, for work or any other reason, he'd always find his way back to Findlay Roads.

"Don't worry. Even if I do have to leave from time to time, I will *always* come back."

"Dad was supposed to come back, too," Kitt reminded.

"I know, buddy. But I'm not your dad." He felt the weight of this statement. Why had fate chosen Gavin and not him? Gavin certainly had brought more light to this world than Burke ever had. He'd been a husband, a father and a defender of his country. In terms of worth, Gavin far exceeded him. It should have been Gavin here, playing Frisbee with his son.

But it wasn't.

"Hey."

Kitt met his eyes.

"Your dad loved you. And if it had been up to him, he never would have left you and your mom." Burke drew a breath. "And if it's up to me, I'll never leave you either. You got that?"

Kitt nodded.

"Good." Burke stood to his feet. Scout rolled to a sitting position. "We should get back to the inn, see if your mom needs any help getting ready for tomorrow."

Kitt stood and pulled Scout up with him. "Uncle Burke?"

"Yeah, buddy?"

"I'll never leave you either. Okay?"

Burke's heart swelled with both affection and sadness. If only his brother could have lived to see his son, to see how much Kitt had grown and what kind of man he would become.

"It's a deal."

THE DAY OF the open house dawned bright and muggy, and Erin was already in the backyard as the sun came up, making sure the tables and tents were ready to be assembled for the event. Sweat pooled at the base of her back as she surveyed the lawn with a sense of uncertainty.

So much of her future depended on this one day and whether she could prove that the Moontide might turn itself around. She didn't even want to consider what life might look like living elsewhere.

She had first come to Findlay Roads as a teenager, after her parents had separated. Her dad had been an army general, moving them around for years until her mom couldn't handle it anymore. After the separation, her mom, having grown up nearby, moved her and Erin to the Findlay Roads area and rented an apartment for the two of them for a few years while Erin finished high school. Eventually, her parents reconciled, but by then, Erin was engaged to Gavin and remained in town to plan their wedding.

That's when she'd started living at the Moontide. It had been her home longer than any other place she'd ever lived. After years of moving from place to place, untethered and often lonely, as an only child and an army brat, the Moontide became her sanctuary. The thought of leaving it after so much time had passed caused a physical ache in her chest.

But within the hour, she no longer had time to dwell on this past history as the locals who were participating in the event began showing up. Connor and Harper arrived first in separate vehicles loaded with food and warming stations for the event. Burke joined them, and they all pitched in, putting up tents and tables. Shortly after they began setting up, the bakery's crew pulled up, followed by the bridal boutique and the musicians Erin had invited.

As the morning wore on, she was tempted

to ask everyone to form an orderly line. Everywhere she turned, someone had a question for her.

Connor needed to know if she had more tables to accommodate the extra food he'd brought. The bridal boutique girls asked if they could switch their mannequins to the other side of the lawn so the dresses didn't pick up the smell of food from the hors d'oeuvres table. But that required shifting the musicians, who had already set up their speakers and instruments using extension cords, over toward the bakery's cake displays. To complicate matters, the early dawn humidity had turned into a midmorning swelter. Erin's shirt was already clinging to her back, and they hadn't even opened the inn's grounds to guests yet.

Not that there were any attendees to open for at the moment anyway. Despite her efforts to advertise the event, there were no long lines, eager for a glimpse at what the Moontide had to offer. Had she really thought there would be?

It was fine, she decided. People would begin showing up soon enough. She refused to be deterred. This was her chance to prove to Aunt Lenora just how much promise the Moontide still held.

"Where do you want these?"

Erin turned to see who was speaking, but the face was hidden behind a very large, decorative potted palm.

"Oh." She glanced behind her. The local florist had already delivered their flowers for the event. Had they overlooked something? "Are you with Findlay Florists?"

The palm shifted, and a face appeared. He looked mildly offended. "No. I'm with On-line Flower Showers. I have a delivery for Lenora Daniels."

"A delivery?" Erin frowned, confused. She hadn't invited any online florists to this event. The idea was to promote local businesses in conjunction with the Moontide. "I didn't order anything."

"Well, somebody did." He looked down. "Allan Worth? He sent a card. It's in the pot."

He didn't wait for Erin to say anything else but shoved the palm into her arms. "Just initial here." He held out the clipboard for her to sign. Inwardly, she fumed but didn't see how she could refuse the gift. She juggled the palm in one arm, scribbled her initials with the pen he provided and then turned, struggling with the large, ostentatious plant.

Who did Allan Worth think he was? More important, how stupid did he think Aunt Lenora was? As if she'd fall for some cheap potted palm.

Well, judging by the size and weight of the thing, she had an idea that it wasn't so cheap after all. But she wasn't about to have this overgrown monstrosity at her open house. Just as she was debating taking the palm outside to the curb, it was lifted from her arms.

"Thanks." She pushed one of the leaves aside and saw Burke through the foliage. "Oh. It's you."

He didn't react to this lackluster greeting. The truth was, she'd done her best to avoid Burke over the last two weeks, and she'd succeeded quite well, not having to exchange more than a handful of words with him. Until now.

She shifted uncomfortably, wishing her stomach would stop doing butterflies. She didn't want to react like this every time Burke came near. She couldn't. She should have learned her lesson years ago. One kiss, and her world felt upended. The conversation with Mrs. Cleary had set her straight.

She and Burke could never be together. She'd known that, in her heart, all along, but hearing someone else speak those same doubts had served to reinforce her opinion. And it was easier just to avoid Burke than try to address her feelings.

"I let the bakery lady into the kitchen," he said. "She needed to wash a few things up. I hope that's okay."

"That's fine."

"Um…" He lifted the palm he was holding. "Where do you want this?"

"The garbage would probably be the best place."

He arched an eyebrow. "Did you have a bad experience with a potted plant in your childhood that I don't know about?"

She quirked her lips at his attempt at humor. It felt like forever since he'd made a joke. "Not quite. But that particular potted plant that you're holding came from Allan Worth. So I can't say I'm keen on having it around."

She noticed a rectangle of white amidst the green and plucked it free. It was a card, sealed and addressed to Aunt Lenora. She was tempted to open it but knew that wouldn't be right.

"Who does he think he is?" She knew she shouldn't be venting about this to Burke, but the knowledge that this "gift" had come from Allan, perhaps as a way to sway Aunt Lenora, grated. "He'll probably expect Aunt Lenora to leave this plant with the property if it sells. He can display it in his precious clubhouse."

"Erin."

She shifted her attention to Burke. He looked distinctly uncomfortable. But then that wasn't really unexpected since he wasn't on board with keeping the inn. She appreciated that he wasn't standing in her way and had even helped out with a few things over the last two weeks. But she didn't mistake his efforts for acceptance of her plan. If it were up to Burke, Aunt Lenora would have signed Allan Worth's offer on the same day he presented it to her.

"I just wanted to tell you—"

"Erin!"

Her gaze moved to Harper, who had approached from behind Burke.

"Do you have any food picks for serving the hors d'oeuvres? Connor forgot them. I can run back to the restaurant, but if you have any here, it would save time. Toothpicks will work fine."

"Sure. There's a box of them in the kitchen pantry."

"Okay, thanks. Oh, and sorry to interrupt," Harper offered before turning on her heel and heading toward the house.

Erin looked back at Burke, who had found a spot for the palm while she was speaking to Harper. "Sorry, what were you saying?"

He offered a smile, although it seemed a little sad. "You're good at this. Directing the troops. Maybe you should have been the army sergeant."

She shrugged. "Comes from being raised as a military brat, I guess."

He opened his mouth but before he could speak, one of the musicians approached. He didn't look happy.

"Where's your electric panel? We plugged in where you said, by the chef dude's tent, but there are too many feeds going into the electric hookup there. I think it blew a fuse."

"Oh." Erin frowned. "It's inside—"

Connor joined them, raking a hand through his unruly black hair. "Erin, the breaker must have tripped when the band hooked up their equipment."

"That's what I *just said*," the disgruntled musician announced.

"Oh, sorry, mate."

"It's fine. We'll run a second extension cord from another outlet in the house. Hopefully that will help balance out the current."

"Fine, but we'll need to reset the breaker."

Erin looked at Burke. She was curious what he had to say, but it didn't look as if she'd get a chance to hear it.

He smiled, and the sight of it instantly made her feel better. And then she cursed her wayward heart for such a feeling.

"Even sergeants need a little help once in a while," he remarked. "Come on, guys, I'll show you where the electric panel is."

Erin watched as the three men walked away, with Burke in their center. Suddenly, Burke stopped, said something to the other two and turned to jog back in her direction. He slowed as he reached her side once more.

"I just had to say before I forget…good luck today."

He turned and headed back toward the others before she thought to thank him.

IT DIDN'T TAKE long for Erin to recognize several things she hadn't counted on with the open house. For one thing, the July heat was oppressive, the air thick with humidity.

Though the Moontide was air-conditioned, thanks to Aunt Lenora's foresight many years ago, Erin hadn't thought to arrange for fans or any means of keeping guests cool while they perused the offerings in the backyard.

Most of the attendees looked distinctly uncomfortable, fanning themselves rapidly with the brochures Erin had printed up for the event. She had an uneasy feeling that most of those mangled leaflets were going to end up in the trash by the day's end, which she would feel badly about for the inn's sake but also for Burke's. He had offered to use his photography skills to take some high-resolution photos of the inn for her to use. All the hours he had spent photographing and editing the images would be wasted.

She also hadn't thought to supply bottled waters or pitchers of ice water either, and after the sixth guest had asked for something to drink, she and Harper had raided the pantry for a beverage dispenser, filled it with ice water and put it on display along with a stack of paper cups. Now Harper was refilling it every twenty minutes as both the guests and the others working the open house kept draining it.

But the heat also meant that most guests

didn't linger too long. They nibbled on a few appetizers, talked to the ladies from the bridal boutique and then soon made their way back to their cars. The musicians had given up playing and now sat in the shade of the backyard's white oak tree, sipping from sodas they'd brought in a cooler.

The wedding cakes on display from the local bakery were listing dangerously, a slow mudslide of icing and fondant slipping toward the table's edge. Erin felt the last of her battered enthusiasm fizzle as she saw Connor wiping his forehead with an already sweat-soaked towel as he encouraged his drooping staff to keep making the rounds with their hors d'oeuvres platters.

"You'd seriously consider holding your wedding *here*?"

Erin's ears picked up a conversation from several feet away. The group of young ladies had only arrived a few minutes ago. They'd sampled some cake and then attacked the beverage dispenser, draining the water so quickly that Harper was stocking it up again even though she had refilled it less than ten minutes ago.

"I don't know. I thought it would be cute."

"Cute? Or quaint?"

"Kathy thought I should check it out," the would-be bride defended.

Her friends, presumably also her bridesmaids, rolled their eyes. "Ginny, when are you going to realize that you don't have to do everything your future mother-in-law suggests? This is *your* wedding. Wouldn't you rather have it at a venue that doesn't look like something out of *Anne of Green Gables*?"

This particular bridesmaid was waving a bee out of her face as she spoke. Erin thought about jumping in, defending the Moontide, but she didn't have the mental or emotional energy at the moment.

"I don't know. Maybe with the right designer, this place could be charming. Put up those cute wooden folding chairs and drape some tulle on them? It would be, like, more intimate?"

"Ugh, you can do intimate indoors, without the insects and heat. Honestly, Ginny, if this is your choice, I'm not sure I *want* to be maid of honor. Like I told you before, just go with the Delphine. I've heard they do phenomenal weddings."

Erin felt tears threatening. As brutal as it was to overhear this criticism, they were right. Why had she ever thought the Moontide could compete with the Delphine when it came to a girl's dream wedding? Maybe she'd have chosen the ritzy resort herself if it had been around when she and Gavin got married.

But then she shook her head. She knew better. No matter how lovely the Delphine's weddings might be, she would still have chosen a smaller, sweeter venue such as the Moontide for her wedding to Gavin. Even if it was too much like *Anne of Green Gables*.

This didn't change the fact, however, that her open house was poised to become a major flop. She watched as another group of guests left the backyard. If she remembered correctly, they'd arrived less than fifteen minutes ago. Her heart sank even further.

"Hey."

She turned to see Burke hold out a glass of water. "You need to drink something."

"I'm fine," she said, but that was a lie. She was hot, thirsty and miserable. Burke didn't say anything, but he kept his arm, with the glass of water, extended. She could see the ice already dissolving in the liquid, and her throat itched with dryness. She finally accepted the drink and took a sip. It was cool and satisfying, and she proceeded to drain the glass without stopping.

He took the cup out of her hands as she finished, and she was relieved when he didn't remark on her stubbornness. Instead, he shifted a little closer to her and assessed the backyard.

"It's okay if you want to call this off."

She bristled. "No."

He drew a deep breath and released it slowly. "Erin, it's not your fault, but it's obvious you're miserable. And so is everyone else."

The words stung all the more because she knew he was right. But she wasn't about to give in, not yet. This might be her last chance to do something to change Aunt Lenora's mind.

"The heat will break soon." She spoke with a lot more confidence than she felt.

"I've been checking the weather. It's not due to cool off a little until tomorrow."

One day. If she had held off the open house for one day, maybe she'd have had a chance. But who was she kidding? It could have been seventy degrees with clear skies and birdsong, and she still wouldn't have been able to pull this off successfully. Maybe it was fate. Maybe the Moontide really was destined to become a clubhouse.

But the very idea left the bitter taste of anger in the back of her throat.

"At least take a break for a little while. Go inside the house and cool off. That's what everyone else has started to do. Aunt Lenora and I offered the use of the library so people can get some relief."

She'd noticed that each of the businesses attending had started breaking off in shifts to go inside. Connor and Harper had begun sending the Callahan's staff off, too, and even as she looked in their direction, she saw Harper shooing Connor toward the back doors so he could take a break. She'd noticed Harper go earlier. She frowned.

"I can't. This is my event, my responsibility. I'm seeing it through."

"Taking five minutes to cool off and get something more to drink, and maybe even a bite to eat, does not make you a quitter."

She wanted to believe Burke was saying all this solely out of concern for her. But part of her wondered if there was something else to his insistence. He'd wanted the open house to fail so the sale of the Moontide could proceed unhindered, hadn't he?

She suddenly felt overwhelmed by these thoughts. It hurt to think of losing the Moontide. But it hurt more to think that Burke was pushing to see it happen.

"Erin—"

"If you don't have any constructive suggestions, I have things to do."

She didn't look at his face, and she didn't stick around to hear his response because she didn't know how many more times her heart could break before there was nothing left to put back together again.

CHAPTER FIFTEEN

BURKE WATCHED ERIN walk away as a knot formed in the pit of his stomach. He knew she was devastated by the way things were going. The open house was turning out to be a failure. The heat of the day, the irritability of the vendors, and the discomfort of the guests marked it as an utter flop.

Burke lost count of how many would-be brides and their entourages had come and gone in an hour's time. None of them lingered very long, and few bothered to ask any questions about the possibilities of the Moontide hosting their wedding. Sadly, those who showed the most interest in the event weren't even there to consider a wedding on the premises. They'd come to get a look at the inn—especially since word of Allan Worth's offer had spread through the community. They were curious to explore the Moontide and reimagine it as a golf clubhouse.

Most of these locals gravitated to Aunt Lenora, to pry for gossip about the inn's possible sale. He was grateful none of them spoke to Erin. He worried such questions would only upset her further.

He could tell she was doing her best to remain upbeat in front of the everyone. She moved from table to table in the backyard, speaking to the other business owners attending the event and also greeting guests as they entered the backyard. She handed out brochures, directed people to the beverage dispenser she and Harper had set up and congratulated brides on their engagements before mentioning a few of the amenities the inn had to offer.

She presented a cheerful face, but he could see how the effort was wearing on her. He'd kept an eye on her as the event dragged on, watching from a distance and taking careful note of how her shoulders grew tighter with each passing minute. He knew she wasn't drinking enough, and he hadn't seen her eat anything at all today. As far as he knew, she hadn't even gone inside to check on Kitt.

Both his nephew and Scout were holed up in the inn's private living area, watching television. It was the easiest way to keep them out of everyone's hair and away from the suffocating weather. Burke and Aunt Lenora had taken turns checking on them a time or two. Scout would occasionally look out the window and woof, as if to establish himself as watchdog, but the two of them seemed relatively content to be away from the activities.

Part of him wished he could stay on the couch with them, but his concern for Erin wouldn't allow that. She would be heartbroken if this failed. She'd invested so much of her life in the inn. Burke still firmly believed it was time to move on, but he understood why Erin couldn't see that. This was her life now, the thing that had filled the gap in Gavin's absence—both while he was living and now that he was gone.

"It's sad to think of this place becoming some sort of snooty clubhouse, isn't it?"

Burke nearly jumped. He hadn't heard the older man beside him approach until he spoke. He was maybe in his early sixties. He had thinning brown hair with a heavy salting of gray and a thick mustache.

Burke didn't know how to respond to his question. In some ways, it *would* be hard to say farewell to the Moontide. But only because it represented a final goodbye to Gavin, as well. Despite his efforts to help Erin today, he still didn't feel the need to hold onto the inn. This place held far too many memories of things lost.

Rather than answer the question, Burke asked one of his own. "Are you here for the open house?"

The other man had the decency to look abashed. "I'm afraid not. I just happened to see it advertised and thought I'd use it as an opportunity to visit this place again."

"Have you stayed at the inn before?"

"Not as a guest, no."

"Oh. Are you a local then?"

The man extended his hand. "Neal Weaver. I used to be the caretaker at the Moontide, a long time ago. Back when your aunt Lenora could still afford one."

Burke's eyebrows rose at the man's familiarity. He didn't recall a caretaker being around when he and Gavin lived at the inn. "I'm sorry, I don't remember you."

"You wouldn't. I worked at the Moontide before you and your brother came to stay here. But I remember you."

"Hmm. Well, I imagine two orphans coming to live here is somewhat memorable." He tried to keep the bitterness from his voice, but it was there.

"Oh, I knew you before all that. Knew your parents, too."

Burke was surprised. "You knew my parents?"

He gave a short nod. "Ethan and Sophie Daniels. Sweet couple, they were. You were such a lovely family."

Burke was flummoxed. "I'm sorry, but how did you know us? I didn't come to Findlay Roads until after my parents died."

"But you did. You were here as a little boy. You all took a vacation and stayed at the inn. You must have been no more than Kitt's age."

Burke blinked. Neal's words jogged his memory slightly. There had been a trip, though he'd been even younger than Kitt. Maybe five?

"I'd nearly forgotten about that," he murmured.

"Well." Neal cleared his throat. "Perhaps your good times got lost in the bad, hmm?"

"Maybe." But it bothered him. How could he have forgotten that vacation, even young as he was? It was coming back to him in snatches now. It had been summer, and the smell of the Chesapeake had been a new experience for him. They'd lived in the Catskills, and he was familiar with the scent of clean, fresh air, but the bay had struck him as a child with its sharper, muskier aroma.

"My dad made a joke about it." He barely realized he was speaking aloud. "Something about the sweat and blood of all the Irishmen who'd founded this town giving the water its smell."

Neal smiled. "That sounds like your dad. He was a history professor, as I recall. He spent a lot of time in the library, reading up on the area."

Burke didn't remember that, but he recalled how much his father had liked to read. When he was younger, he'd been in awe of his dad's library and the shelves filled with books he had read. Burke, at such a young age, couldn't conceive of reading them all. They had burned in the fire. Every last one.

"And your mom, she was a delight. How she loved you boys. When your dad got tied up in the library, she'd take you for long walks by the bay. Had picnics with you by the lighthouse."

This startled him since it was a pastime he enjoyed. Was it rooted in his subconscious? Did he gravitate toward picnics at the lighthouse because he remembered, on some level, the times spent with his mother there?

"She was always taking photos, too. I guess that's where you got your knack for photography. I've seen your pictures a time or two over the years. Beautiful shots. It must be something, to have traveled all those places."

Burke didn't know how to respond. He knew his mother had taken a lot of photos while he was growing up, but he had never connected it to his own enjoyment of photography. They'd lost most of their family possessions in the fire, so there had been no mementos to mourn over, no images to study and reflect upon.

It took some effort for Burke to return to the conversation and focus on the older man. "How come I don't remember you from when I lived here in town?"

Neal rubbed a finger beneath his nose, as if his mustache tickled him. "I moved away less than a year after you boys came to live here. I came back a time or two to visit family but didn't move back to the area until a few years ago. I imagine it was tough on you two, after losing your parents. I wish I had been here while you were growing up."

"Yeah," Burke agreed. "I wish so, too."

"Well, feel free to look me up anytime. I'm semiretired. I work part time down at the marina. If you can't find me there, I spend a lot of my spare time at the community center. I'd be happy to talk some more. I know it was just that one summer, but I have to say, your family made an impact on me. I'm a bachelor, no wife, no kids. Seeing how happy you all were...well, I've never regretted being a single man, but there was something about your family that made me wish I'd known what it was like to be part of something like that. Even if it was only for a little while."

Emotion clogged Burke's throat. How long had it been since he thought of his family that way? He'd spent so much time mourning what he'd lost. When had he forgotten to appreciate what he'd had, even for a brief time?

Involuntarily, he thought of Erin. Her loss had been different than his own but no less painful. And he'd never once heard her speak with regret about her time with Gavin. She wasn't bitter. Sad, of course. And reluctant to move on, perhaps. But he had a feeling, if he asked her if she'd trade her time with Gavin, knowing she'd lose him, that the answer would be a resounding no. And he realized that he wouldn't want her to. She may have chosen Gavin over him, but maybe that was because God knew that Gavin only had a limited time on earth. So he had deserved the best of everything while he was here.

But Erin...she had become stuck, just as Burke had. She was mired in her mourning, living in a past that no longer existed. Maybe it was time for them both to find their way out of the dark and look to the days ahead. It wasn't a betrayal of those they'd lost. If anything, it was a way to honor their loved ones whose lives had been cut short.

Now was the time for him to embrace the loved ones he still had and stop grieving those he had lost. And maybe, just maybe, he could convince Erin it was time for her to stop grieving, too.

DESPITE ERIN'S BEST EFFORTS, the open house had been a failure. The musicians had left early, grumbling as they packed up their equipment about the event being "a waste of time." The bakery staff was apologetic, even though none of it had been their fault. Even after setting up a fan in the wake of the band's departure, the cool air had failed to save the wedding cakes from melting into a deflated lump of sugar. They salvaged what they could and distributed it to be eaten, but Erin refused. She didn't think her stomach could handle eating anything—it was too twisted into knots. The only group that seemed to benefit from the open house had been the bridal boutique. They'd booked multiple consultations and handed out all their fliers.

Connor and Harper sent most of their staff home while they remained to assist with the cleanup. Erin felt terrible about having dragged them through this event with her. They'd been generous enough to provide the food, and Connor was paying his employees out of his own pocket for helping out. And it had been a disaster. Not to mention the fact that she was exhausted.

But more than that, she was soul sick. While losing the inn had been a harsh possibility two weeks ago, now it felt even more like a stark reality. Aunt Lenora was going to get rid of this place, her home, her sanctuary. This thought, coupled with the utter failure of the open house, nearly caused her to burst into tears.

She held it together for as long as she could, thanking people for coming as they left, expressing her gratitude to everyone who had stuck it out. By the time Harper and Connor had finished up in the kitchen and packed away all their serving platters and sent their crew home, the day had slid into evening. She was physically drained, depressed and ready to lock the door against any more people. For the first time, she was relieved the inn had no guests. She wanted to pretend this day had never happened. That way none of this would be real.

Connor must have read her expression because he pulled her into his arms for a warm hug. They were both sticky with sweat, but she didn't mind. She needed the support.

"We can try again," he offered. "When the weather turns cooler."

She pulled back and forced herself to smile. "Yeah, maybe." She didn't want to sound pessimistic, but she didn't have that much time. And Connor surely knew that. She appreciated that he wanted to help, but Allan wouldn't wait until summer's end for an answer. And Aunt Lenora likely wouldn't want to delay her decision that long either. She had already pushed him off for the past two weeks to give Erin her chance at the open house. She'd had her shot to bring things right. And she'd failed.

"I appreciate all your h-help." Her voice trembled with the tears so near the surface. Connor looked at her with sympathy.

"I know what it's like to lose a place you love, that you gave your heart to and poured your soul into."

She nodded. Connor had lost his first restaurant and nearly the second one that had been his father's. And he'd still managed to rise from the ashes. Now, Callahan's was not only a wildly successful restaurant in Findlay Roads, but there was talk of opening a second location in D.C. Connor had thrived, despite the adversity he'd faced.

But Erin didn't know if she could do the same. The inn had never been hers. And it wasn't as if she wanted to start over with some other B&B. She simply didn't want to lose this place.

Harper stepped up and nudged her husband aside so she could give Erin a hug of her own. "Call me if you want any help to finish the cleanup tomorrow."

"That's okay. You've helped out a ton already," Erin said. In fact, she'd probably prefer to be alone tomorrow, licking her wounds.

"I don't mind," Harper insisted.

Erin didn't want to argue. She just wanted to be alone.

"I'll call if I need you."

She exchanged goodbyes with her friends

and then saw them out the door. Next, she made sure Kitt was in bed. Aunt Lenora had taken charge of him as the night wore on, seeing to it that he ate dinner and took a bath before bedtime.

Erin peeked in his bedroom, not wanting to disturb him, and saw Aunt Lenora dozing in the rocker by his bed while Kitt breathed deeply beneath the covers. Scout was sprawled out along the foot of the bed, one paw resting protectively on Kitt's leg. She relaxed slightly. She still had Kitt. No matter what life might take away, if she had her son, there was still some promise to the future.

The question was…what did the future look like? Aunt Lenora had made it clear that she intended to see that Erin and Kitt were provided for. Erin found this unnecessary. Erin was trying to save most of Gavin's life insurance money for Kitt's college fund, but enough could be spared to buy a small house for the two of them. Property values in Findlay Roads had increased exponentially in recent years, but she was sure she could find something reasonable.

With a sigh, she eased the door closed. She considered dragging herself to her room and simply falling into bed, but she wanted to make sure the inn was closed up tight for the night. She hadn't seen Burke since they'd wrapped up most of the cleanup. She assumed he'd headed to bed, given the late hour. Or maybe he'd even gone out. There was no reason he should just hang around the inn, especially since the old building made him uncomfortable.

She moved slowly down the staircase, savoring the quiet, except for the creaks and groans of the settling house. She checked the front entry and the side one, tidying up a bit as she moved from room to room. When she reached the back door, she found it unlocked and frowned.

A single light illuminated the veranda. She eased open the door and stuck her head outside. The temperature had dropped only a few scant degrees since the sun had gone down, and humidity was still thick in the air. She felt smothered by it. But then the heat was forgotten as she caught sight of Burke sitting on one of the porch chairs and looking out into the night.

His profile arrested her attention, with the sharp slope of his clean-shaven jaw and the way his hair fell over his temple. Her heart fluttered at the sight, but she ignored it, more

interested in why he looked so pensive. It was
as if he was lost in some distant memory. She
hesitated and then gathered the nerve to slip
onto the porch and join him.

CHAPTER SIXTEEN

BURKE DIDN'T HEAR Erin come outside, so he was startled when she first took the seat beside him. She didn't say anything at first, and neither did he. He was content with that. There was a lot on his mind, a lot to consider. Ever since his conversation with Neal, his mind had been retracing memories, trying to recall what else he might have forgotten over the years.

He'd escaped to the back porch about an hour ago, needing the quiet to manage his concentration. And while he couldn't say he'd been able to pull up any more memories, he'd relived the ones that had surfaced.

He couldn't imagine how he had forgotten that summer, or why Aunt Lenora hadn't brought it up. Perhaps she thought it would wound him further, but in truth, he'd found it healing. All those families he had witnessed over the years—all those times he'd been miserable and overcome with jealousy for what they had and he didn't…but he'd had those things, once. Yes, they'd been taken from him. But he'd *had them*.

Love wasn't less precious when it was lost. Perhaps it was more precious because it had been fleeting. His time with his family, short though it had been, had created the foundation for who he was and wanted to be. It was those memories that should have defined him, not what he had lost. It had been a lesson that was a long time coming, but he finally understood.

And with that understanding came a clarity he had never known.

He loved Erin. He had always loved her. And he wanted to believe that she loved him, too. They were both wounded and felt a deep obligation to be faithful to Gavin's memory. But perhaps they had both lost sight of who Gavin was and what he would have wanted for them. It certainly wouldn't have been his wish to see them live without love. Would he have begrudged them a lifetime together, when his own time had been cut short?

Burke didn't think so. His brother had spent such a large part of his life caring for others—from their childhood when he'd watched out for Burke and tried to walk him through his grief and loss, to providing for and promising himself to Erin and even to protecting his country. That was who Gavin was. And maybe, just maybe, to deny themselves happiness was in itself dishonoring all that Gavin had lived for.

He turned to Erin then and said the thing that was foremost in his mind.

"I love you."

It was a bold declaration, but he didn't know how else to say it. He wanted to be bold. He wanted to live life without letting his fear of loss rule him. He had spent too many years building walls, holding himself back from relationships because he was so certain that if he loved something, he would lose it. It was a theory he'd seen proven true over and over—from his parents to his love for Erin to his brother. Every person he'd loved had left him, in some way or another. But that was just life. If he wasn't willing to live it, then of course, death couldn't hurt him.

But he also wouldn't experience all the things that made death such a threat.

Erin's eyes were wide. She looked as if she'd been jerked awake unexpectedly. He took the opportunity to lean in, gather her face in his hands and kiss her soundly on the lips. She remained frozen for several heart-beats while his mouth explored hers, and then she pushed him away, somewhat violently, and scrambled to her feet.

"What are you doing?" she demanded.

"Erin, I'm in love with you. I don't want to deny it any more. I can't. I have loved you since I was seventeen years old. Some days, I buried it so deeply that I was convinced I was free of it. I lived for years like that, be-lieving my feelings for you had been the re-sult of teenage hormones. But that was just a lie I told myself to ease the heartache of missing you. That's why I left Findlay Roads. And that's why I so rarely came back while you were married to Gavin. Because see-ing you brought the truth painfully close to the surface—I was in love with my brother's wife." He swallowed. "But Gavin's not here anymore. I would give anything to bring him back, I swear. But I can't say it means I don't love you. Because I do."

She was still wide-eyed. "What about Tessa?"

He shook his head. "I care about her. But I'm not sure I ever loved her. She was safe. Sweet. There were no risks with Tessa. That was the point. I had less to fear where she was concerned. But with you... I'd risk everything if it was for you. Because it's *always* been you."

She took a step back. "Burke. Don't. We can't. I'm married to Gavin."

"Gavin's gone, Erin." The words still pained him. He suspected that they always would. "But you and me…" He pointed a finger at her and then at himself. "We are still here."

She shook her head, but he could tell she was thinking about what he'd said. He stood but didn't move toward her.

"Do you love me?"

The question drew her gaze back to his, her green eyes growing wider. "W-what?"

"Do you love me?" he repeated. "Because if you do…that's all that matters."

"I have Kitt to think about."

"I adore Kitt. And I believe he's pretty fond of me, too. My first choice would always be to have Gavin raise him. But if Gavin can't do it, then I'd like to step into that gap and be his dad."

She stared at him. "Do you have any idea what you're saying? You run, Burke. It's what you do. You protect yourself by not getting too attached and by staying away. You feel sorry for us, I get that. But I'm not going to let you talk me into some relationship just because you have a misguided sense of duty."

Anger flared at her words. "Duty? Why would you think this is about duty?"

"Because Gavin was your brother, and you weren't here when we needed you, and now you think you can make up for that by saying you love me." Her eyes filled with tears as she spoke. "You're right, love is a risk. But you're a bigger risk than most where it's concerned."

He tried to remain patient, but her words struck him in an almost painful way. "You know me better than that. Don't try to mask your own issues by hiding behind mine."

"*My* issues?"

He gave a short nod.

"How dare you turn this around on me!"

"But it is on you, Erin," he threw back. "Because no one can force you to let go. You have to do that for yourself."

"Let go of what?"

"Of this!" He gestured toward the inn's back door. "Of the Moontide, of Gavin, of this little cocoon you've created for yourself to avoid getting your heart broken again."

Her jaw had dropped, and he felt a twinge of remorse but not enough to stop. He'd held back so much with Erin for so long. For fifteen years. He didn't think he had it in him to keep silent any longer.

"Holding on to the Moontide won't bring Gavin back. And it's no way to live your life. You have to move forward. You can't hold on to this place just because of what it represents."

Her eyes flared to life. "That's so easy for you to say when you hate this place. You ran away because you couldn't handle your grief, and now you're accusing me of holding on to mine?"

He shook his head. "I don't hate this place. I never did. And I didn't run because I couldn't handle the grief. I left here when I turned eighteen for *you*."

She folded her arms across her chest. "What do you mean, for me?"

"Because I loved you, and you chose my brother. That's why. And if I couldn't have you, I wasn't going to stay here and watch the two of you in love. Or worse, be tempted by you every day he was gone on a deployment."

Her cheeks grew red, but he continued, taking several steps forward and causing her to take two back.

"I love you. And I want to marry you. But I won't live in my brother's shadow or have his ghost in my bed. And by living at the Moontide, that's exactly what would happen. I don't hate this place. In some ways, I'm kind of fond of it. But it's never quite felt like my home."

He drew a deep breath, trying to steady himself, and then went down on one knee. "I want to create a new home and new memories. With you. With Kitt. I want to put down roots and leave the past behind."

Erin's hand went to her mouth as she stared down at him.

"I know how much you loved Gavin—how much you still love him. I love him, too. I would never do anything to dishonor his memory. But I won't live my life as some sort of punishment for the loved ones I've lost. I've done that for too long. I want to start *living*. For myself. For you and for Kitt. And I want you to have that, too."

He stopped and took a breath. "What do you say?"

She stepped back, putting distance between them.

"No," she breathed, dropping her hand back to her side. "No, I can't."

He was disappointed, but he couldn't say

he was all that surprised. After all, he'd heard those words from Erin before. "Why not?"

I love you. Choose me.

That's what he had asked her, so many years ago along the shores of the Chesapeake. And her response had been the same then as now.

"I'm sorry...but I can't."

He released a breath of defeat and then stood.

"Fifteen years ago, you said no because of Gavin."

He bowed his head.

"Fifteen years later, and Gavin's dead. But you're still saying no because of him."

He didn't wait to see if she had a response. Instead, he brushed by her and headed back inside.

BURKE HAD A good idea of what was coming when Aunt Lenora said she needed to speak to him the next morning. Kitt and Erin were still in bed, but Burke had been unable to sleep after all that had occurred the night before. He'd gone into the kitchen to make himself some coffee and discovered Aunt Lenora had beat him to it. She poured him a cup and then said, "It's time you and I had a talk."

They settled themselves at the kitchen table, a sealed container of Erin's homemade croissants between them, though he had no appetite at the moment. Aunt Lenora wasn't one for preambles. She wasted no time in telling him what was on her mind.

"I'm selling."

Burke leaned back in his seat and eyed her with consideration. "Are you sure this is what you want?"

She studied him with the same concentration he was bestowing on her. "I would not have expected you to ask me that, given your feelings for this place."

He frowned. The words shamed him somehow, though he wasn't quite sure why. "It's just that you and the Moontide have always gone hand in hand. I guess, given your history, I'm surprised you'd actually go through with selling it."

"If it wasn't for Gavin and Erin, I would have sold it a long time ago."

He raised his eyebrows in surprise.

"Gavin loved this place. He and Erin had dreams of buying it from me one day and running it together. I knew it would likely be a challenge for them, but together, they were up to the task."

Burke felt that familiar pang of loss. "And now that Gavin's gone, that dream is dead." Burke realized why he was feeling shame. Because he didn't love the Moontide as Gavin had. "I'm sorry, you know."

"For what?" Aunt Lenora asked.

"I've said it to Erin and to Kitt. But I don't think I ever said it to you. I'm sorry you lost him. I'm sorry I didn't come back right away, after he died."

Aunt Lenora leaned forward. "You run away when you're hurt, Burke Daniels. You did it when you were fourteen, and you did it when your brother died."

He felt a twist of pain, Aunt Lenora's words striking too close to a truth he hadn't wanted to admit. "What do you mean?"

"When you came to live here, you were like a wounded animal. Like that dog you adopted. Skittish. Wary. Unwilling to be hurt again." She gave a little snort. "The dog recovered far faster than you did. Some days, it was all I could do to keep tabs on you, when you hid in the attic or went to Fallon Point to look out at the bay after school."

"You knew about that?"

"I knew. I wouldn't be much of a guardian if I wasn't keeping an eye on you."

He was stunned. He had always thought Aunt Lenora hadn't known nor cared what he did. He'd done his best to never cause her grief. He hadn't rebelled or lashed out. He'd maintained average grades and had a handful of well-behaved friends. He didn't go to parties, and he didn't get close to people. Erin was the closest friend he'd ever had. He'd always assumed that Aunt Lenora didn't care what he did, as long as he kept out of trouble.

"I…didn't know that. I always figured that as long as I kept my nose clean, you didn't care."

She frowned. "Of course I cared. But you were like that dog of yours. Every time I tried to approach, you backed away. I thought you just needed time to lick your wounds, to heal." She sighed. "But you never really did. And when you turned eighteen, you ran. Again." For the first time in all the years he'd known her, Aunt Lenora looked…vulnerable. "I'm sorry I failed you. I didn't know anything about raising children, much less two wounded and grieving teenage boys."

His heart caught in his throat, and the words came out falteringly, "You did just fine. You showed Gavin and me more caring than anyone else. You gave us a home."

She clasped her hands on the table. "I know you've never seen this place as your home. Gavin did. But not you."

The knot remained lodged in his throat. "I'm not sure I could see any place as home, after my parents died." He drew a breath. "And I'm sorry, that I wasn't able to be more like Gavin."

"More like Gavin?"

"Yeah. That I couldn't… I don't know. He just, he had a way…" Burke broke then, the tears for his brother rising unexpectedly. "He was a healer. Gavin had that gift of making the worst situation better because he had faith. I could never be like that. And I'm sorry. I know you loved him better, that everyone loved him better…and he's the one that's gone."

He lowered his head and let the tears flow, so overwhelmed by his grief that he didn't realize Aunt Lenora had moved from her chair and come to his side until he felt her lay her head on top of his.

"Oh, dear child." He felt the weight of her small frame, leaning on him. He'd grown accustomed to her not touching him. It had never been her way. But feeling her so close to him now was soothing. "I never loved him better. Just differently. *You* were the one who captured my heart."

These words stunned him. He straightened, and so did she.

"Me?"

She gave a short nod. "You and Gavin were so different. He saw the light in the world and tried to preserve it. I think that's why he joined the army. He wanted to protect what he valued. But you…you see the truth. The only problem is you don't always know how to live with that truth. Gavin may have made the world brighter, but you, sweet boy, make it matter."

He swallowed, too shocked and moved to respond. Lenora released a ragged sigh, but he sensed some deeper emotion in it.

"You love Erin," she stated.

He considered denying it. Wouldn't it be better for him to keep that information to himself, especially given that Erin had turned him down? But then, like Aunt Lenora had said, it was time for a new chapter. And maybe a clean start meant being honest, not only with himself but also those who loved him. *Loved him.* He hadn't realized until this moment just how much he needed to know he was loved.

"I have loved her since I was seventeen years old," he admitted. "I left here and didn't come back much because it was too painful to see her with Gavin. She belonged with him," he rushed to explain. "They were meant for each other. But I couldn't bear to witness it. I wish… I had. I wish I'd had more time with him."

Aunt Lenora nodded in understanding. "You ran," she said again. "But I think, perhaps… you're done running."

Her words settled on him with the weight of a benediction. "I think you're right. I'm ready to be here, in Findlay Roads, for good."

Aunt Lenora smiled. "I've waited a very, very long time for that. So let me be the first to say…welcome home."

ERIN SLEPT IN late the following morning. At one point, she roused enough to hear a faint knock on her door and the creak of it opening, but she kept her head buried beneath the covers and soon enough, her intruder closed the door again and let her be. She slept fitfully, a subconscious tangle of dreams and nightmares causing her to toss and turn.

In one, Gavin was beckoning to her from the lighthouse but no matter how hard she ran to him, she never gained any ground. In another, Burke stood on the shore of the bay. She stood watching him for a long time as he looked out over the water. And then he turned and began walking away. She tried calling to him, but he didn't turn around, and she couldn't will her legs to move to follow him.

She woke up from that particular dream drenched in sweat, her heart thumping heavily. After stumbling to the bathroom and draining a glass of water, she returned to bed and fell back into another restless sleep.

By the time she finally stirred, her stomach was growling loudly and the bedside clock registered the time as well past noon. She frowned in dismay at her laziness and then reconsidered.

If the inn would be closing, she'd have no guests to worry about, no duties to tend to in the future. She might be able to sleep in more often. It was a bittersweet thought. Besides, she reminded herself, the inn hadn't closed yet. Unlikely as it seemed, maybe Aunt Lenora would reconsider.

She hopped in the shower and tried to keep her thoughts focused on what else she could possibly do to help the Moontide. But her mind kept returning to Burke, to the way he'd looked at her the night before and to the things he'd said.

I love you. I want to marry you. I want to put down roots and leave the past behind.

And the way he'd kissed her, as if she was his sole reason for existence. She shivered at the memory but then pushed it away. She had told Burke no. Again. She had her reasons. She believed she was doing the right thing.

But why did the right thing hurt so much? Of course, it had hurt fifteen years ago when she'd turned him down. But that had been for a good reason, too.

Gavin. She'd made the right choice then. Surely she was making the right choice now.

She stepped out of the shower and dried off, dressed in her favorite pair of jeans and an old T-shirt of Gavin's and pulled her hair into a ponytail without bothering to dry it. It was too late in the day already to waste time with primping. She hesitated before heading downstairs, worried about the embarrassment of facing Burke. But she couldn't hide in her room forever and decided it was best to meet the awkwardness head on, as if nothing had ever happened. Burke would follow her lead, as he'd done over the years, and they'd say no more about it.

Though she felt confident about this, she was no less disappointed in the idea of keeping Burke at a distance, as she'd done for so long. They'd been friends once, very good friends. She'd cherished having that back, but she'd been foolish to think it could last. She would always have to keep Burke at arm's distance. She wouldn't be able to resist temptation otherwise.

She reached the first floor and headed for the kitchen, ears tuned for conversation and wondering what Kitt had been up to all day. The house seemed eerily silent. She stepped into the kitchen and found it empty. Despite her rumbling stomach, she wasn't sure she could eat—at least not until she had reassured herself Kitt was being taken care of.

"Aunt Lenora? Kitt?"

She didn't call out Burke's name, but neither of the others responded. She wandered through the house, soaking up the atmosphere. The leftover evidence of the open house had been cleaned up, and the inn looked much the same as it always did. The sight was reassuring, even if it did make her sad. What kind of changes would Allan make?

In the library, she paused to run a hand over the fireplace and let her gaze roam around the room, viewing the setting with a new appreciation. It was hard to imagine the inn as anything other than a B&B. It had been a place for families and travelers for as long as she'd lived in Findlay Roads. After another minute spent memorizing the details of the room, she headed back to the hall.

She wandered toward the parlor and finally discovered Aunt Lenora, watering the plants blooming on the windowsills. Belatedly, Erin remembered the gift Allan Worth had sent the day before and wondered what had happened to it.

"Where's Kitt?" Erin asked.

"With Burke. He took him and Scout for a walk. They were both restless after being cooped up inside yesterday, and it's cooled off quite a bit."

"Oh." Erin didn't have a response to this. It was thoughtful of Burke to get Kitt and Scout out of the house, but it also made her wonder if he was avoiding her. Not that she could blame him if he was.

"Erin."

Erin focused her attention on Aunt Lenora as the older woman said her name.

"I think it's time we talk."

Erin felt her shoulder stiffen into a rigid line of tension. She knew what was coming.

"Please. Give me another chance. I messed up yesterday, I know. But if I could just try again—"

Aunt Lenora reached out and took Erin's hands in her own. She ignored Erin's pleading and tugged her toward the settee. They both took a seat.

"This house has been part of my family for generations."

"I know. Which is why I don't understand why you want to give it up."

Aunt Lenora looked around, a strange smile on her lips. It was as if she and the house were silently communicating. Erin felt oddly out of place.

"It's time it had a new story."

"I don't understand."

The older woman returned her gaze to Erin's. "You don't have to. I believe this is the right decision."

"And what if it's not?" Erin's words came softly, but they echoed in the overwhelming silence. "What if you're wrong?"

Aunt Lenora's expression was not without pity. "I could be," she admitted, "but I don't think I am."

"Then let me buy the Moontide from you. I have Gavin's life insurance. It's not as much as Allan is offering, but wouldn't you rather see the inn stay in the family?"

"No."

It was such a stark and immediate refusal that Erin felt a tug of desperation.

"What about Kitt? If you won't consider me then please consider him. What if he wants to run it someday?"

"Oh, Erin. There is a whole wide world out there, just waiting for Kitt. I wouldn't want him to decide to remain here out of some sense of obligation to me, or to you, or even Gavin. The money from his life insurance is for your future, not to be used to save this old place."

"And what do you think Gavin would say, if he was here?"

The pity in Aunt Lenora's expression shifted to something harder. "He is *not* here, Erin. He has not been for a long time. Keeping yourself chained to this place will not bring him back. It will cause you to waste the best years of your life in self-imposed punishment."

Erin shook her head. "You don't understand me at all. You don't understand Gavin or what this place meant to him."

Aunt Lenora arched one fine, gray eyebrow. "I understand far more than you know. I know that you love this place. I have loved it, too. But it's time for a new chapter. For all of us, including this old house."

But Erin was not ready to give up. "Aunt Lenora, please, if it's about the money—"

"It has never been about the money. The money will be helpful, it will allow us to establish a new life beyond this place. I already have a house in mind for us to rent until we can find something permanent. But the money is not why I'm selling. And that's why you will not change my mind."

Erin heard the finality in this declaration, but she was still not willing to give up.

"Please." Tears rose to her eyes. "I will ask you one more time. Please don't sell this place. Please don't give it up, when it is so precious to me."

Aunt Lenora's face softened. She leaned forward. "I am sorry, Erin. I know it pains you, and I am the most sorry for that. But this is the best thing. I am sure of it."

Erin felt the weight of sorrow settle onto her shoulders. She had lost. First Gavin and now the inn, her last tangible connection to him. She sniffed and sat there a moment longer, absorbing the finality of this blow. She knew she shouldn't be angry with Aunt Lenora. The inn was her property. It was her choice to sell it. She had been gracious in letting Erin and Kitt live here all these years, both before Gavin's passing and particularly afterward. But at the moment, none of that generosity mattered. Erin felt nothing but anger at the older woman. She pushed back her chair and stood.

"Then, if you'll excuse me. I have to consider how I'll share this news with Kitt."

"We can tell him together, if you like."

"No." Erin rejected this suggestion. "No, I think it would be better if he heard it from me."

Aunt Lenora gave a nod of acquiescence. Erin turned then, hurrying from the room before her tears began to flow in earnest.

CHAPTER SEVENTEEN

ERIN WAITED UNTIL after dinner that evening to talk to Kitt. In fact, she didn't bother going downstairs for dinner at all. She was still angry at Aunt Lenora, and she didn't want to see Burke either. She managed to avoid them both for the rest of the afternoon, staying holed up in her room—the room she'd always shared with Gavin, silently mourning Aunt Lenora's decision. No one came to check on her, and she suspected Burke was keeping Kitt distracted in order to give her some space. She appreciated his thoughtfulness, but it didn't ease the sting of knowing she'd have to face him sooner or later.

Erin peeked her head into the hall after she heard Kitt's tiny footfalls on the stairs and the notable creak of his bedroom door. Seeing no one about, she slipped out of her room and went to Kitt's bedroom. She found him with an array of plastic green soldiers spread out in front of him. Scout wasn't with him, and she realized how odd it seemed without the dog around. In such a short time, Scout had become a member of the family, Kitt's silent companion, even if he was technically Burke's dog.

As she stepped inside the room, her eyes automatically flicked to the framed photo of Gavin, in his army dress, on Kitt's nightstand. The sight of him left her feeling ashamed. She had failed him, failed their dream. And now she had to figure out how she was going to break the news to her son.

"Hey, sweetheart."

Kitt looked up as she went to sit down beside him.

"You're awake," he noted.

"I am. I've been awake. I just…needed some time."

Kitt nodded in understanding. "That's what Uncle Burke said."

She couldn't help it. Her stomach flip-flopped at this confirmation that Burke had seen to it she was left alone to grieve for the day. She shifted her focus to her son, trying to push away thoughts of Burke.

"What are you doing?" she asked.

"Playing," Kitt replied as he placed several of the toy soldiers into a toy Jeep.

"Hmm." She watched him for another couple of minutes as he moved the toys around, clearly unfazed by her presence. She finally reached out and ran her fingers through his hair. He didn't react, still playing.

She sighed.

"Kitt, there's something I have to tell you."

She didn't need to instruct him to put the toys away. He pushed the Jeep and its occupants aside and then placed his hands in his lap, looking at her expectantly. She drew a breath and looked away, trying to gather her emotions so she didn't end up crying in front of him.

But it was a lost cause as the tears trickled down her cheeks.

"Kitt, I'm sorry."

She broke then, the trickle of tears becoming a torrent. She sobbed for a couple of minutes, inwardly berating herself for losing it completely in front of her son. But Kitt seemed to understand because the next thing she knew, he was climbing into her lap, wrapping his arms around her and patting her cheek.

Of course, this only made her cry harder. She wasn't even entirely sure why she was weeping. She was certainly devastated about the inn, but this violent emotion came from something deeper. Perhaps it went the whole way back to her childhood, being moved around from place to place as an army brat and feeling as though her needs came second to her father's career. She cried and cried for the things she'd lost until her chest hurt, and her eyes burned. And then, almost as swiftly as it began, the tears stopped.

She drew a deep, shuddering breath and held Kitt tightly to her. He hadn't budged during the entire episode. She planted a few kisses on the crown of his head, which was damp with her tears.

"I'm sorry, sweetheart. I'm not sure what came over me."

"You're sad," he said, his voice soft and concerned.

The funny thing was that she wasn't sad. At least, not as much as she had been. The crying fit had relieved some of the pain in her chest, the pressure of grief. For the first time in a long time, she felt cleansed of mourning.

"I'm better now," she reassured him. "Much better." She squeezed him tightly and drew a deep breath. "But I have some bad news." The words came easier than she had expected. "Aunt Lenora is selling the Moontide. It means that we can't live here anymore."

She ducked her head to see her son's face. His expression was thoughtful. "We'll have to leave." It wasn't really a question. Kitt had clearly been expecting this announcement.

She brushed the hair off his forehead. "Aunt Lenora already has a house in mind that she'd like us all to rent together, until we can find something more permanent."

"Uncle Burke, too?"

She paused. Burke. What would happen with Burke? Especially now?

"I don't know," she admitted. "Uncle Burke was only going to live here for a little while, remember? Just until he could figure out what he was doing next."

"But he loves us," Kitt pointed out. "And we love him."

Erin stiffened at her son's logic. She didn't love Burke. She couldn't love him. Her head wrestled this point with her heart. "Your uncle Burke will always love you," she replied lamely.

Kitt frowned. "Can Scout come live with us, too?"

"Scout is technically Uncle Burke's dog, and I don't know if the house we'll be renting allows pets. So I think he's better off with Uncle Burke right now."

She refused to acknowledge how much this hurt her, an additional blow to her already ravaged emotions. She'd grown attached to that dog, and she knew that Burke couldn't very well take it with him on his travels. Maybe, after they were better settled, she could offer to take the dog off Burke's hands. Once he was traveling again, he wouldn't be able to care for Scout anyway.

The thought of Burke leaving and not knowing when or if he'd come back tore a hole through the remainder of her spirit. She had to bite down hard on her lip to keep from breaking into tears once more.

"Scout needs us," Kitt unexpectedly announced. "So does Uncle Burke. And we need him, too."

Erin bit down so hard on her lip that the skin broke, and she tasted the bitter tang of blood. She didn't answer Kitt but shifted him off her lap so she could stand and grab a tissue from the nightstand to blot against her stinging lip.

"Mom?" She looked down at her son, who stared up at her with wide-eyed optimism. "It's going to be okay."

He looked so much like Gavin in that moment that she expected her heart to break all over again. She was stunned when she realized she felt a twinge of wistful longing but not the painful ache she expected.

She scooped her son up into her arms and squeezed him tight.

"As long as I have you, Kitt, then yes. It's going to be okay."

ONCE AUNT LENORA made the decision to sell, things proceeded swiftly. Allan Worth was obviously eager to finalize the sale, and as soon as the paperwork was signed, Aunt Lenora began the tedious work of packing up a house that had been in her family for generations. She was ruthless as she directed Burke on what to box up, donate or place in storage. He followed her directions to the letter and kept himself busy with all the tasks she'd given him.

Because the busier he was, the less time he had to think about Erin or wonder how she was doing. They were still living in the same house, but they were no closer than if they were two separate guests staying at the inn. They saw each other for meals, kept their conversation to a minimum and went about their assignments on their own.

From what little he saw of her, she seemed despondent. He hadn't asked Aunt Lenora how it had gone when she'd told Erin about her decision, but based on how Erin had avoided them all that day and her subsequent silence, he could guess her feelings well enough. Not that he'd expected differently. He knew Erin's feelings wouldn't change. She'd made that clear fifteen years ago, and it was even clearer now. She was still clinging to what she'd lost, unwilling to open her heart to love a second time.

Or maybe just unable to consider love with *him*.

Her rejection still hurt, in a far deeper way than Tessa's had. Maybe, deep down, he had known that he and Tessa weren't meant to be. But with Erin, he no longer had a single doubt. He felt as if he was missing out on something precious, a love so incredible that it had been worth the wait. But whatever longing he experienced, Erin obviously had made a different choice. He would have to live with that until the end of his days.

But he'd decided not to run. He'd made an offer on the house at Fallon Point, and the seller had accepted. He'd live there alone, unless you counted Scout, who was coming with him. The house Aunt Lenora had arranged to rent for a few months for her, Erin and Kitt had a firm no-pets policy.

In a way, Burke was glad for that. It gave him the excuse to take Scout with him with the offer that Kitt could come and visit the dog, and him, anytime he wanted. It would give him a reason to keep spending time with his nephew and maybe, occasionally, he'd be able to talk to Erin as well.

He didn't tell Erin about purchasing the house on the point, though. He let Aunt Lenora share that news. It wasn't as if they talked much these days anyway, he thought as she brushed by him in the upstairs hallway without a word. Sometimes, he wondered if he was really a ghost, haunting the halls of the Moontide.

And no matter how hard his heart beat when Erin came near, she seemed not to hear it at all.

Findlay Roads Courier
Local News

On August 1, the Moontide Inn closed its doors to guests for the final time. The inn has been a landmark in the Findlay Roads community for generations, dating back to 1789, when it was first built by Irish immigrants, Cormac and Grainne O'Beirne. The Moontide passed hands several times during the nineteenth century until it was purchased by Hugh Daniels in 1901. Several generations of the Daniels family have lived in the home since that time, ending with "Aunt" Lenora Daniels, a lifetime Findlay Roads resident.

Ms. Daniels recently sold the inn to Allan Worth, owner of the Delphine Resort on Dublin Avenue, so that he might expand the resort's offerings with a clubhouse and golf course that will take over the inn's acreage. When asked how he felt about acquiring the longtime local treasure, Worth responded, "I couldn't be more thrilled that the Moontide has come into my possession. The upcoming renovations will boost the economy of the area and continue to elevate Findlay Roads as a resort destination."

Ms. Daniels declined to comment, but her great-niece by marriage, Erin Daniels, replied, "I trust Allan knows what a treasure the Moontide is, and he will treat it with the same love and care that previous generations have instilled in it. I'm sure many future Findlay Roads residents will continue to value its place in the community."

Erin Daniels is the widow of Sergeant Gavin Daniels, hometown hero who passed away two years ago in a car accident while driving to the airport to return to his army base. Gavin Daniels, along with his brother, Burke Daniels, had lived at the inn as teenagers after their adoption by "Aunt" Lenora. When asked what her late husband would have thought of the inn being sold, Ms. Daniels said she didn't know what his thoughts on the matter might be, were he still living.

The Moontide Inn is located at 1214 Eamon Lane.

CHAPTER EIGHTEEN

ONE WEEK AFTER they'd all moved out of the Moontide, Burke to his house on the point and Aunt Lenora, Erin and Kitt to the house they were renting together, Burke received a call from Tessa. It was unexpected, but when she tactfully mentioned all his boxes still sitting in her garage, he realized he'd better clear them out. Besides, now that he had his own place again, there was no reason for his possessions to be taking up space at Tessa's. He planned to spend the remainder of the summer fixing up the house and settling in before he jumped back into some work projects in the fall.

As he pulled up to the cottage Tessa had inherited from her grandmother, he considered how much could change in the span of a couple months. This house was supposed to have been his home. He'd looked forward to it, settling down, finally making his peace with this town and putting down roots here.

And he'd done just that but without Tessa at his side. He'd learned his heart's true north was the same as it had been fifteen years ago, even if Erin was no more in love with him now than she'd been then. He'd come to some sort of peace about that, too, even if he still longed for what could never be.

But at least he and Tessa had been able to part amicably. While he still felt great affection for Tessa, he was not in love with her and wasn't sure now if he ever had been. Or at least, if he had, it was a pale thing compared to what he felt for Erin. He should have known when he moved back here that he had never really shaken Erin from his heart. He'd tried. He'd traveled the world, immersed himself in different experiences, made an effort to date other women, to fall in love, to move on.

But the truth was, it was her. It didn't matter where he put down roots. She was his home. She was the one who anchored him. He didn't mind giving up his dream of a life with Tessa. And he certainly didn't mind if the Moontide was sold.

But Erin?

Her rejection was the thing that made him feel untethered, lost. He couldn't dwell on that right now, however. He turned off the car and stepped outside into the late summer sunshine. He barely made it to the porch when the front door opened. Tessa must have been watching for him.

"Hi," she greeted.

"Hey." She looked no better and no worse since he'd seen her last. There was still a strange and sad hollowness to her eyes. "How are you?"

"I'm fine. How about you?"

"Good." He didn't know if he believed that Tessa was fine, but he no longer felt as if they were in the type of relationship where he could press her on the subject.

So he said nothing as she stepped inside and gestured for him to follow her. They ended up in the garage, where they'd stored most of his possessions. He had never had much stuff, given the nomadic nature of his job, and he hadn't really accumulated a lot since moving back to Findlay Roads.

He had a few seasonal clothes in bags, and a small box of the mementos left from his childhood. He and Gavin had lost most of their family keepsakes in the fire that had claimed their parents' lives. There were two more boxes filled with various items from his travels and not much more than that. He'd sold his limited collection of dishes and household goods since Tessa already had everything they'd need. Aunt Lenora had offered him quite a few things from the Moontide so he shouldn't have to spend too much money to stock the point house.

He and Tessa didn't speak much as they carried everything to the car in two trips. He didn't mind the silence. He was used to it, after Erin.

As he prepared to close the car door, Tessa said, "Rumor has it that you bought that pretty little house up on Fallon Point."

He arched an eyebrow. "How did you know about that?"

She shrugged. "We may have grown a lot in recent years, but Findlay Roads is still a pretty small town. Or at least, it gossips like one."

He nodded. "Yeah, I guess I'd forgotten that. It's good to know that no matter how far she progresses, some things never change." He was surprised to realize he spoke with fondness. Tessa must have heard it in his voice because she cocked her head.

"That doesn't bother you?"

He shrugged. "Not really."

She studied him. "How do you feel then, about Aunt Lenora selling the inn?"

He hesitated, and she smiled her warm, reassuring smile. It was one of the reasons he'd felt so comfortable around her, so early on in their relationship. Her smile had a way of putting him at ease.

"You don't have to sugarcoat how you feel, Burke. And you don't have to tell me either, if you don't want to."

He relaxed a little. "Truthfully, I'm fine with it. I think it's time. The inn…it needs a new purpose." He felt the parallel in that statement. The inn needed a new purpose… just like he did.

"But?"

He caught her eye. "But what?"

"There's something you're not saying."

Her intuition unsettled him. "You're not supposed to be able to do that anymore."

"Do what?"

"You're not supposed to know if I'm not saying everything. Not if we're not going to be husband and wife."

She appeared startled, and he laughed softly.

"I'm just kidding, Tessa. It's a joke."

But it occurred to him that maybe Tessa

wasn't ready to treat their relationship like that—as something in the past. He knew he'd moved on pretty quickly, but even though Tessa had been the one to end things, maybe she wasn't as far along in her feelings as he was. He rushed to fill the awkwardness.

"Erin is pretty torn up about it. It's been her home for so long, and she shared her life with Gavin there. She's devastated at the thought of losing it. But it's not as if the inn isn't going to be there anymore. I know it won't be the same, but she can still go there, if she needs to. Maybe she'll have to take up golf to have a reason to visit, but the old place will still be part of the community." He laughed, but it died off when Tessa didn't join in.

"Burke. I know I shouldn't say anything, but…" Her eyes were filled with some emotion he didn't recognize. "My father's not converting the inn into a clubhouse."

He frowned. "What?"

She licked her lips and wrapped her arms more tightly around herself. "He plans to level it as part of the golf course."

Burke felt as if the wind had been knocked out of him. He leaned against the car.

"But, he said that he planned to convert

it into a clubhouse. I thought he liked the house."

"He does."

"So he lied?" Burke prickled with irritation. He may not have had any great love for the inn, but Allan lying about his plans seemed manipulative.

"No, it really was his plan, at first, to keep the house. But his contractor did the numbers, and it's cheaper to just level it and build elsewhere rather than renovate the inn and bring it up to the appropriate construction code for his plans."

Burke's fingers tightened into fists. "Did he decide this before or after Aunt Lenora signed the paperwork?"

Tessa hesitated, and he had his answer without her uttering a word. He swore, slamming his palm on the roof his car.

He shook his head. "That building is a historical icon, Tessa. It has stood for over two hundred years. It's been through wars, marriages, births, deaths. It houses hundreds of chapters of history within its walls."

Tessa frowned. "I thought you didn't care about the inn or what happened to it."

"Maybe I'm not its biggest champion," he insisted, "but that doesn't mean I want to see it torn down, as if it never existed. Your father has no right."

She didn't say anything, but her expression conveyed her sadness.

He expelled a breath. "Sorry. It's not your fault, I know that. It's just…not what I expected."

"I understand." She didn't say anything for a moment. "But Burke, if the inn truly doesn't matter to you, then why are you so upset? I mean, I get that you want to see a landmark preserved, but you seem pretty passionate about it. And in all the time I've known you, you've never spoken about the Moontide with any great sentimentality."

The question made him uncomfortable. He knew Tessa hadn't asked it to get under his skin, but it did.

"Does it have something to do with Erin?"

The question struck too close to home. Just how much had Tessa observed? She'd had plenty of opportunities over the last year to witness him and Erin together, but he didn't think he'd paid Erin any particular attention during that time. At least, no more than any brother-in-law would have provided to a sister.

Or maybe Tessa was simply asking for the

obvious reasons—the fact that Erin would be losing the inn she loved so much.

"Erin loves that place. It was hard enough for her to see it sold. But finding out it's going to be demolished will wreck her."

"Hmm. I see."

Tessa's tone said more than it should have, and he grew uneasy. He tried shifting the conversation.

"I know he's your father, Tess, but he doesn't deserve everything he's gotten from this town."

Allan had swooped in and bought up land for his resort as property values began to rise. He'd put the Moontide out of business. And now, to add insult to injury, he was going to rip it down, a fact he'd failed to mention when Aunt Lenora agreed to sell it to him.

"What will you do?"

This unexpected question made him stand a little straighter.

"What *can* I do?" he asked. "The deal is done. The Moontide doesn't belong to Aunt Lenora anymore."

Tessa frowned. "I'm sorry. I… I didn't want you to find out from someone else."

"No, I know. I'm glad you told me. I just wish…" He trailed off. He'd never been one for wishing. Wishing wouldn't bring his parents back, it wouldn't erase the years he'd felt unwanted and unloved. He didn't believe in wishes. But if he did... "I wish there was a way the Moontide could continue to stand, to be part of the community, like it has been for years."

Tessa didn't respond, and he knew why. She was thinking that it was a useless wish when Allan Worth already had plans to level the place. She looked away, and he was again struck with the feeling that something still weighed on Tessa.

"I should probably get going." He looked at her for a long moment, even though she wouldn't meet his eyes. "But, Tessa, thanks. Not just for telling me about the Moontide or storing my stuff but...for the last year and a half. You reminded me that I was worth loving."

She didn't look at him, but on impulse, he leaned down and planted a kiss on her cheek. "I hope you get everything you want, Tessa," he said.

She ducked her head, but he caught a glimpse of her eyes, shiny with tears.

"You, too," she choked out.

And then she turned and fled toward the house before he could say another word.

BURKE DIDN'T KNOW what he intended when he pulled up to the Delphine Resort. A valet greeted him as he got out of his car, but he brushed him off.

"This won't take long. I just have to speak to Mr. Worth."

The valet looked impressed at Burke's confident assertion. "I can place your vehicle in the private lot—"

"That won't be necessary. Just keep it nearby please." He walked off before the valet could offer anything else.

He knew exactly where Allan's office was located, thanks to the multiple visits he'd paid to the Delphine during his and Tessa's engagement. He also knew that Allan was in town for most of the summer, running his other business in D.C. remotely, so he hoped he'd be able to catch the other man in his office.

His luck was rewarded as he stepped through the door leading to the suite of offices for the Delphine's staff and glimpsed Allan at his desk, the phone pressed to his ear. Burke headed in that direction. The offices at the Delphine were more relaxed than Allan's firm in D.C. He'd only been to that building once, with Tessa, but it felt like there were several layers of security and office personnel before they were allowed entrance to Allan's office.

Allan looked up as he stepped inside the office and stood, arms crossed.

"Julien, I'm going to have to call you back. Yes, we'll talk soon. Bye now." Allan placed the phone in its cradle and offered a smile. "Burke, how nice of you to drop by." Allan's tone was strained, and Burke doubted very much that the father of his former fiancée was glad to see him.

"You lied."

Allan looked distinctly uncomfortable at this accusation. "I hardly think that's a fair—"

"You're demolishing the Moontide."

Allan frowned. "How did you hear about that?"

"It doesn't matter. It's the truth, isn't it?"

Allan had the grace to look abashed. "That wasn't my original intention. I liked the history of the place. But after consulting with my contractor and local code officials, it just didn't make sense, financially, to use the inn for the clubhouse."

"So you decided to tear it down?" He shook his head. "You couldn't find another option?"

"Burke, why don't you take a seat, and I'll talk you through the logistics—"

"Are you kidding me?" Burke felt a swell of ire. "I'm not one of your employees, Allan. I just want to know when you decided it was cheaper to bulldoze the inn than preserve it. Was it before, or after, you asked Aunt Lenora to sell? Did you know before she signed the contract and turned the deed over to you?"

Allan fidgeted. "These kind of plans are rarely that easy, or simple."

"It seems like it was easy enough to decide to destroy a local landmark."

Allan's humiliation turned to irritation. "This kind of sentimentality is what prevented that inn from being successful. If it had been treated it as a commodity instead of an heirloom, Lenora wouldn't have had to sell the place."

Burke took three steps forward and leaned down over Allan's desk, resting his knuckles on the surface. "Aunt Lenora had her own reasons for selling, and not all of them were financial. Don't underestimate the fact that the Moontide has been a part of the Findlay Roads community for a long time. The Delphine hasn't."

It was obvious Allan's patience was wearing thin. "I own the property now. Neither you, nor Lenora, have any say in what happens to it. That decision rests with me."

Though Burke still felt affection for Tessa, the more Allan spoke, the more relief he felt at not having him for a father-in-law. "You seem awfully certain about this happening."

"Why shouldn't I be? I've gone through all the proper channels. Demolition is set to begin next week."

Burke's stomach dropped at this bit of news. This timeline severely limited his window of opportunity to forestall Allan's plans. He straightened.

"Can't you hold off a little while?"

"Why?" Allan asked. "The sooner it's done, the faster I can move forward with my plans for development."

"Of a golf course."

If Allan noticed the disgust in Burke's tone, he didn't react to it. "Yes."

He thought of Erin. She'd had such a hard time saying goodbye to the Moontide. She'd be devastated to learn it was being torn down.

He swallowed his pride, for her sake, and tried to appear humble.

"Allan, please. Don't do this. At least, not right away. Give it more time and consideration. The Moontide may not mean much to you, but to some of the people of this town... it's everything."

"You mean Lenora. And your brother's widow."

He tried not to flinch, but Allan saw what he wanted to.

"You know, I wondered at Tessa's choice when she agreed to marry you. It's obvious now how you feel about Erin. I certainly hope you were smarter about how you behaved while you were engaged to my daughter."

Burke's fist flexed at this insult, not only to Erin but to Tessa as well. "I'm not even going to deign to comment on such a narrow-minded opinion."

Allan made a face that came suspiciously close to a sneer. "You Findlay Roads locals. So much pride and so little sense."

"You have a pretty low opinion of a town that has benefited you greatly."

Allan pushed back his chair and stood. "Don't mistake me. I have benefited from this town, and I'll continue to do so. But this place needs a vision to keep up with the recent growth of tourism."

"A vision? Like yours?"

"Don't sound so skeptical. The Delphine managed to take away most of your family's little B&B business, didn't it? How's that for vision?"

Burke ground his teeth together, not trusting himself to speak. When he didn't rise to the bait, Allan relented slightly.

"Listen, Burke. I didn't purchase the inn with the intention of tearing it down. But that's how it's worked out, and I can't apologize for dreaming of something better for Findlay Roads."

"Something better? Like a *golf course*?"

He shrugged. "It will bring in more tourism, and that's good for everyone."

"Not so good for the Moontide," Burke pointed out.

"I'm sorry you choose to view it that way, but that's the price of growth." Allan resumed his seat and turned his computer screen.

Burke recognized the action as the dismissal that it was. He made his way to the door but couldn't resist throwing one last comment over his shoulder.

"There are some things in this life that you can't put a price on."

And with that, he left the room.

BURKE SAT DOWN at his desk in the Graham suite and flexed his fingers over his laptop. He was better at photography, but when the occasion called for it, he could put words on paper well enough.

And this occasion certainly called for it.

He closed his eyes, drawing inspiration from his memories of the Moontide: the Galway room with its walls painted a pale blue, the cream-colored wainscoting, the pewter candlestick holders and the Chinese porcelain figurines on the mantle. There were several scuffs on the walnut desktop and a deep gouge on the surface of the desk. The brass bedstead was a little tarnished, and one of the windows was cracked.

The inn had seen better days, perhaps, but none of that mattered now. Its imperfections were like lines on a weathered face. For all the Moontide had lived through, it had earned those scars. Who was he to be critical of them? They were all little details that he'd ignored as a teenager and taken for granted during his last few weeks living there. Now, in hindsight, he cherished them.

He didn't regret that Aunt Lenora had sold the Moontide. It was time. But he did mourn the fact that it had gone to a man who didn't appreciate its true worth. Allan saw the inn as something disposable, an obstacle to his so-called vision. He didn't recognize that the place was a historical treasure, a local landmark. It had been a haven for weary travelers, a sanctuary for slaves on the Underground Railroad, a Civil War hospital and especially…a home.

Burke was grateful for Erin's open house that had prompted him to take an impressive collection of photos of the inn before they'd moved out. Now all that was left was to write the words. But in many ways, that was the more difficult task. His own relationship with the Moontide was complex. So how to put it in words for others to understand?

He would find a way. He might not have Allan's money or influence, but he wasn't without resources. He'd already talked to several editors who were interested in the inn's story. But publishing the Moontide's history was only the second part of his plan and one that would take time.

He didn't have time. He'd done some investigating and confirmed what Tessa had said. Demolition on the Moontide was slated to begin next week, pending approval from the city council. That part of his plan was phase one—halting demolition.

He wasn't doing this just for the Moontide or the town, either, and he knew it. It was for Erin. To spare her whatever heartbreak he could. If she wasn't meant to be his, then he would learn to live with that. But he was still determined to look out for her, to watch over her, to take care of her. Just as he'd told Kitt that he would.

He opened his eyes and faced his laptop screen. And then, he began to type.

CHAPTER NINETEEN

BURKE SAT IN the back of the room at the town hall, observing the proceedings from a distance and doing his best to keep his nerves in check. He'd attended a few town councils in his life, joining Aunt Lenora several times while he was still in high school. She had thought it important that he and Gavin learn how local government operated, especially since, as a small business owner, she had necessary dealings with the system.

Burke recalled his utter boredom at these events as elected officials droned on about right-of-ways and boundary disputes. He'd never had much invested in the workings of the local council...until now.

His gaze shifted from the council seats to the right, where Allan Worth's assistant sat in one of the folding chairs placed in neat rows to accommodate citizens who wished to involve themselves in local affairs. Allan's assistant, Tate Cummings, tapped his foot impatiently on the linoleum floor of the town hall building where the council met the first and third Tuesday evening of every month. Tate checked his watch and then began tapping his pen on the chair in front of him in a loud, staccato rhythm.

Councilwoman Rosalee Hastings shot him a look of disapproval which he obviously missed. She cleared her throat loudly, which finally drew Tate's attention.

"If you find yourself uninterested in the town's agenda, you might consider removing yourself from the premises."

Tate coughed, finally getting the message.

"Uh, sorry, ma'am. Please, don't mind me."

Burke's lip twitched. It was just like Allan to send a minion to perform the tasks the older man couldn't be bothered with. Allan was highly successful, and he was used to delegation. Burke was hoping that worked in his favor tonight. Tate wasn't a bad guy, but he certainly wasn't as silver-tongued as his boss, and he lacked the ability to think on his feet.

Burke was counting on this as Ms. Hastings finished up the discussion on a permit for a new sewer system and moved to the next item on the agenda. The reason Burke had come to the council tonight.

"Next item on the agenda is Allan Worth's proposal to demolish the Moontide Inn in favor of expanding his Delphine Resort by adding a golf course to the site. Mr. Worth has already purchased the property from its former owner, Lenora Daniels."

After a brief glance around the table at her other council members, Ms. Hastings turned her attention back to Tate, who was already on his feet and moving to hand out the golf course proposal.

Burke had stolen a look at the paperwork earlier, while Tate was speaking to a young woman before the meeting began. It was impressive, with detailed drawings of the proposed golf course and a list of how the development of the property and the influx of additional revenue from golfing enthusiasts and vacationers would continue to benefit the town's economy.

"As you are already aware," Tate was saying, "the Delphine has done much to bolster the Findlay Roads economy. Since its opening last summer, it has drawn an unprecedented number of guests to the town."

Nate Donahue, seated at the far end of the

council's table, cleared his throat. "I hardly think the Delphine is solely responsible for our tourism boom. We've seen a steadily growing uptick in tourism for the last ten years. That distinction is thanks to many different initiatives, outside interests and efforts on the town's behalf."

"Especially Sawyer Landry's," Jessica Murphy said. "His growing fame as a country music star and his annual concert series here in town has done much to grow our reputation."

"Of course, of course," Tate agreed. "But with the Lodge having closed last fall, all of these visitors need somewhere to stay when they visit. The Delphine has filled that need by providing a quality resort right here in town. By expanding and building the golf course, we'd be growing the town and its opportunities even further."

Councilman John O'Shea huffed at this. At the age of seventy-six, he was the oldest of the council's members. "I'm not sure we need more growth at this point. We want to maintain our small-town feel. Adding a golf course to that monstrosity of a resort seems excessive."

Even from his position in the back of the

room, Burke could see Tate's frown. Clearly, Allan hadn't warned him to expect any opposition.

"Um, well, surely you can see the benefit—"

"Benefit to whom?" John countered. "To the town? Or to Allan Worth, lining his pockets at the expense of our heritage?"

This was just the kind of opening Burke had been hoping for. As John finished speaking, he rose to his feet and started toward the front of the room.

"Councilman O'Shea raises a good point. Which is why I have a different sort of proposal for the town to consider."

All five council members turned their heads in his direction. From the corner of his eye, he saw Tate Cummings do the same.

"Burke?" Tate's tone was one of confusion.

"Mr. Daniels. It's good to see you," Ms. Hastings commented, her tone welcoming. The last time they'd spoken had been nearly a year ago, when she'd expressed her condolences over Gavin's death and welcomed him back to town. "I assume this matter is of some interest to you, given your family's history with the inn."

"It is," Burke confirmed and then began handing out the folders he'd prepared. Each one contained a copy of the article set to run in *Traveler* magazine next month, along with the photographs he'd taken of the Moontide and the idea he wanted to share.

"As you are all aware, in recent years, the Moontide has lost much of its business."

"If you're planning to blame that on the Delphine—" Tate began to protest, but Burke held up a hand to cut him off.

"I'm not. Allan Worth may have used the Moontide's situation to his advantage, but he was not responsible for the loss of income. The truth is that the house is old, and it needs a lot of upkeep and repairs, which was a deterrent to guests. Aunt Lenora did what she could, even took out a mortgage on the place though it's been in her family for generations. My sister-in-law, Erin—" he stumbled briefly on her name, his emotions striking him hard "—has also done her best over the last few years to keep the inn running, though it's been more than difficult. When Allan offered to buy Aunt Lenora out, it seemed like the perfect solution."

To him, anyway. But not to Erin. He feared she would never forgive him for voting to sell the inn, especially given its imminent destruction. He knew he couldn't win her heart.

But he would do whatever he could to restore their friendship, to love her as a brother-in-law if not as his wife.

"Burke?"

His attention jerked back to Ms. Hastings. She was looking at him with concern, and he realized that he'd trailed off, mired in his thoughts for Erin. He had to pull himself together. This was his only chance to save the Moontide…and his friendship with the woman he loved. His gaze swept the table and saw that the other members of the council were now reading through the contents of his folders with what he hoped was interest.

"Allan Worth was not entirely forthcoming about his plans for the Moontide. He told Aunt Lenora he was going to convert the inn into a clubhouse. He never once mentioned its demolition."

This statement caused the members of the council to confer amongst each other, murmuring in disturbed tones.

"So you're here because you don't like Allan's plans for the inn?" Tate snapped. "Do you mean to tell us your aunt wants the inn back?"

Burke shook his head. "No, that's not what I'm saying." He drew a breath and sent a quick, silent prayer heavenward. "But I'm raising the question about what is better for the town. Is the loss of the Moontide, a building that has stood over two hundred years and is rich in local and national history, acceptable in comparison to what will be gained? A golf course."

John O'Shea let out a hearty, "Amen!" It gave Burke the courage to continue.

"The Moontide is the oldest surviving building in this town. The only other one that comes close to it in age is St. Peter's Church on Elm Street. But St. Peter's wasn't built until 1832. That is twenty years after the attack on the town during the War of 1812. The Moontide was around shortly after our country became an independent nation, and it is our last witness to some of the struggles Findlay Roads faced in the early nineteenth century. After St. Peter's, the next oldest buildings weren't around until 1891."

He realized that the entire room was silent, hanging on his every word. He sensed the other attendees at tonight's council in the chairs behind him leaning in, listening to hear what he had to say next.

"The Moontide was a station on the Underground Railroad. It saw countless men and women on the road to Canada and their freedom during the mid-1800s. It was briefly used as a hospital during the Civil War. It operated as a boardinghouse for Irish immigrants before being converted to an inn around the turn of the century. It housed visiting soldiers heading off to war during the World Wars." He stopped to draw a breath.

"It has sheltered weary travelers, welcomed the birth of countless babies, hosted innumerable weddings, seen the best and worst of history pass within and beyond its walls. It gave me and my brother a home when we had none. Do we really want to tear it down and level it with golf turf?"

There was no reply, but he sensed the emotion in the room. They were with him. Jessica Murphy was even rummaging in her purse for a tissue to wipe away tears.

"You've got to be kidding." Tate's pasty expression had a sheen of sweat on it. "Your aunt agreed to the sale of the inn. This is just your way of getting back at Tessa for standing you up at your wedding."

The audience at their backs drew in a collective breath at this low blow.

"Mr. Cummings, I hardly think that kind

of accusation is appropriate," Ms. Hastings chided.

Tate had the decency to blush. He slid a glance at Burke. "Sorry."

Burke gave a nod of understanding. He felt bad for Tate. Reporting all this back to Allan Worth wouldn't be a fun task.

"Well, boy, you've certainly got our attention," John said, drawing him back to the moment, "but don't get us all lathered up for nothing. Tell us what you propose we do about this situation."

Burke grinned. "I'd be happy to."

"Aunt Lenora?"

Erin stepped through the house they'd been renting since their move from the Moontide and tried not to flinch at the unfamiliarity of the place. It was a nice enough house with beige walls and earth-tone laminate wood flooring, shiny chrome fixtures and pristine white windows. It was also boring and lacked character and made Erin ache for the Moontide's flaws and features of worn wood, old paintings and chipped antiques.

"Here!" Aunt Lenora's voice could be heard somewhere nearby.

"Where are you?" Erin called, cursing the

thin walls that shifted sounds outside of their actual location.

"In here!" Aunt Lenora called again. "In the storage room!" she clarified.

Erin made her way toward the back of the house, to the room they'd designated as a storage area. It was meant to be a den/home office, but they had no need for one of those anymore so they'd stacked boxes in there until they could be moved into storage or until they found a new home.

When she stepped into the room, she found Aunt Lenora with various cardboard cartons piled around her, half of their contents spilling onto the floor. Erin's jaw dropped.

"What are you doing? We just organized all this stuff."

"I'm looking for the photos Burke packed up," Aunt Lenora announced, the words coming out in disjointed puffs as she breathed hard from exertion. "I want to start working on some albums for Kitt."

"But we haven't even unpacked all of the essentials yet," Erin pointed out. "We still have crates of household items in the garage."

This didn't seem to bother Aunt Lenora who struggled to pull an oversize box down from a closet shelf. Erin hurried to help her.

"Aunt Lenora, sit down before you break something."

The stubborn old woman finally relented, stepping back to allow Erin to take over. The box was even heavier than Erin anticipated, and by the time she wrestled it to the floor, she was breathing as heavily as Aunt Lenora had been a moment before.

The older woman now sat on one of the unopened boxes as she tried to catch her breath.

"You shouldn't be trying to move boxes like this on your own. Why didn't you ask for my help?"

Aunt Lenora shrugged. "I may be eighty-nine and feeble, but I'm not entirely helpless."

Erin's mouth twitched at Aunt Lenora's candor. "No, I suppose not."

"Erin, do you know how I came to take over the Moontide?"

This question was so unexpected that Erin blinked several times, wondering if she'd misunderstood. And when she realized she'd heard correctly, she didn't respond. She had no wish to discuss the Moontide. The loss of it was still a bitter wound in her heart, not healed over. She had managed to temper her resentment toward Aunt Lenora, and her anger at Allan Worth, but somehow, she still had not been able to release her feelings of betrayal about Burke. This, perhaps, was the greatest pain of all.

She'd lost the Moontide, yes, and that cut her deeply. But she'd also lost her best friend in the process and hadn't even realized what a tragedy that was until it was too late to go back. Burke had said he wanted to marry her. Why? He had ruined everything with those words. He knew she couldn't be his wife, not after Gavin. But because he'd been selfish enough to ask that of her, she saw no way that they could mend things and be content as friends.

"I had a young man, once." Aunt Lenora had obviously decided to say what she wanted without Erin's acknowledgment.

The shock of this statement made her ask, "You...were in love?"

"You sound surprised."

"No, I just...it's only...well, okay. Maybe a little," Erin admitted. Years ago, when Erin had first gotten engaged to Gavin, she'd asked him if Aunt Lenora had ever married. He'd said no, that she'd always been a spinster. Aunt Lenora herself had never once brought up the idea of a romance, in all the years she'd known her, and despite their relatively close relationship, Erin had never found it appropriate to ask.

Aunt Lenora didn't seem in the least offended by Erin's amazement.

"It was a very long time ago," she said, as if this made up for never mentioning it before this.

"He came to stay at the inn with his family for a few weeks as sort of a final vacation before he was shipped out to Germany during the war." She looked past Erin, at some distant point over her shoulder as though she could see her beau standing in the doorway.

"I found him loathsome, at first. I was an only child and quite spoiled. You see, I had chores around the inn, but my parents didn't reprimand me if I chose not to do them or simply disappeared for the day. Clark and I didn't start off on the best foot, you might say. He needed clean towels, and I couldn't be bothered to get them for him. So he reported me to the person he assumed was the management. Typically, this would have been my mother, but she was out for the day, and my grandmother was filling in. She gave me quite the schooling for my behavior, and of course, I blamed it on Clark."

Aunt Lenora sighed, almost dreamily.

"It was impossible to stay angry with him, though. He had the most delicious wavy brown hair and gray eyes. Absolutely mesmerizing."

"He sounds like a looker."

"Oh, he most certainly was. And it didn't take long before I was finding excuses to see if his family needed anything." She chuckled to herself. "I believe those weeks may have been some of the hardest I ever worked at this old place."

Erin smiled, but it slipped as Aunt Lenora stopped laughing.

"I volunteered to show him around the town. We became inseparable. By the time his family's stay was up, we were in love. He asked me to marry him, and I agreed, though we didn't tell our parents. We exchanged letters for months until the last letter I received came from his sister. He was dead from a German bullet. She knew he'd had feelings for me and passed along the news."

Aunt Lenora shook her head. "I vowed that I would never love again and determined to spend the remainder of my days, tending to the inn." She raised her head and looked Erin in the eyes. "And so I did. I had opportunities, other chances at love, but I scorned them all until it was too late. My youth disappeared, along with any suitors I might have had. One day, I woke up and I was an old lady, clinging to the memory of love rather than living it. Sometime in the last fifty some years, it has occurred to me just how much of life I might have missed out on by tying myself to the inn."

Erin's eyes filled with tears, though she wasn't exactly sure who or what she was crying for. Aunt Lenora and her lost love, her lost youth? Or Gavin and herself?

"I know you thought it was unfair of me to sell the Moontide when you love it so much. But sometimes, we must let go of the things we love in order to make room for new things. For new loves."

Erin felt the tears begin to slip down her cheeks. "All I have ever loved has been tied to the Moontide."

Aunt Lenora leaned forward. "Love isn't tied to any one place or thing. Because it cannot be tied down. You know the old saying, if you love something, let it go? It's because you can't hold it. It's like a bird, it must rest in your hand. Hold it too tightly, and you crush it. Set it free, and it will come home to nest in your heart."

Erin wiped at her eyes. "I don't know how to let go."

Aunt Lenora patted her hand. "You let go by giving in."

"To what?"

"To the love that's waiting for you."

Erin thought of Burke. Was it really so simple? Could she let go of Gavin, and still cherish his memory, by loving Burke?

"You make it sound so easy."

"Oh, it isn't easy," Aunt Lenora said. "Love is a risk because life is fragile. You know this lesson better than most." The old woman leaned in once more. "But tell me this. Would you trade your life with Gavin, erase it from existence, because you experienced the pain of losing him?"

The answer left her lips before Aunt Lenora had even finished speaking. "No."

Aunt Lenora leaned back with an approving nod. "To know love is to know pain. But it does not mean you stop living."

Erin sat there, letting those words sink in.

"And I don't think Gavin would have wanted you to stay at the Moontide, tied to his memory, without him there beside you."

The words settled on Erin's shoulders, a weight of sadness. But they were not so heavy as they might have been. She had grieved a man she loved more than life itself. Surely she was strong enough to grieve the Moontide, too.

She cleared her throat and looked at Aunt Lenora. "Let's see if we can find those photos, hmm? Maybe we can assemble a photo album of the Moontide over the years."

Aunt Lenora beamed. "What a perfect idea. And Burke took so many photographs before we left that we can include those."

Erin didn't comment, but she began sorting through the boxes to find which ones the inn's mementos might be stored in. She started when she felt Aunt Lenora's hand rest gently on her head.

"You see?" the old woman said. "The Moontide will live on, through its memories."

And maybe, Erin realized, that was what mattered most.

ERIN SAT ON her usual bench within view of the lighthouse and observed as a father and his little boy walked hand in hand around its circumference. The sight made her wonder if Gavin would have walked with Kitt like this one day, had he not been taken from them. But while the observation made her a little sad, it didn't break her heart like it once would have.

The August morning was already warm and muggy, which may have been why the lighthouse was more deserted than usual, even though it was a Monday morning. She'd skipped coming at her usual time on Sundays and had decided to spend those hours with Kitt instead.

It was strange, not feeling the burden of the inn. It left her at loose ends. The Moontide had provided some much-needed distraction over the last couple of years. She wondered if perhaps that was part of her difficulty in letting it go. She did love the place and had treasured every moment there. But the daily care for its upkeep and her efforts to boost its revenue had consumed a large part of her thoughts and time. She realized now that maybe she was afraid to give up the Moontide because it would require her to face everything she'd been avoiding—moving on. And while the last month hadn't been easy and she'd experienced her fair share of grief over the inn's loss, she had also come to a sort of peace about it.

The Moontide had been a home for her when she needed it. But it wasn't her home anymore. That was with Kitt. With Aunt Lenora. And...

She refused to think about Burke. Though she missed him, she was still smarting at how he had encouraged Aunt Lenora to sell the inn. Granted, she knew he'd been doing it because he believed it was the right thing. And maybe it was, given the personal revelations she'd experienced over the last week. But she couldn't forgive Burke. Because if she did, she had to face that she'd made the biggest mistake of her life in letting him go.

The man and his boy had left, and Erin now faced the lighthouse alone. The flag fluttered slightly, as if feeling too lazy to fly proudly today.

"This is the last time I'll be here for a while," she said aloud. "I've been telling myself for a long time that I came here for you. But really, we both know it was for me."

She lowered her head and toyed with her wedding ring. She'd never taken it off. Not once since she'd learned of Gavin's death. She drew a breath and raised her head.

"Years ago, when you were in army basic, Burke and I became...very close. I was young and unsure, and I missed you so much. I felt a little, I don't know, abandoned? I think it just stirred up all my old insecurities from being shuffled from place to place because of my dad."

She sighed.

"The point is, Gavin…as much as I loved you… I fell in love with Burke, too, a little. When you asked me to marry you, and I accepted, I think I broke his heart. It's my fault he left and hardly ever returned. I didn't mean for it to happen, and I promise you that I was never unfaithful to you, not even in my thoughts. I buried any feelings I had for Burke so deeply that I thought they'd ceased to exist. But over the last few months…ever since he came to live at the Moontide…" Speaking the inn's name didn't bring as much pain as it once had. She was learning to let go.

"Those feelings resurfaced." She swallowed, willing herself to say the words out loud. "And I fell in love with him, all over again, and deeper than before."

It was still difficult to admit this aloud. Surprisingly, not because of how she felt for Burke but because she'd kept it in for so long. She felt foolish for not unburdening this to Gavin sooner. He was gone, and she didn't know whether he could even hear her confession or not. But by imagining he could, she realized that Gavin wouldn't have condemned her for loving his brother, now that he was gone. His heart had always been bigger than that. If he couldn't be here, at Erin's side, he would have given his blessing to her and Burke.

"It's too late, though," she whispered. "Burke asked me to marry him, and I told him 'no.'"

Her wedding ring felt heavy on her finger at this admission.

"So I'm not here to tell you I'm marrying Burke. But I am here to tell you that I know it's time to move on. I think that's why I clung to the Moontide so desperately—I wasn't ready to close that chapter of my life and look to the future."

Despite her best intentions, tears rose to her eyes.

"I will always love you, Gavin. Nothing will change that. It isn't dependent on the Moontide or the town or whether I fall in love with someone else. You will *always* be my first love. But wherever you are right now, if you have the chance to fall in love again… I'd want you to take it. I miss you. So much. But I miss you a little less now than I once did. I was afraid that made me a bad person, an unfaithful wife. But I think it just means I'm healing."

She wiped at her eyes. "So I'm moving forward. I applied to a culinary school in Baltimore, to earn my degree as a pastry chef. Connor said as soon as I'm ready, I can come back to work for him. But I want to take a little time to focus on school and Kitt first. With Aunt Lenora's help because of the B&B's sale, we'll be all right, at least for a year or so.

"And I won't be coming here to the lighthouse as often. It's time for me to start some new traditions, with Kitt."

She closed her eyes and just sat there for a minute, savoring the sound of lapping water from the bay and the scent of the tide. Her heart was heavy but not entirely in a bad way. It was full, of memories, of loss, of hope. This was in some ways her final goodbye to Gavin.

She opened her eyes and stood to her feet, moving closer to the lighthouse. She leaned against it and looked out over the water. And then, slowly, she removed her wedding band, resting it in the palm of her hand. Its golden circumference caught the sun and glinted sharply. She ran her thumb over it.

"The only thing left to say is thank you. Thank you for protecting your country.

Thank you for giving me Kitt. Thank you for loving me and offering me a home and a place at your side. Our marriage wasn't perfect, but I never regretted a single minute of it. It was a joy to be your wife."

She raised the ring to her lips and kissed it gently before carefully tucking it into her pocket.

"Goodbye, my love."

And then she turned and walked toward her car without looking back.

CHAPTER TWENTY

By the time Erin arrived back at the house Aunt Lenora was renting, any remaining tears had dried. She felt...at peace. It was a new and unexpected emotion, but one she believed would last.

She grabbed the mail from the mailbox as she pulled into the driveway and carried it inside without looking through it. The day was warm, and she was thirsty so she dropped the mail on the counter on her way into the kitchen.

"Kitt?" she called as she opened the cupboard for a glass.

Aunt Lenora shuffled into the room. Erin had to admit that moving out of the Moontide had been good for the woman. She still moved like the eighty-nine-year-old woman she was, but she stood a little straighter and her eyes were a little clearer. Erin hadn't realized how much the inn had become a burden for Aunt Lenora. If she had, she might have looked at the Moontide differently much sooner.

"I picked up the mail on my way in. It's on the counter." Erin gestured toward where she'd dumped the pile of envelopes. The mail haul had been respectable since they moved, as word of the inn's sale spread. People had written from as far away as Alaska to share their memories of the Moontide. Erin left most of that correspondence to Aunt Lenora. It seemed to bring the older woman a sense of closure, as well as joy, to read the letters. But for Erin, it would only cause her to look back instead of forward.

"There's fresh lemonade in the fridge," Aunt Lenora said, guessing Erin's need for a drink, "and Kitt's with Burke."

This statement gave Erin pause. "Burke is here?"

"No. He came to pick up Kitt about an hour ago. He's taking him to his new house on the point, to help do a few projects. Mostly, I think Kitt and Scout will probably keep each other company so Burke can get some work done."

"Oh." Erin knew Burke had purchased a house on Fallon Point, but she hadn't been to see it. In fact, she and Burke avoided each other as much as possible since the move. She assumed he was angry with her over her rejection, and she couldn't bear to see the resentment in his eyes.

She'd been surprised to learn he was staying in Findlay Roads, after all that had transpired, and that he had even gone so far as to purchase a house. It showed a level of commitment she hadn't expected from him. And she was touched at the effort he was putting into his relationship with Kitt. He stopped by several times a week to pick up her son and take him and Scout to the park or out for ice cream or to his new house. Erin usually made herself scarce when she saw him pull up and let Aunt Lenora see Kitt out the door and welcome him back inside when he returned.

Erin took a long sip of lemonade, savoring the sugary sweet taste that masked the sharp tang of citrus.

"Erin."

She turned, curious about the tone in Aunt Lenora's voice. It was filled with expectation. She held up a large manila envelope. Even from a few feet away, Erin could see the culinary school's logo on the exterior.

"It's addressed to you."

She set the lemonade on the counter and

moved to take the envelope from Aunt Lenora. By the weight of it, she knew it had to be an acceptance letter and welcome packet. Tearing it open, she pulled out the paper, gave it a brief scan and grinned.

"I'm in. I'll be starting pastry school next month."

Aunt Lenora clapped her hands together and then drew Erin into her arms. It was an unexpected gesture since Aunt Lenora rarely showed affection in this way, except with Kitt. She wrapped her arms around the old woman's shorter, thinner frame and hugged her.

"Congratulations," Aunt Lenora whispered, then pulled back to look in Erin's eyes. "Gavin would be thrilled for you."

"Thank you." She marveled that the mention of Gavin's name did not stir the grief it would have even a month ago.

Aunt Lenora moved away to continue sorting through the mail while Erin perused the folder containing her orientation information.

"Oh. Oh my."

Erin looked up. "What?"

But Aunt Lenora ignored her, her attention focused squarely on a magazine she held in her hand.

"Aunt Lenora? What is it?"

When she still received no response, Erin moved to Aunt Lenora's side and looked down at the front page of *Traveler* magazine. She gasped at the familiar sight of the Moontide featured on the glossy paper.

Findlay Roads Local Inn Finds a New Purpose, by Burke Daniels.

The words were prominently displayed amidst the titles of other articles.

"Burke did this?" She grabbed the magazine from Aunt Lenora's hands, unable to contain herself. She flipped through the pages until she found the article as Aunt Lenora took a seat at the table.

Findlay Roads' local treasure, the Moontide Inn, has withstood wars and rebellion and served as a safe haven for many during its 200 plus years.

"Read it aloud," Aunt Lenora instructed.

"Oh, sorry." Erin repeated the article's opening line and then continued, "From the exterior, you might never guess the secrets held within these walls, but the Moontide Inn has experienced its share of history over its lifetime. All of that was nearly lost recently when the inn was slated for demolition."

Erin's jaw dropped. "What? The inn was slated for demolition?"

Aunt Lenora frowned. "Allan Worth. He didn't intend to keep the Moontide as a clubhouse. It made more sense to level it."

Erin experienced a surge of anger. "He *what*? And you knew that was his plan?"

Aunt Lenora shook her head. "Not until after the sale was final. There was nothing I could do at that point. My hands were tied."

Erin went to the kitchen table and sat down. Her own hands were trembling at the idea of the Moontide's destruction. She had said her goodbyes to the place, but she wasn't ready to see it destroyed.

"Is it…? Is Allan…?" She couldn't even bare to voice the words aloud. Fortunately, she didn't have to. Aunt Lenora answered her unspoken question with a swipe of her head.

"No. Allan is no longer in possession of the inn."

Erin's jaw dropped a second time. "He's not? But…the restoration that's been going on…"

"By the town and the historical society. He donated the building and a small bit of land back to the town."

Erin was floored. "He did *what*?"

Aunt Lenora's smile was just a little too gleeful. "I don't pretend to know the particulars, but apparently Allan was facing some difficulties with permitting and such for the golf course. After he donated the inn to the town, all that red tape went away. Or so that's what Mrs. Cleary says."

"Why didn't you tell me about the demolition?"

Aunt Lenora's smile faded. "Burke asked me not to."

"Burke?"

"It was him. He was the one who managed to pull it off. He learned of Allan's intentions and he spoke to the town council, convinced them to declare the inn a historical landmark, which would prevent Allan from tearing it down. What choice did he have except to turn the Moontide over? They're converting the inn into a museum and local offices for the historical society. So clever of Burke." Her smile was back, filled with pride.

Erin rested her palm over her chest. Her heart was racing.

"Burke managed to do all that?"

She nodded.

"Why didn't he want me to know?"

Aunt Lenora looked at her with something

that appeared suspiciously like pity. "He was afraid of hurting you further."

"But…he saved the Moontide from being bulldozed to the ground. Why would he think that would hurt me?"

"Because you already resented him for encouraging me to sell the inn. He was afraid if you found out how close it had come to being torn down that you'd be even angrier with him."

She blinked. "I'm not angry with him."

Aunt Lenora arched an eyebrow.

"Well, not anymore at least," Erin clarified.

"Hmm. I'm not so sure he knows that."

Erin looked down at her hands, resting in her lap. There was a faint white line, paler than the rest of her skin, where her wedding band had been. It would fade with time, she knew. Just as the worst of her grief and guilt had faded.

"I thought he was angry with me," she murmured.

"Oh, you foolish girl." Despite the words, Aunt Lenora's tone was warm with caring. "He is in love with you."

Erin raised her head. "I know. But I turned him away. Not once but twice. He has to hate me for that now."

Aunt Lenora sighed, as if weary of young people's mistaken assumptions. "Have you had one conversation with him in the last month? Just one?"

Erin furrowed her eyebrows together. "Well... no. Not really."

Aunt Lenora harrumphed, as if to say *I rest my case*.

Erin considered. Could Aunt Lenora be right? Could Burke still love her? Could he forgive her? Was there still a chance?

Her eyes fell on the article before her, and she began reading once more. Tears welled in her eyes, and she had to blink them away in order to continue the article. Burke had done a stellar job of telling the inn's history, including his personal connection as a child, visiting Findlay Roads with his family and then later, as an orphaned teenager in need of a home. And finally, he mentioned Gavin and her, as the last in a long legacy of married couples who had made their home at the inn. By the time she finished reading, she was steadily wiping the tears from her eyes.

"Do you think it's too late?" she asked, not bothering to tell Aunt Lenora what she referred to.

The older woman's voice was strong with confidence. "It is never too late, where love is concerned."

AUNT LENORA SAID Burke planned to drop Kitt off at home before dinner, so Erin had plenty of time. Even so, she hurried, stripping off the jeans and T-shirt she wore to shower and then dressing in a flowing, peach-colored sundress. She pulled her hair back into a ponytail, swiped on some lipstick and sprayed a touch of body splash on her wrists before giving herself the once-over in the bathroom mirror. She could have done more, but she was in too much of a hurry. She looked pretty, she decided, if not gorgeous—it would have to do. She couldn't wait any longer.

With a quick explanation to Aunt Lenora about where she was headed, she barely had time to register the older woman's pleased smile before she was out the door and in the car, navigating toward the point.

She slowed once she found Burke's street and hesitated when she reached the turnoff to his lane. The house was a little more secluded than she had thought it would be, but she found she liked it. It had a slightly rural feel as she headed down the unpaved drive and ended up in front of a breathtaking Cape Cod–style house with a wraparound porch. It was obviously in need of some repairs, but Erin fell in love with it at first sight. It was a home for a family, a house for a couple in love to grow old in. She parked the car on the grass and opened her door.

She heard Scout's bark announcing her arrival well before she caught sight of Burke and Kitt around the side of the house. As she approached, she saw Burke had a paintbrush in hand as did Kitt. They were applying a coat of paint to the railing.

Burke's face revealed his surprise as she approached, and it was all she could do to keep from running straight into his arms. Scout stopped her as he leapt around at her feet, his tail wagging furiously. He jumped up, placing two paws on her waist, and strained to reach her face so he could cover her in wet kisses.

"Scout, down," Burke called in a warning tone, but Scout was disinclined to listen. Erin laughed, bent down for a face full of slobbery kisses and then scratched him behind the ears.

"You're a good boy," she approved, and Scout's tail wagged even harder.

"Mom!" Kitt whined. "I'm not ready to go home yet!"

Burke was walking toward her, his lips turned down in a frown. "I could've brought him home sooner if you wanted. You didn't have to drive out here to get him."

She looked at Burke, the wariness in his expression, and felt a moment's doubt. What if Aunt Lenora was wrong? What if he was too angry to forgive her? She'd broken his heart twice, choosing Gavin over him, even when Gavin was no longer an option. But she'd come this far, and she was past the point of letting fear hold her back.

"I didn't come for Kitt."

"Oh?" His face registered another display of surprise.

"No. I came for you."

He blinked, his jaw sagging slightly. She reached for his hand, tugging the paintbrush free and tossing it onto the grass. And then she didn't waste any more words, she stepped up to him, drew his head down to hers and kissed him.

She could feel his shock, electric and sharp, or maybe it was just the rightness of finally giving in to how she felt.

It took him a moment to recover from his

surprise, but once he did, he kissed her back, pulling her tightly against him and wrapping his arms around her, holding her close. Her heart soared at how tightly he held her. It wasn't too late.

Why had she ever thought it would be too late? He had waited fifteen years for her, not wanting to come between her and Gavin, giving her the space and distance that she needed for her marriage to thrive. But she knew, so clearly, that she and Burke had been destined for one another. She had loved Gavin, loved him body and soul, holding nothing back.

But in his absence, another room had opened in her heart, one to fill with her love for Burke. It wasn't a betrayal to love him. Perhaps it was a tribute to Gavin, in some way. Because Gavin had loved her so truly and so well that she was no longer afraid to put her faith in loving again.

She only pulled away from Burke when she needed to catch her breath. He stared at her.

"Erin…"

"Wait. I have to say something first."

She rested her palm against his cheek as he fell silent, stroking her thumb across his cheek.

"I need to thank you."

"Thank me?"

She nodded. "For waiting. For your patience and understanding. For what you did to save the inn. For making Kitt smile again and adopting Scout. For taking care of Aunt Lenora and knowing that what she needed wasn't necessarily what I wanted. For staying away for so many years so I could love Gavin without distraction." She drew a breath. "For loving me so well and so steadily that I almost didn't realize your love was the thing getting me through the last couple of months."

She licked her lips. "Do you still love me, Burke?"

He pulled her against him once more. "So much it hurts to breathe."

She sighed, feeling as if everything in her world had finally shifted into place with a soft and satisfying click. The breeze kicked up, tickling the back of her neck, and for a moment, she wondered if it was Gavin, giving his blessing.

"This house better be big enough for us, Scout and Aunt Lenora, too," Erin said.

His smile was so bright that she had to laugh and press a kiss to his lips. Scout barked, and Kitt tugged at the skirt of her sundress. She hadn't even heard him approach.

"Does this mean I can stay, Mom?"

She and Burke stepped apart to draw Kitt into their embrace.

"Sure, buddy," Burke answered, "I think this means we're all going to stay here. Together." He looked at Erin, his expression still awed.

"Just like at the Moontide?" Kitt questioned.

Erin looked at her son. "Even better." She turned her eyes toward the view of the town, her gaze falling on the lighthouse. It stood in silent approval, unchanging. Just like the Moontide. Thanks to Burke.

"We're going to be a family," she whispered.

"We're already a family," Kitt pointed out.

Burke rubbed a hand over Kitt's hair. "That's right. We are. Now, let's get back to work on turning this place from a house into a home."

And then he took Erin's hand as Scout and Kitt scampered ahead of them toward the house...and their future.

EPILOGUE

IT WAS A little strange to be back at the Moontide when it was no longer home, but Erin had
to admit that the renovations had breathed
new life into the inn. The historical society
was hosting this reception to show off the
great lengths they had gone to in order to repair and restore the old building. The walls
were painted a linen cream color with Colo-
nial blue accents. Paintings and photographs
adorned the walls—some were even ones
Erin recognized from her years living there.
Aunt Lenora had donated quite a bit to the
historical society, and Erin was pleased to
see these items returned to the home that had
housed them for so long.

Erin shifted her gaze to Aunt Lenora now
to see how she was reacting to the changes.
The old woman was obviously pleased, her
eyes bright and a smile permanently af-
fixed to her mouth. She had her arm linked
through Burke's as they were greeted by

members of the historical society and provided with a pamphlet that detailed the inn's history and recent changes. There was even a framed copy of Burke's article on display, and Erin's heart sped up when she saw it, feeling a swell of pride.

They had been married less than three months, and she continued to feel a thrill every time she looked at him. As if her gaze drew him, he looked over his shoulder to find her, his face brightening when she smiled at him.

Her heart was so full, she feared it couldn't contain her joy. They had begun the necessary paperwork for Burke to legally adopt Kitt, and her son had started referring to Burke as Dad on occasion, as if trying out the sound. Aunt Lenora had moved into the house on the point with them, and she was enjoying all the holiday festivities at their new home now that the winter months were almost upon them.

Erin and Burke's wedding had been a very quiet, private affair. Given Burke's recent engagement to Tessa, it didn't seem quite right to flaunt their nuptials. The ceremony had been simple but precious and had included a special tribute to Gavin. They hadn't invited any of their friends. Instead, they were hosting a holiday get-together at their new home next week to invite people to share in their new life together.

Erin was enjoying the thought of the upcoming Christmas holiday, especially since she had a special present for Burke. Her doctor had confirmed her pregnancy just this week, but she had decided to hold onto the news for a bit so she could tell Burke on Christmas day. She was a little wary of how Kitt would receive the news, but she had a feeling he'd be thrilled with the idea of a brother or sister. And she'd be able to finish out her classes at the culinary institute in time for the baby to be born.

Of course, Aunt Lenora fussed over her in a way that made Erin suspicious the older woman already suspected her news, but she didn't want to share it with anyone else until she had told Burke.

Kitt tugged his hand free from hers as he caught a glimpse of Neal Weaver in the crowd. Neal had been a regular feature at their new home as he helped Burke take care of some remodeling. The older man had become like a father to Burke and a grandfather to Kitt, for which Erin was grateful, given her own dad's distance.

And Kitt had blossomed in the months since the move, the aura of soberness gone. He'd become more animated and had made a few friends since the school year had begun, though he still maintained that Scout was his best friend in the whole wide world.

The way Kitt had grown made her realize that Aunt Lenora was right. It had been time for a new chapter—both for her and for the inn. She wasn't sure any of the miracles of the last couple of months would have taken place if she'd still been living at the Moontide, tied to it and the past.

Now, however, she walked through the old house with new eyes, appreciating all the care and detail the historical society had gone to in creating the Findlay Roads museum. The parlor was dedicated to the first settlers in the area, including Donal Findlay, the town founder. There was a copy of the land deed he'd obtained to found the town, along with detailed descriptions of what Findlay Roads had been like during those early days.

Each room in the first floor of the house featured some of the major milestones in the town's history, and Erin was fascinated to find that a wall of the dining room had been excavated to reveal the secret passageway slaves had used to hide in the attic during their journeys north on the Underground Railroad. She rested her hand on the glass that enclosed that space and felt a shiver of gratitude that she had lived in this house that had seen so much, for as long as she had.

She continued through the rooms, occasionally greeting townspeople as she passed. She spotted Mrs. Cleary and waved, but the woman turned her back.

Erin didn't let it bother her. She knew Mrs. Cleary thought it shameful that she and Burke had married when Burke was Gavin's brother, and so soon after he'd been set to marry Tessa, but Burke had said it well when he told her he didn't care what other people thought. She knew Gavin would have given his blessing to them, were he able, and that was all that mattered to her.

When she entered the library, she paused, noticing a brass plaque hanging by the door. She expected this one to mention Allan Worth again—so many of the inscriptions did since Allan had donated the Moontide to the society. It chafed a little, seeing his name stamped all over the inn, but it hurt far less than see-ing the old house destroyed.

This commemoration, however, was dif-ferent, and her eyes filled with tears as she read it.

This room is dedicated to one of Find-lay Roads' most precious sons, Army Sergeant Gavin Daniels, who lived here with his wife, Erin, and his son, Kitt, before his untimely death. He was a be-loved husband, a loyal brother and a true friend.

She wiped at her eyes and then sighed as she felt Burke's arms come around her. He pressed a kiss to her temple.

"Aunt Lenora donated the money for it, but she asked me to write the inscription. I hope I did him justice."

Erin turned in his arms so that she could face him. "You do him justice every day by the way you love me and Kitt."

He sighed and rested his forehead against hers. "Does it bother you? Being back here?" he asked.

She wrapped her arms around his waist. "I'm surprised to say, not even a little. I love this place. I'm so grateful it's still standing. But it's no longer my home."

Burke opened his eyes, and they were so close that she could see every dark fleck within the blue.

"My home is wherever you are," she whispered.

He touched his lips to hers. "And right here in Findlay Roads is where I plan to stay."

* * * * *

Get 2 Free Books,
Plus 2 Free Gifts—
just for trying the Reader Service!

Get 2 Free Books,
<u>Plus</u> 2 Free Gifts—
just for trying the *Reader Service!*

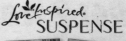

LIS17R3

Get 2 Free Books,
<u>Plus</u> 2 Free Gifts -

just for trying the *Reader Service!*

Get 2 Free Books,
Plus 2 Free Gifts—
just for trying the Reader Service!

Get 2 Free Books,
Plus 2 Free Gifts—

just for trying the Reader Service!